MIDSUMMER

THE COURSE OF TRUE LOVE NEVER DID RUN SMOOTH

MIDSUMMER
BOOK ONE

JENA DOYLE

DIRTY WORDS PUBLISHING LLC

For my ancestors of order... Thank you.

PROLOGUE
IVY

Now

It was a sham wedding.

I might as well be honest about that.

I *hated* Alexei Fairfax. I always had. I always would. Yet, as I traced over the scars on my palm, a permanent reminder of what we'd done together all those years ago, there could be no doubt I loved him more deeply than I ought to. More deeply than this marriage would require.

Our lives were so entangled and chained together that we would never be free of one another. I had stopped trying long ago.

"Ivy?" my sister, Kit, called from the doorway. She gave me a hesitant smile and took a few steps inside, her dark hair twisted up on the back of her head. "Wow, you look stunning. Absolutely stunning."

She raked her steel eyes over my heavy wedding dress and the lace trailing down my arms. With my hair in soft curls and waves, I looked every bit the American princess my name proclaimed me to be, but it was a lie. Lex wasn't my Prince Charming, nor was I his one true love. This was politics. We were stuck like mice on one of those poison pads, tempted by the smell of peanut butter but realizing too late there was no way out. Perhaps there had never been.

"You look beautiful, too," I told her, looking back out the window to the beginnings of the party below. The Potomac River glistened in the afternoon light, and boats littered the channel with paparazzi hoping to get a picture of the Washington-Fairfax wedding.

The event of the season. Of the year.

More photographers and news stations waited downstairs than I wanted to think about, and my stomach churned. This was always the worst part, right before I went on stage. The butterflies. The shaking limbs. The sweaty palms. And that didn't even take into account everything else that had gone wrong up until now.

"Did he bolt?" I smiled, imagining it.

She laughed. "Not a chance. You know he won't back down from you. He never has."

"Tell him I'm planning to murder him in our marital bed."

Kit hummed an amused noise. "I bet he already suspects that."

I cleared my throat and looked down at the scars on my palm, right along my lifeline. I traced over a particular grouping as the aching chasm in my heart deepened. Miri wasn't here. Carter wasn't here. That hurt the worst. Not that I expected them to come, not after everything that's happened. It was too unbelievable, and given the danger heading straight for us, I didn't blame them.

If I could, I would have left myself years ago.

Just me and Lex again. Like always.

"Ivette," my mother said, waltzing into the room with the confidence and prowess a former president should have. She stopped when she saw the look on my face. "Why so glum? It's your wedding day. At least pretend like you're excited."

Ah, yes. *Pretend.* Pretend this was my idea. Pretend the relationship between Lex and me had been real from the start. Pretend I wanted any part of this.

I should. Lex was a handsome, powerful man, and we had all the money in the world. Our marriage would be broadcast to over twenty-seven countries, but the sinking hollow feeling in my gut only worsened.

It seemed so trivial now, compared to what we were up against. All of this and all of *them,* so insignificant.

"Look at me, child," Evelyn Washington said. I forced my chin up and tried to smile, hoping she couldn't see the fractures through the duct tape. "You're making the right decision. You both are." She straightened her spine. "I know this isn't what you wanted, but we all have to make choices we don't like for the good of the country." She touched my cheek, the way she used to do when I was a little girl, and gave me that pitying smile. "I've been where you're standing, and I wouldn't change my decision."

It was the wrong time to compare her and my father to me and Lex, especially since I'd spent the better part of this week discovering the depths of how much she had manipulated my life. Sure, they had a powerhouse political alliance, and the Washington name had become synonymous with America itself. We were royalty in the States. But my parents weren't in love and never had been. Their hatred for each other might rival that of mine for Lex.

I shouldn't be marrying him.

It repeated in my head like a mantra.

I shouldn't be marrying him.

We're already married.

Both of us...to other people.

My mother gave me a peck on the cheek and announced I had fifteen minutes to get downstairs if we wanted to start this thing fashionably late.

All I could think about was *them.*

All I could hear was the sound of Carter's laughter and the thrill of Miri's whisper. All I could see were future versions of Lex and me at each other's throats, desperate to hurt each other in the worst way possible because we were so sick of the fighting and the grind and the hustle. My parents had beaten each other down relentlessly over the years. I wanted no part of that.

As soon as the door shut behind my mother, I made up my mind.

I knew what I had to do.

ACT I

Love looks not with the eyes, but with the mind,
And therefore is winged Cupid painted blind.
-Helena, Act I, Scene I

I

IVY
AGE SEVENTEEN

I'd known Lex my entire life. With only six months age difference between us, we'd come out of the womb with each other's names etched into our souls. There was no succinct memory I could point to and say, "This...This was when I met Lex Fairfax." But there were moments that stuck out, times when I could tell fate had tethered us, even as children.

Like a true Washington, my father, George, had been president for eight years, serving two terms before my mother had taken over the mantle, becoming one of the first Washington women to claim the title. Lex's father, Kellan Fairfax, had been vice president both times, and some of my earliest memories were of me and Lex wrestling backstage at political events.

In those days, I only had eyes for his older brother, Marcus. He was two years our senior and thus more refined and worldly, as much as a child could consider someone else such things. I'd always been a type-A know-it-all with a fondness for lists and ten-year plans. Marcus starred in every single one, and when I imagined what my wedding would look like, he was the one standing at the end of that long aisle.

Most importantly, he made me feel safe when we had to be on stage. I had hated the media attention and all the eyes on me. They'd flash my face across magazines and television programs while I had to smile and pretend like it was totally normal for children to be as famous as we were.

That's the price we pay for being Washingtons, my mother would have said.

Then I don't want to be a Washington, I would have told her. I'd meant it.

Lex had taunted me about it backstage during their first inauguration, cutting down to the bone as he always did, like he was born pre-wired to trip my triggers.

"If you're scared, just say you're scared." Even at ten years old, he had incinerating hazel eyes and the beginnings of cheekbones that could cut glass.

"I'm not scared," I'd told him. I just hated people looking at me and the cameras taking pictures. They'd put my face on a magazine cover and say something horrible about my haircut or clothes. The paparazzi were ruthless, even to children, but especially to my family. They lived to tell stories about us, and I had hated that, too.

But at that moment, I'd hated Lex most of all.

"Yes, you are." He narrowed his hazel gaze at me. "You're lying right now. You know how I know?"

My heart raced, and I tightened my hands into fists while I tried to keep myself from launching at him and clawing his eyes out.

"There's a bright red X on your neck." He came closer and poked at the side of my throat, his finger icy cold on my overheated skin. "X marks the lie."

It wasn't a scar or a mark or anything like that. Just the way my pale skin flushed when I got nervous, a rosy-pink pattern forming in the shape of an X right over my pulse. It had been there as long as I'd been alive.

I had glared at him, wishing his head would explode. This was not the first time he had challenged me, and even so young, I'd never back down from him.

Yes, I was a girl, but I could kick his butt, and he knew it.

"Shut up!"

"Don't tell me what to do, X." He'd taunted me with the nickname.

"Stop calling me X." I had raised my voice and disturbed my baby sister Abigail, who started crying from the commotion.

"Stop being a ridiculous baby, X," he'd teased. "X marks the lie! X marks the lie! X the Liar!"

It had set me off, and I threw myself at him, aiming for his throat as I snarled. Lex twisted one hand in my hair and smacked at my face with the other. I shoved my thumb in his eye as we grappled until our parents broke us up. Half the time, we were just releasing pent up tension, but even I could admit, there was a healthy respect mixed in with our aggravated competition. He was the only person who could match me, wits for wits, temper for temper.

Such was our life for the entirety of our parents' term, and by the time we were juniors in private school, our parents had won another election together, and I'd fallen in love with Lex's brother. It was innocent teenage adoration. Marcus and I texted all day, talking until the sun came up and falling asleep listening to each other breathe. When we woke the next morning, the call still connected, we'd laugh at how badly our parents were going to kill us when they got the phone bill. He and I had a lot in common. We understood what it meant to wear the burden of history on our shoulders. As the eldest children, we had a "responsibility to uphold the family image."

We longed for a normal life, whatever that meant. One away from the flashing paparazzi cameras, the headlines, and the politics. Away from the fake smiles and niceties. Maybe in a log cabin where no one would ever find us, where we could stare at the northern lights every night.

Just once, I'd like to show up at Mount Oberon's Academy, the fancy boarding school where our parents sent us, and not worry about what someone would tell reporters that year. I'd stopped having roommates two terms ago because the girl I lived with sold pictures of me to *The Puck,* a well-known gossip magazine obsessed with my family. She'd made enough money to move her parents to an impressive villa in Tuscany after my mother threatened to have them thrown in Gitmo.

I'd thought she was my friend. I'd thought we'd be roommates until we graduated. Now, I kept to myself. My brother, Jon, was only a grade behind me and my sister, Kit, only two. She would be in my building this year, which made it easier with my siblings around. And Lex? Well, things would always be the same. He hated me, I loathed him, and in that mutual disdain, we had a healthy competitiveness that drove us both to the top of the class. (Much to my chagrin that I had to share yet another thing with him.)

Two months into our junior term, the secret service showed up unannounced in the middle of debate club to escort Lex, my siblings, and me back to the White House. My knees locked into place and dread soured my stomach as I registered the stoic expressions of our bodyguards. They couldn't meet my eyes as they stuffed me inside the SUV and shut the door.

"What's going on?" Kit asked from the third row. Jon lifted his gaze, too. Of the five Washington children, the three of us were born back-to-back. The younger ones, Henry and Abigail, had come much later, my parents' last ditch effort to save their drowning marriage. Since I was the eldest, they all looked to me for direction.

I shrugged. "I have no idea."

"It's probably nothing." Lex waved it off and lit a cigarette, cracking open the back window to tap the ash out.

"Why would they come get us in the middle of the afternoon if it was nothing?" I narrowed my eyes.

"I don't know, X. Maybe someone fired a missile at Uranus"—he pronounced it *your-anus*—"and finally destroyed that giant stick that's been living there your whole life."

"Shut up, Lucifer." I gave him a dirty look and crossed my arms. *Jerk.*

After that, we sat silent in the Range Rover on the hour drive back to DC while my thoughts ran wild.

All the president's children, and all the president's men…Where's Humpty Dumpty?

I didn't have any missed calls from my mother or her assistants, which should have eased my anxiety but only made it worse. This situation was more important than contacting the children, and that said something.

This is bad.

An hour later, we parked outside of the White House residence, and the arrangement of the cars in the parking area unnerved me. Both of my parents were here, which was not unusual. It was our house. But both of Lex's parents were also here, and there were a few other cars I didn't recognize.

The secret service agent helped me out of the SUV and touched my shoulder to guide me toward the entrance. The humid August air stuck in my throat as I went, almost like fate was giving me its own warning, coalescing in my gut like cement and growing heavier with each step I took.

I stopped when I set eyes on Lex's mother, Anna, seated on the couch in the parlor and curled into herself with a tissue pressed to her face, her cheeks red, her blond hair falling out of her chignon as she sobbed in my mother's arms.

Mother immediately looked at me, her steel-gray eyes red-rimmed with tears. The alarms in my heart blared. It was the first time I'd ever seen her cry.

My father stood in a dark corner, holding a whiskey tumbler in one hand and his forehead in the other. Vice President Kellan Fairfax sat stricken on an end chair, his salt-and-pepper hair in disarray, his dark eyes pale and motionless. He didn't even look up when we arrived.

Lex stiffened next to me. Kit and Jon froze.

"What's happened?" I found the courage to ask.

Somehow, I already knew. All this family here, the Washingtons, the Fairfaxes. The only one missing was—

"Where's Marcus?" Lex's voice cracked, but he took a deep breath and cleared his throat to try again. "Where is he?"

"Oh, *malysh,*" Anna said, her cheeks streaked with tears as she shook her head. "Marcus is dead. He's dead! He's dead!" She wailed and fell into the arms of my mother, who rocked her, cooing and whispering something too low to understand.

I didn't hear much after that. The buzzing sound of shock between my ears made it impossible to understand words. Kellan mentioned a boating accident, and my father said they were flying his remains back on a chopper. But they could have been the parents from *Charlie Brown,* mutated into unintelligible noise.

Marcus is dead. He's dead.

Then, as soon as the thought crossed my mind, another more despicable voice followed with—*At least, it's not Lex.*

I could exist in a world without Marcus. We'd lived apart for a lot of our lives due to the age difference between us. But Lex? I didn't know who I was if there was no Lex. I didn't know how to *be* if he wasn't also a part of this world. I blinked, shocked with myself.

What? Where did that come from?

I swallowed down the thought, determined not to let it take up any more space in my mind.

Marcus is dead. He's dead.

"Ivette," my mother said, bringing me back to the present. "Take the children upstairs to your room."

Silently, stoically, I grabbed my sister's hand and led her to her room. Jon went to his, but I...well, I couldn't be alone. Lex turned the handle on my door, walked inside, and sat down on my bed. Wordlessly, I followed. What could I say to him? What could he say to me? We'd lost a huge part of who we were, and I couldn't feel anything... nothing except relief that it wasn't him.

And what did that say about me?

Marcus is dead. He's dead.

I went to sit next to him, our bodies connected from shoulder to elbow and hip to knee. We'd spent ages hating each other, but in that small intimate connection, the history of the universe existed between us. Like we'd been born in stardust together and traveled through space and time to arrive here on Earth in these bodies. It was nothing sexual, only companionship in this loss we both endured. I'd always called him my enemy, and tomorrow, we'd go back to our regularly scheduled programming. But that night, we needed each other.

That's when it hit me, alone in that room with Lex.

Marcus. Is. Dead.

He's gone.

He's never coming back.

The last time I talked to him? That was it. That's all I'd get. The last time I saw him? That was the last time I'd *ever* see him. Period.

My chest tightened, and I grabbed Lex's hand, intertwining my fingers in his so tightly that his nails dug into my skin.

"He's dead," I blubbered, tears spilling over my cheeks and sobs racking the back of my throat.

Lex opened his mouth, but for the first time in his life, he didn't have anything to say. He put an arm over my shoulders, pulled me in to his torso, and pressed a kiss to my temple. Wails poured out of me, the utter despair of this lance in my heart ripping me in two. I wept into the tentative truce between us while Lex silently sat there, holding me through it.

2

LEX

AGE SEVENTEEN

I stared at the silver urn on the pedestal in front of my brother's portrait, willing myself to cry. I should cry. Over a thousand people crammed into this church and not a dry eye between them. The organ blared, the choir sang, and my mother sobbed.

Me?

Nothing. All I felt was numb.

How could this happen?

I'd talked to him two hours before he went sailing with his friends. I didn't think to press him for more information. One spontaneous thunderstorm and a capsized boat later, my brother could fit inside a flower vase.

How cruel. All the wild shit I'd done. All the horrible things I had not an ounce of remorse for. And this? This is what fate had in store?

I could see it in my father's eyes, in my mother's.

It should have been you, they said.

I know, I wanted to tell them. *It should have been me.*

It repeated in my head during the entire ceremony: as I stood poker-faced next to my mother and shook thousands of hands, as I listened to the priest bemoan the will of an unknowable God, as I said my final goodbyes to Marcus's spirit and felt it leave my heart forever.

My mother wanted me to attend the wake and listen to people talk about Marcus like they knew him. They didn't know shit.

Bunch of fucking sycophants, all of them, I thought, yanking my tie as I stomped toward the Potomac River. *Vampires sucking the life from my family.*

The Washingtons had generously offered their ancestral family home to us, so we didn't have to worry about planning such a tragedy. But everyone knew it was so they could show a public sign of unity and smush the Washington and Fairfax names together even more.

Our families had a political alliance going back centuries. There had been three such administrations over the course of America's two hundred and fifty years, the one belonging to our parents rounding out number four and five, respectively. It went back to the first son of George Washington, Thomas, who'd won the fifth presidency with my ancestor, William Fairfax. Since then, we've been close.

I hate that most of all.

Which was why I was alone, sitting on a bench, staring at the sunset over the river, and chain-smoking cigarettes until my lungs bled.

"I knew I'd find you here."

Great. Just what I need.

"What do you want, Ivy?"

"To check on you."

She sat next to me, reaching for the pack of smokes so she could put one between her lips. I lit it for her. "I didn't know you picked up my filthy habit."

She coughed as she exhaled. "I didn't, but if there ever was a good day to start..."

"I don't need to be checked on," I scoffed. "Especially not by you."

I mostly didn't care about anyone or anything except for myself. I didn't care what my parents thought or what the public said. *The Puck* took pictures of me and called me a delinquent because of my tattoos and sour disposition. I gave them the finger and told them to go fuck themselves. This nonchalant attitude had worked most of my life.

But Ivy?

Something about this stuck-up ginger got under my skin and made my blood boil. I never had this reaction to *anyone* else. I shouldn't care about the things she said or the way she said them, but anytime I was around her, I spewed the most vile shit just to see what she'd say in response.

It had started as a joke, a way to pass the time at those boring political events I had to attend. But now? I hung on her every word. I craved that X on her neck as much as I hated everything else about her.

"Everyone needs to be checked on, even self-centered jerks." She held out a piece of gum, perhaps in a peace offering—like the one we'd given each other a few nights ago, the one we'd spent cuddled together in her bed. It had been entirely G-rated, of course. I hated Ivy as much as she hated me, which was why we'd quickly dissolved that rare act of kindness the following morning and never spoke of it again.

I took the gum and stuffed it in my mouth.

"I'm sorry you lost your brother," she whispered. "I can't imagine what that...If I even think about..." She couldn't finish, and I looked away, not wanting her to see I was a heartless bastard who had not a single tear to shed for his only sibling.

"Sorry your dream boy died," I said. "Guess you'll have to rethink your ten-year plan."

"Can we not?" She winced and cleared her throat, hanging her head between her shoulders. "I'm tired of doing this with you."

Ivy didn't itch for a fight the same way I did, not today.

Too late.

Fury boiled in my gut—at her, at the world, at whoever had taken my brother out on that boat and didn't bring him back. Perhaps at my brother most of all, for having the good sense to die and leave me here to deal with this bullshit on my own.

"Why?" I snapped. "Afraid I'll hurt your feelings?"

"Yes," she said. "You're grieving, and so am I." She pushed to her feet, balling her hands into fists.

There it is—that rosy-pink X on the side of her neck, the splotchy proof of her fury and racing heart. I itched to wrap my hand around it and squeeze.

"I wanted to tell you I was here if you needed anything," she said. "But I can see you're back to your old self. So, I'll just fuck off."

A tiny sting of disappointment pierced my heart when she gave up so easily and turned away from me. She was my best combatant. She had razor-sharp claws to match my razor-sharp tongue.

Come back.

"Wait," I said.

She turned and crossed her arms, raising an eyebrow.

I'd never know why I did what I did next. Maybe it was that night between us, when we'd held each other until we fell asleep. Maybe I needed to feel something. Maybe I needed her to react the way I knew she would.

I grabbed her shoulders and collided my lips with hers.

They were so soft and warm, unfurling tension in my chest as the heavy weight of my pathetic existence dissipated for one euphoric second. Things changed in that moment on the banks of the Potomac River, and even if I couldn't name it at the time, a fundamental part of my soul altered into something undefinable.

She stiffened and shoved at my shoulders, squealing like a trapped rabbit. The sound made me stop, and I pushed her back, gasping for air as reality sank in.

I'd kissed Ivy Washington. I kissed—

A sharp burst of agony thwacked through my cheek, into my jaw, and down my neck before my brain caught up.

She slapped me...*hard.*

"The next time you kiss a girl," she huffed, her hair pluming around her face, "it had better be because she wants you to. Not because you're pissed at the world."

She left me there, alone and shaking and furious. But the feel of her palm colliding with my face burst through a mental barrier I hadn't realized I'd put up. I looked out over the river, the sky a brilliant array of blushes and violets matching the mark on Ivy's skin.

The tears finally came.

I let them.

I didn't handle Marcus's death well. I'd like to say I learned from his lesson and stayed away from any behavior that could result in my untimely death. Instead, I became more self-destructive. I did a bunch of shit I wasn't proud of, and thankfully, I never got caught. By the end of that summer, my parents were done with me.

"You need discipline." My father sat at the head of our dining room table, his hands crossed over his dinner. I'd been avoiding my family for weeks, but he'd cornered me tonight. And now, here we were. "You need someone to get you into shape."

For what?

"You need space to heal, baby," my mother said in Russian, sipping a glass of wine. Was that her fourth or fifth tonight? She'd been slurring her words since dessert. And they wondered where I got it from?

Hypocrites.

"Space to heal," I repeated. *Whatever the fuck that means.*

I met my father's stern, unyielding gaze as he said, "I won't have you be a disappointment to this family any longer."

He meant the drugs and the tattoos and the photographs with different people every night. I'd taken a bad situation and made it worse by acting out. They'd decided the best way to deal with that was to send me to some shithole boarding school in London for my senior year, hoping the change of scenery would do me good.

"I'm sorry it wasn't me," I told him. "I know you wish you had Marcus back. Believe me when I say we all do."

"Oh, Jesus Christ." My father groaned and shook his head. "This again? It's nonsense, Alexei. You're a Fairfax. Start acting like it." Done with the conversation, and apparently my bullshit, he stood and stalked away, leaving me with my drunken, depressed mother.

I lit a cigarette and glanced back at her, and she ran a finger under her eye.

Does she see shame or apathy when she looks at me?

"I promise you," she said, "I won't let him do to you what my parents did to me. Turn eighteen and you're free."

Born the great-granddaughter of the Tsarina Anastasia Romanov, Grand Duchess Anna married my father as part of a political alliance, a way to seal some stupid trade agreement. I wanted to believe she meant her promise, and even if something smelled foul, I took her at her word.

What a idiot I was.

3

IVY

I didn't see Lex again after he kissed me. He didn't return for senior year, and even if a small (read: *incredibly* small) part of me worried about him, I'd been too pissed off to care. No one had ever kissed me before. Not Marcus. Not anyone.

Only Lex.

The night we'd found out about Marcus's death, we'd held each other through our grief. A few days later? He'd tried to make out with me, to turn me into one of those girls he snuck into his room at Mount Oberon. Even if I didn't have conflicted feelings about his brother, I wouldn't have stood for that disrespect.

And yet...why did I like it?

I didn't like it. Not one bit.

Liar. X marks the lie.

My hand went to the burning spot on my neck, and I cursed him again.

The grief I harbored for Marcus swelled in my chest. I missed him. I missed his texts and his late-night phone calls. I missed his smiling face at our family functions and how he helped me face my fears by telling me to be afraid but to do it anyway.

I didn't even know he sailed. Then again, how well did I know him? When his girlfriend spoke up at the funeral, I realized I'd been a stupid fool. Marcus was all talk when it came to me. He strung me along, and that hurt worse.

Now he was gone, and Lex was gone, and I raged at both of them for it.

That's when I met Miri. The granddaughter to the British crown through the king's second child, Miri had all the fame but none of the responsibility. Like me, she knew what it was to stand in front of hundreds of flashing bulbs, smiling until your cheeks hurt and your retinas burned, even as your toes cramped from the heels you'd shoved your feet in because they were made by some intolerable fashion-forward asshat. The queen had sent her to the States after a car accident killed her parents and left her orphaned.

She strut into my dorm room on that first day, her dark hair pulled into a ponytail and her pink frilly dress poofed around her, matching luggage in tow. "Hello, darling."

I'd never met anyone I was more intimidated by. With her perfect grin and soulful chestnut eyes, I didn't know if I wanted to be her or marry her. Probably both.

"I'm Miriam," she said. "But you can call me Miri."

I knew *of* her. Everyone did. But despite the titles our parents held, I'd never met her before. I smiled and offered, "Ivy."

"I know." She walked to the twin bed on the other side of the room and sat, crossing her legs. "We're to be roommates."

"There must have been a mix-up at the registrar. I usually have a single."

"You didn't want me here?" Her brows furrowed, and she tilted her head.

"No. It's easier to be by myself. Friends are"—I sighed and ran a hand over my neck, covering my X—"difficult to come by."

"Well, how fortuitous," she said. "I don't have any friends, either."

I snorted, amused by her charm and lack of boundaries.

"It's a bit karmic, yes?" she said. "You and me?"

"Sure," I agreed, playing along with her.

"We should set some ground rules about the room."

"Okay," I said. "What did you have in mind?"

"Well, for starters, if you're going to bring someone back, do me the courtesy of letting me know. I'll give you your privacy if you do the same for me."

I tried not to laugh.

Someone?

I was seventeen, and I'd only been kissed by one person—my archnemesis, Lucifer incarnate. There would be no bringing anyone back to my room.

"That's not necessary," I told her. "I don't date."

"What? Like never?"

"Never."

Her eyes widened and she dropped her jaw open, clearly shocked by my admission. "Why the bloody hell not?"

I shifted in my seat. "Kind of hard when the secret service has to do a background check anytime someone gets within five feet." It wasn't totally the truth, but if I told her about Marcus, she'd feel bad. Usually, everyone felt bad when I talked about Marcus.

Miri tilted her head again and ran her gaze over me from head to toe, her hands on the mattress edge as she leaned her weight forward. She tucked bottom lip under her teeth like she wanted to say something but purposely held back.

As for other rules, Miri didn't have a bedtime or any kind of routine. She got up when she wanted, ignoring silly things like breakfast or first session. More than once, I'd had to get out of bed to turn her alarm off because she slept right through the damn thing.

Despite these personality quirks, we grew close that year. We had similar positions about things like dirty laundry (a pile on the floor) and taking plates back to the kitchen (once a month was fine, right?). For the first time since Marcus died, I'd found someone other than my siblings who understood me.

Miri reminded me of the bite of lingering winter air on a cool spring morning. She wore floral patterns and bright pastel colors, but she had a tempestuous dark side to her, especially when it came to sex. She didn't see the point in forming lasting attachments, not when her soul and spirit were free.

She wanted to have lovers in every country, all over the world. Men, women, it didn't matter. She loved people, and she loved to be loved. She wanted to be the gorgeous independent starlet with a hundred children who lounged by the pool in her seventies, looking not a day over forty, amused by the gossip over whether she was a witch because she never aged.

I fell for her instantly.

"What about Quinton Rockefeller?" she asked months later during study hall. We sat in the library, our books spread out on the table in front of us, though studying was the least of what we were doing. She was gossiping, and I was reading the latest edition of *The Puck.*

"In love with his car," I said, flipping the page.

"Ivy Washington Eating Her Feelings?" read the headline. *"Sources close to her say she's depressed after the death of Marcus Fairfax, son of Vice President Kellan Fairfax. They were close and his death hit her hard. She's put on at least forty pounds."*

I ignored the stab in my gut and the hot flash in my cheeks. They'd taken an unflattering shot of me from an awkward angle and slapped right there for everyone to see. My blood pumped through my veins, deafening in my ears. Was I really so out of shape? And even if I was, did my body define my worth in the eyes of America?

"Ivy?" Miri said. "Are you listening, darling?"

I blinked back tears and closed the magazine, forcing a smile as I tried to remember the question. She snatched the tabloid out of my hands and read the headline for herself.

"I don't know why you entertain this rubbish," she said. "Marcus Fairfax? Oh, that was the vice president's son, yeah?"

I cleared my throat and dug my fingers into my eyes, hating that I still cried over him, ashamed that I couldn't shake this hole inside my chest at the thought of his wasted future.

At least, it wasn't Lex. At least, I still have him.

I tried to shush that voice and trap it in a dark part of my soul, never to return to the light of day. Shame burned through me, hot and scalding, and I swallowed against a dry throat as I smothered the agony in my chest.

"Didn't he have a boating accident or something?" She glanced back up at me, watching my reaction carefully.

"It capsized." My voice shook, and I cleared my throat. "He hit his head underwater."

"Oh." She crinkled her nose as she read the headline again. "These bastards." She flipped to another page. "Look at this. Princess Miriam hates her American life and wishes to return to England, but the king says to stay away. Is she being ostracized?" Miri rolled her eyes and tossed it into the closest trash can. "Do yourself a favor and never open one of those again."

I pulled my politician mask up around me, shutting down my emotions and pretending like it didn't sting to know other people made entertainment out of my grief. The public could be so cruel and heartless.

She grabbed my hand and squeezed. "You know, my parents died when I was fourteen."

"I remember," I said. "My parents went to the funeral."

She tightened her fingers around mine. "What they didn't print in the papers, the true story, is that I was in the car with them when it happened."

I didn't know this part. They said she'd been in a different car and her parents were alone.

"I survived because I ducked down to hide from the photographers. When the car crashed, I was knocked out, and when I woke up, I was outside the vehicle, fifty meters away." She took a deep breath, leaning in closer to me. "The police said I must have crawled out the window after the accident. I was too undamaged to have been thrown. But I would have remembered if I did."

I narrowed my eyes.

"To this day, I don't know what happened. Maybe someone pulled me from the wreckage. Maybe I did crawl. But I do know things happen for a reason, Ivy." She shrugged, her lips pulling into a sympathetic smile. "Some of us live. Some of us die. Who's to say who will be next? But you and me? We're still here. And death's a fickle bitch, so let's not worry about the opinions of others, yes?" She wiped away the tears on my cheek and brushed my hair behind my ear. "We have more important things to attend to...like whom you plan to invite into your bed."

She obviously meant it as a joke, and I choked out a laugh, wiping away the hint of tears at the corners of my eyes.

"We've gone through every eligible guy in our age group," she said. "Let's discuss the ladies."

"Miri, part of the reason I don't date is because of this. Anyone I bring into my life is going to be on the front of some magazine. Our entire relationship will be on display."

"It doesn't have to be a big deal, you know." She narrowed her beautiful brown eyes and gave me a saucy look, curling her lips into an adorable, devilish grin. "Kissing. Touching. Sex. It's fun. It's them that makes it a thing." She gestured to everyone around us, everyone who *wasn't* us.

Another, more terrible, thought ricocheted through my mind, one involving Miri and a tangle of sheets and her soft delicate skin pressed so firmly against mine. Maybe I wanted to kiss *her*. Maybe I wanted her to show me how much of a big deal it *could* be. My cheeks burned as I zeroed in on her mouth, her full, pouty lips that looked so bitable and soft.

No, I chided myself. *She's your roommate. Stop that.*

I clenched my thighs together, trying to soothe the churning ache between them, and hushed thoughts like that away, determined to find someone else to help me figure those things out.

Her phone buzzed and she startled, taking a step away from me so she could grab it and look at the caller ID. She sighed and righted herself before running a hand through her wild curls and bringing the phone to her ear.

"Hello, Gran," she said.

Gran.

The queen of England. The one Miri had to answer to. The one pulling all of her strings.

"Oh, I'm fine," she said, grinning softly to herself.

Even if Miri wanted to kiss me (or more) in return, I couldn't have thoughts like that about her. I was young and naive. She was... well, she was *everything*. Miri and I were better as friends. Her Gran would never allow anything else, nor would my mother.

Knowing that did not make it easier to pretend that I hadn't thought about it or that I didn't keep thinking about it anytime I masturbated. I'd stood idly by while she went through partner after partner every day, suggesting I should do the same.

"We're young," she said. "Play the field while you can."

For a late bloomer like me, that talk with Miri reset my expectations and my determination. It was almost like I had something to prove, like I needed to confirm to myself that I *wasn't* in love with my best friend and I *didn't* pine for her every goddamned day. I threw myself into trying to lose my virginity, and by the end of the month, I had managed to make out with three separate individuals and even gave a blow job to a guy in my theater class. He'd wanted to go down on me afterward, but I still had trouble trusting people I didn't know, so I declined. Miri berated me about it for the rest of the year. By graduation, I hadn't made much progress, and Miri had given up on me.

"You're a lost cause," she said, "and I won't be bothered with it anymore."

"Well, thank God." I snorted out a laugh. "It was starting to get old."

We spent the final night of term at a party in a friend's dorm. In the morning, she'd head back to the UK for a very important dinner with the king and queen, and I'd go home to Mount Vernon. We both planned to attend college at Thomas Washington University in the fall. It would only be a few months apart, but even that felt like a lifetime.

"You don't know what you're missing. But—" She giggled as she leaned in closer to me. "It's your life. Do who you want."

We were shit-faced, stumbling our way back to our room. What time was it? I hadn't checked in ages. Frankly, I was surprised she was still with me. I thought she would have found someone else to mess around with by now.

"I told Quinton I'd meet up with him tomorrow if he gave me a joint tonight. But I'm leaving in the morning, so the joke's on him." We laughed as we walked. "Let's smoke it before we go. For old time's sake."

"I have that press thing as soon as I get home." I fumbled with the lock on our door.

"Even better," she said. "Everyone will think you're the coolest Washington. Maybe they'll finally leave you alone."

"Har har." I pushed the entry open, and she walked ahead of me, dancing her fingertips down the side of my arm and sending goose pimples over that entire side of my body. Grabbing my hand, she tugged me inside and let the door close on its own behind us.

The soft glow from the lamp next to my bed illuminated the dark space, casting Miri in shadows as she twirled to face me, her rose-colored skirt puffing around her. I leaned against the wall to watch, admiring the way her playful expression made my heart beat a heady staccato.

"Why are you looking at me like that, darling?"

I shook my head and sighed, crossing over to my bed so I could collapse on top of the pillows. "No reason."

"Lies," she said. "Now I'm even more intrigued."

"You could be out with anyone right now. Why are you here with me?"

"Because I love you." She bounced over and hopped into the bed next to me, turning on her back so we both stared up at the ceiling. "You're my best friend, Ivy, perhaps my only friend, and it's our last night together."

Miri interlaced her fingers with mine next to my thigh and turned her head to face me. I turned mine to face her. We were so close that her breath coasted across my lips and nose. She smelled like her perfume and wine and whatever it was that made her *Miri*.

At first, the expression was friendly—a coy smile on her lips, the drunken haze in her eyes. Then she rolled on her side and scooted closer, her features softening. The yearning thing between us blazed to life inside of my chest, aching and pulsing with need for her.

"Will you let me kiss you?" she whispered, so low I barely heard her.

I balked, my jaw falling open. I didn't know how to answer that. *Yes. Probably. Maybe? No? Maybe yes. Maybe no.*

"Do you want to?" I tripped over the words, voice shaking, every part of me unsure and trembling in anticipation of her rejection.

"Yes."

"Then yes."

She rolled into me, devouring my lips as if she'd been as starved for me as I was for her. I kissed her back, my head whirling and my heart racing. When she climbed on top of me with her knees on either side of my hips, I pretended the surge of energy to my cunt had more to do with the alcohol than the beautiful girl. I had convinced myself these bubbling emotions in my chest had been a product of hormones, an influx of oxytocin at the proximity to her. Nothing more.

But now? No, this was different. As I moaned into her mouth and ran my hands over her body, greedily touching whatever I wanted, I let myself admit I was bisexual. I liked kissing boys, but I definitely loved this.

When she broke away to drag her tongue down the side of my neck, all the sexual neurons in my brain fired. I'd let Miri do whatever she wanted to me, and afterward, I'd do whatever I wanted to her.

She cupped my breasts, pushing them up so she could bite the tops, and I arched into the contact, desperate for more of her, desperate for this. My thighs trembled when she ducked down farther, tugging at the fabric of my panties and yanking them over my ankles.

Once they were off, she trailed kisses over my thighs and toward my pelvis. I'd never been this exposed to *anyone* else before, and when she ran her hands toward my pussy, my legs quivered under her palms.

She giggled and looked up at me, dipping her fingertips between my legs and ghosting over my most sensitive spot. "Are you nervous?"

I nodded, but my mouth was too dry to talk.

"Oh, darling," she said, pressing a small kiss to the inside of my knee. "You're beautiful." Another kiss closer to my pussy. "And I love you." A nibble on the skin right *there*.

She smiled and licked me, and when she circled her lips around my clit, I jerked off the bed from the jolt of hot, fiery electricity that went up my spine. I pressed my palms into my eyes and laughed at myself.

I'm a mess.

She echoed my joy and did it again, but this time, I moaned and urged her on. I tunneled my fingers in her hair, praying this feeling never ended.

With Miri, it was effortless. I didn't have to worry about whether she would run and tell someone about this. I knew she wouldn't. She would protect me, protect *this*. And when she pressed two fingers against my entrance, against the place no one had ever touched me before, I nudged her on.

It was right with her. We were friends, roommates...soulmates. It was only as she pushed inside of me and brushed the flat of her tongue over my clit again that absolute happiness filled every inch of my soul. She was here. She was giving this to me, this intimacy, this pleasure.

One finger became two, slowly in, and slowly out. Then she found the spot inside of me that had me arching my back and moaning her name.

"Yes," I said. "God, yes."

My climax hit me hard and unexpectedly. I'd heard most women didn't orgasm their first time, and whether it was because it was Miri or because she knew what she was doing, I didn't care. I sank into it with a fury. I let it pull me under its weight, and when I resurfaced, Miri kissed the insides of my legs and grinned. "How was that, darling?"

"Amazing," I said, breathing down the intensity of my hormones. My focus caught on the soft shade of chestnut in her hair, the moonlight filtering in through the windows and making it glisten and shimmer. It reflected the same glint in her mahogany eyes.

Was there anyone more beautiful in the world than her? Could there ever be?

She crawled up my body and kissed me, tasting like sex and alcohol and me. I wanted to return the favor. I wanted to taste *her*. I flipped us so she was under me, and she let out a squeal that made me chuckle and run my hands down the sides of her body. I ducked under the hem of her skirt and inched the fabric higher. When I brushed against skin, she smiled into the kiss and pulled back to look at me.

I lowered my shoulders under her knees and licked her the way she'd done. This was the first time I'd ever gone down on a girl, but I listened to her reactions and paid more attention to the spots that made her clench her fists. Turning her on turned me on, and I wanted more.

"Right there," she murmured when I sucked at a sensitive spot, and she said, "Yes, fuck yes," when I fingered her. I made her come, and she scraped her nails against my scalp, clamping her legs around my head. I'd become the most powerful person who had ever existed because *I,* a mere mortal girl, could make HRH Princess Miriam fall apart.

I collapsed next to her, giggling and smiling at the levity of the night.

"How could you think I'd be anywhere else?" She shook her head and gave me another delicate wet kiss.

"I love you, Miri."

"I love you, Ivy." She kissed me again. Sated and sleepy and drunk on the passion of this newly discovered desire, we fell asleep in each other's arms.

4

LEX

LONDON

My therapist told me to find a creative outlet—photography, drawing, writing. Something to channel the rage burning inside of me. Trying to fuck it away would only land me in a messy custody battle, and trying to snort it away would put me in an urn next to my brother. Apparently, bottling it up wasn't healthy, either.

As with a lot of things in my life, I ended up where I did because of a girl. I don't even remember her name. Kylie, maybe? Karli? Something with a K and an I. It didn't matter because the point was I wanted to fuck her. She was hot and had great tits, and I wanted to see what my cock looked like in between them.

I had begrudgingly agreed to a double date with her friend, whose name I definitely forgot as soon as I learned it, and her friend's boyfriend. I hated the term *date,* as I had taken up Ivy's stance on relationships since Marcus died, but if it ended with my cock in her ass, I'd suffer through worse.

Except as soon as we got there, Karli (Kolbi?) ran into her ex and his new girlfriend. "Do you think she's prettier than me?"

"Uh—" I didn't know the right thing to say. *No, right?* "No."

She rolled her eyes. "You took too long."

I was about to tell this bitch to fuck off when the other half of our double date scooted into the barstools across from us. Karli's forgettable friend and a tall, lanky dude wearing a Chicago Bears hat. I only noticed him because of the logo. It was strange to see an American football team represented this far away from the States, especially one that had never been any good. But I knew the Brits were into some American sports, so I didn't comment.

"Don't bother," Karli said. "We're leaving."

"What?" I said. "We just got here."

"Hey!" the dude said in an accent I hadn't heard in months. "You're American?"

"Yeah," I said, delighted to have someone from home to talk to. "DC."

"Chicago." He narrowed his deep indigo eyes on me. "I know you."

"Lex." I held out my hand.

"Oh, shit," he said. "Lex Fairfax. That's right. Jesus, man." He shook it and introduced himself as Carter.

"Are we friends now?" Karli said. "Can we go?"

Carter and I followed the girls out of the pub and down the block. Karli and Carter's date walked ahead of us, chattering on about the encounter with her ex.

"You been in the UK long?" he asked.

"A few months. My parents sent me to St. Thomas after the thing with my brother."

"I heard," he said. "Condolences."

"Yeah, thanks." I cleared my throat, ignoring the uncomfortable knot that formed in my chest anytime I talked about Marcus. *It should have been me.* I choked that down, filing it away in the darkest part of my heart. "What are you doing over here?"

"I'm in a student exchange with the Royal Theater Group."

"Theater?" I pulled out a cigarette and lit it, offering him one. "Like Shakespeare and shit?"

"Yeah," he said, taking the smoke.

"Which one are you doing right now?" I couldn't remember the last time I'd seen a play, much less Shakespeare.

"*Henry the Fifth*," he said. "It's running next week if you're interested."

I had probably read it sometime at Mount Oberon, but like a lot of my life before Marcus died, I'd smoked that memory away. "Are you Henry?"

"I am," he said, beaming with pride.

I sized him up. He was about the same height as me, maybe an inch shorter at most, and had the same build. At this age, we both had long, lean limbs and matching narrow torsos that only hinted at the muscles of a manhood to come. He stuffed his dirty-blond hair under his baseball cap, his dimples catching in the light when he smiled.

Carter was truly beautiful, down to his fluffy warm soul and big stupid heart. Maybe the camaraderie came easy because we were both from the States, or maybe it was the effortless carefree way he carried himself. Everything about him drew me in. Once I was in the tractor beam, I couldn't get out. I didn't even try.

He had been performing on stage since he was a child. He loved football, cheesy horror flicks, and anything with Tom Hanks. His father, a chiropractor, and his mother, a yoga instructor, had divorced last year. He was the oldest of four children, the younger ones all girls that he'd raised after his parents split.

"Little sisters are the worst, man," he said, running a hand over the back of his head. "You wanna know what's wrong with you? *Really* wrong? Ask a little sister. They'll gut you alive."

I thought of Kit and the supernatural way she pinpointed the weakest part of anyone in her vicinity, thereby exploiting it for her own benefit. That, of course, made me think of Ivy, and I rubbed at my cheek, remembering the last time I'd seen her.

"Who do you want to win the Super Bowl this year?" he asked after we'd found another pub that suited Karli's tastes.

"I don't follow football," I said.

"What? Dude! C'mon." His features dropped. "You're killing me."

"I take it you're a Bears fan." I gestured to his hat.

"All the way."

I lit up another cigarette and took a drink of my beer as he went on about some guy I'd never heard of being the G.O.A.T. Fucking hell, but my therapist was right. I did need an outlet, but it wasn't some stupid shit like photography or drawing.

It was a normal friend.

How ridiculous to come halfway across the world to find one from my own backyard.

He made me laugh in a deep belly guffaw that poured out of me in big, hearty waves. We talked about sports and superhero movies, and not once did he bring up my family or my brother or any of the other bullshit people usually asked about. Perhaps that could have been because we were in a foreign country and no one gave a shit about my last name. Or maybe that's who Carter was at his core, warm and kind and empathetic—the way a crackling autumn fire invites you to snuggle up next to it with blankets and hot cocoa.

It was the exact opposite of me. I was the dark void of a black hole, and I wanted to suck all that light right out of Carter Scott. Devour it whole.

It was sometime around beer number four that we remembered we'd been there with dates.

"Oh, shit." Carter looked down at his phone. "I've got six missed calls from Mindy."

I had a text from Karli saying she'd had a good time, but it wasn't going to work out. I figured that was polite considering I'd ignored her most of the night in favor of her friend's boyfriend.

"Are you two dating?"

"No," he said. "Just a hookup."

"Guess you lost out, huh?"

"Nah." He gave someone across the bar a nod and a wave. "I think we can still score if you're into it."

I was, and we ended up hammered back at a girl's place.

I rubbed my face as my hookup slinked down to her knees in front of me, wrapping her lips around the tip of my cock, the world tilting on its axis considering how much I'd had to drink. I refocused on Carter, sitting on the couch to my left, his girl riding him while he dug his fingers into her hips.

This wouldn't be the first time I'd fucked in the same room as someone else. It wouldn't even be the first time I partner-swapped, if the girls were into it. My parents were liberal, and I'd gone to one of those snooty new age boarding schools. I didn't like labels, but I did like sex. All sex. With everyone. Boys. Girls. Cute little enbies. As with everything else, I didn't give a fuck what society thought of where I stuck my dick.

But Carter Scott still managed to shock the shit out of me. After I fucked my girl into a coma, she passed out on the chaise at the far end of the room, leaving me, Carter, and his brunette to our own devices. I lit a cigarette and let my head fall back on the couch, my mind struggling to focus on reality.

You know, the one where I'd met a guy at a bar and went back to some random girl's apartment with him. The one where he currently had a finger on this girl's clit and her tongue down his throat.

They stopped and looked at me, catching me staring.

Carter smiled, making my cock twitch at the sight of those dimples. The girl echoed his grin.

An invitation...don't mind if I do.

I stood, anticipation flaming through me as I walked closer and stabbed the cigarette in a nearby ashtray. I sat down next to my new buddy and watched the girl's tits bounce as she rocked against him.

"Do you want her?" Carter asked. "You can have her if you want. Right, sweetheart?"

The girl bit playfully at her finger and nodded.

"Hmm." I had different plans entirely. "How does she taste?"

"Like heaven," he said.

"Let's see about that. Turn around."

She did, bringing her back up against Carter's chest and her knees on the outside of his thighs, her sweet pussy exposed and ready for me. I kneeled in front of them, spearing my fingers through her folds and tracing my greedy hands over the spot where his cock slid into her.

I licked her clit, and she groaned, her fingers going for my hair. I did it again, taking my time in one long languid stroke. She squirmed, writhing and bucking into the touch, but it was Carter's reaction that fascinated me. I licked closer to his shaft, not quite touching it, but just enough to tease.

I wanted him antsy. I wanted him waiting for it, knowing it would come, and I laughed out a breath when he shivered. This time, I sampled everything—from the spot where his balls met his cock all the way up her pretty little slit. Their collective groan sent a zing of pride down my spine, and I watched as Carter's legs trembled.

"Fuck me," he said in a slow groan.

"Yes," she said, rocking her pelvis into it. Then the sound of a muffled ringtone cut through the air and she froze. "Shit. That's my dad. They're supposed to be in Paris."

She sprang off Carter like the world had caught fire, his cock bouncing out of her and nearly smacking me in the chin. The girl scrambled to her purse, found her phone, and disappeared behind a closed door at the end of the hallway, leaving me alone with this gorgeous throbbing problem inches from my face.

I looked up Carter's body from my spot between his knees, and his eyes darkened, something sinful passing behind those indigo irises as an eyebrow rose halfway up his forehead.

Another invitation?

I licked my lips, tasting both her and him, and my heart pounded as I waited for him to give any indication that he wanted me to take care of it on my own. Who knew when that girl would be back, and the one on the chaise snored so loudly, the ceiling could come crashing down and she wouldn't wake up.

"Do you want your dick sucked, Chicago?" I ran my hands up the insides of his thighs and blew on his shaft again, making it jump.

He pushed his hands into his hair, highlighting the muscles in his chest and his arms, and let out a long sigh. "I've never done anything with a guy before."

"I'll stop if—"

"No," he quickly said, making my skin burn. "Don't stop."

I didn't. I jabbed my forearm into his lower stomach and grabbed his balls with my other hand. He made a deep noise when I licked him from root to tip and sucked him deep, a noise that I knew would live in my head from that day on—half moan, half growl, all Carter.

I wanted him disheveled and clenching the couch cushions, a slave to his pleasure and knowing I was the one who made him that way. I wanted to taste him and consume him and find that thing that made him shine so brightly. Maybe I could use it to rekindle my own will to live.

He fisted his fingers in my hair and bucked his hips into me when he came in hot spurts down my throat. I let him use my mouth the way he wanted, swallowing down everything he gave me, and when he was done, I sat back on my haunches and grinned.

All that pale Irish skin had turned splotchy and red, reminding me of the fiery X on Ivy's neck, and his chest heaved while he panted down his release.

"God damn," he said. "I can't believe that."

"Don't sweat it, man," I said to him, giving him a little pat on the center of his chest. "Everyone experiments. It doesn't mean—"

"Come here." He pulled me up his body and kissed me. No hesitation. No qualms about me being a guy. Although I did just have his cock in my mouth, so we were well past propriety.

He cupped the back of my neck and dove his tongue into my mouth, his smoky sandalwood scent pluming around me. Then, he rearranged me so I sat next to him and he hovered over my torso.

"My turn," he said.

"Wait," I cut in. He froze and looked up at me as he sat between my feet, his arms splayed over my thighs with his big palms across my stomach. My angry cock throbbed at my protest, but I had to say it. "I didn't do that so you'd do it to me."

"Then why you'd do it?"

"Because I wanted to see what it looked like to break you apart."

He curled his lips into a brief smile before he darted out his tongue and flicked at my tip. An electric pulse shot through me, making me hiss, and I damn near jumped off the couch. "That sounds good enough to me."

He sucked me in deep, and I let out a groan from somewhere in the pit of my gut. My head fell back on the couch as a wave of fiery euphoria sizzled through my blood.

Good. Fucking. God.

For someone who'd never sucked dick before, Carter figured things out quickly. His mouth was hot and warm and soft, and when I told him to suck faster and harder, he followed directions. I ran my fingers through his soft blond locks and exploded down his throat in an embarrassingly fast amount of time. When he was done, he released me with a loud *pop*. I grabbed the back of his neck and yanked him up my body, wanting—no, *needing*—to taste myself on him.

I should have felt ashamed at the way I so callously corrupted such a bright, innocent soul. But that thing, that *whatever it was,* tugged deep down inside of my chest. It reminded me of the time I'd kissed Ivy on the banks of the Potomac River, like a vibrant foreboding, as if there was a part of me that was also a part of Carter, and this night had poked that dormant side awake.

The sound of a door opening broke our connection, and he sprang off me, wiping his mouth with the back of his hand.

"Shit," the girl said. She snatched up my shirt and pants on her way back over to us. "You two need to go. Now."

"What?" Carter said. "It's two in the morning."

"My father is going to be home in ten minutes. He can't find you here." She shoved my clothes at me and picked up Carter's to force them into his arms. "Come on. Go! Go!"

We made quick work of getting dressed, laughing as we shoved our legs into our pants and pulled our shirts over our heads. She opened the door, but her father was already on the other side, raising his hand to put the key in the lock.

Busted.

She shoved us around the old man, and he stormed inside, slamming the door and squawking at her drunk friend to get up. Carter and I stumbled into the night, barely able to stop giggling long enough to figure out where we were.

I couldn't remember the last time I'd felt so light. Since Marcus died? Never?

"I'm just a few blocks up that way," Carter said, matching my pace as we headed toward the major intersection.

"I'm out near Kensington." I grabbed my phone and texted my driver my location. He replied his estimated ETA was five minutes. Then a brief moment of awkwardness fell on us while we played *call me* chicken.

"You should come to the show next week," he said. "It's one of the better ones, as far as the histories go."

"Yeah?" I shoved my hands in my pockets. "Yeah, maybe."

Another heartbeat passed.

I should ask for his number. I should ask him to come back to my place and see what other parts he'd let me lick.

But I didn't know what that pulsing, aching thing inside me was. It terrified me.

"When are you going back to the States?" I asked instead.

"The end of the semester is in two weeks. I'll go back to Chicago for the summer, then I'm off to TW."

"No shit." The hairs on the back of my neck rose. "Me, too."

He narrowed his eyes. "Are you fucking with me?"

"No, man," I said. "My whole family went there. It was either TW or Harvard, and the winters in New England are almost as terrible as the winters in the Midwest."

"Bite your tongue, blasphemer," he said.

Amusement tickled through me.

"All right," he said. "Stop dicking around. Give me your number."

"What?"

"Give me your number." He shoved his phone in my hand. "I'm not a superstitious person, but being in a foreign country and finding the only other American going to the same college as me next semester? Fate is obviously trying to tell me something. Put your digits in my phone and let me call you when I get to TW."

I pursed my lips but did as he asked, sending myself a text so I'd have his number, too.

"Happy?" I put the phone back in his hand.

"Extremely."

Whatever I would have said next died on my tongue when my driver pulled up next to us.

"You want a ride?" I asked.

"No, it's a nice night. I'll walk."

I opened my door to get in, my heart suddenly an anvil in my gut. "I guess this is goodbye."

"Come to the show," he said. "Maybe I'll give you an encore performance afterward."

"A night with the king?" I blew out a teasing breath. "I'm not worthy."

I memorized the way the moonlight twinkled in his eyes when he flashed me that killer smile one last time. "See you around, DC."

"Later, Chicago."

5

LEX

I wanted to go to the show. If I had been left alone, I would have, but life had other plans for me.

Two days after I met Carter, my parents arrived on a diplomatic trip to meet with the king and the rest of Parliament on climate change. The night I was supposed to go see the performance, my father dragged me to a royal dinner, which was a fancy way of saying I had to sit quietly and make nice faces at those society deemed worthy enough to be in the king's presence.

I'd met most of the royal family before and the princes were off at college, so I didn't think there'd be anyone of interest to me. We were halfway through the first course when the door opened and one of the staff announced, "Her Royal Highness, the Princess Miriam."

We all stood, and I rolled my eyes, annoyed she was late and I was the only one my age here. All anyone wanted to ask me about were my future plans in politics, which, at eighteen, were nonexistent.

Miri wasn't a duchess in those days, not until she officially joined the royal household. She stopped my heart all the same in her bright pink evening gown with her long brown hair in waves down her back. She reminded me of a goddess in a Botticelli painting, or maybe Venus herself, appearing out of the sea foam to make me fall in love with her the moment I set eyes on her.

I cleared my throat and tried to act like I didn't give a shit about anyone in this stupid room. I was pissed I had to be here instead of at Carter's show, and not even a hot girl could smooth it over. Even if she made my heart race when she took the seat next to me. Even if she smelled like gardens and sunshine in the spring.

"Good of you to join us," some old guy said. Miri paused for a heartbeat and timidly met that dude's gaze before forcing a smile and straightening her spine.

"Pardon my tardiness," she said. "My flight from Washington, DC was delayed." She put the linen napkin on her lap and took a drink of water. "I've only just arrived from the airport."

"Oh, what brought you to our hometown?" my mother chimed in, sipping at her wine.

"School," Miri politely said. "My uncle, the duke of McCormick" —aforementioned old dude—"arranged for me to board at a private institution there. Just for the year. Just to...clear my head."

"There's a lot of that going around," I muttered.

"Alexei," my mother snapped, giving me that look that said I needed to mind my manners. Like she was the one to talk. We'd only been here two hours, and she'd put away at least a bottle of claret by herself.

Miri's honey-brown gaze fell on me, mischief brewing behind her curious expression. "What? You too?"

Her tease made my mother squirm.

"Miriam," McCormick said. "Apologies, Madam Fairfax. My niece can be quite vocal about her disposition. Most young women would relish the opportunity to study abroad."

I sensed Miri had a million retorts, but she said none of them.

"As always, dear uncle, I concede to your wise counsel. Perhaps an overture to walking up stairs next?" It was a taunt at the recent viral video of him tripping up a flight of steps on his way to a meeting, but she'd said it in such a lighthearted, innocent way that the entire table took it as friendly banter. Someone else made a crack at McCormick's expense, and the conversation went on around us.

"Alexei went to boarding school around DC," my mother said. "Which one did you attend? Perhaps you know some of the same people."

"DC's a big place, Mother."

"You're Alexei Fairfax, yes?" Miri said. "Your brother was Marcus?"

Bringing up Marcus, especially in front of my mother, was like dumping lava on ice cream. We'd be a melted, sopping mess in point five seconds.

It should have been me.

My mother took another long pull on her drink, and I stabbed at a cucumber on my plate, stuffing it into my mouth with a loud crunch, trying not to give in to the demon hissing at me from the depths of its cage in my heart.

It should have been me. It should have been me.

"I was roommates with Ivy Washington at Mount Oberon," Miri explained.

The cucumber lodged in my throat, and I coughed, reaching for my water so I could gulp it down.

"Oh, we know Ivy," my mother cooed, a bright smile widening cheek to cheek. "She and Alexei are old friends."

I tried to clear my windpipe, resisting the urge to balk at the casual way my mother called us friends. We weren't friends. I hated Ivy Washington. I always had. The last time I saw her, she'd slapped the shit out of me.

"Friends?" Miri said, her eyes twinkling. "You don't say?" She gathered salad on her fork and brought it to her mouth, shooting me a playful look that said she knew the truth but had decided to go along with my mother's claim. I could only imagine what Ivy must have told her. She'd probably painted me as some kind of monster who skinned puppies and ate their still-beating hearts. But Miri carried along with polite conversation, entertaining the stories of Ivy and me as children, running through the residence while our parents talked shop, our siblings somewhere in tow.

Miri thrilled me. She played the princess part so well that I almost believed it. But it was that roguish look in her eye that intrigued me the most, like it was all a joke, and she was the only one in on it.

After dinner, the politicians and royal figureheads convened in the parlor while the queen escorted the spouses and children to another room for tea. Miri broke off from the herd and slipped out of her shoes, prancing on the balls of her feet down a dark corridor of Buckingham Palace, her heels dangling from one hand and the fabric of her skirt in the other.

Then she stopped, turned to me, and smiled, nodding like I should follow her.

I didn't even think about it. My feet moved on their own.

She led me through several rooms and down a stairwell hidden behind a massive oil painting, the service access judging by the plain white walls and matching railings. We descended two flights and went out a side door, cool night air hitting me in the face as spring gave way to summer in England. We sulked to a corner of the palace where the east wing met the main corridor and ducked farther into the shadows.

"What the fuck are we doing out here?" I asked.

"*We* are not doing anything. *I* am smoking weed. *You* are keeping me company." She plopped a joint between her lips and sparked a lighter. I took the opportunity to light a cigarette myself, resisting the urge to laugh. *Look at this. Bonafide royalty. A pothead.*

"I need a good buzz to get through the rest of that charade." She ran her fingers over her forehead. "Did you hear the way he talked to me? Like I'm some invalid. Like I don't know my own mind."

I inhaled deeply on my cigarette as she rambled about how horrible her family could be. They'd shipped her off to boarding school without talking to her about it, and now her uncle wanted to act like he'd known it would be good for her all along.

"I'm eighteen," she said. "Old enough to petition Pop for my estate. He's said he'll give it to me."

"What will you do with it once you have it?"

She passed me the joint, and I took it, handing my cigarette to her in exchange.

"Take care of it. I'm going to college in the States this fall, but after that? I'll join the royal household and take up my duties as my father's daughter. Rebrand the Stuart name." A sparkle glinted in her gaze as she spoke of it, like she'd wanted it forever.

"Sounds ambitious."

She paused and cast a skeptical look at me. "Ivy doesn't have great things to say about you."

I cracked a smile and shook my head. "No, I bet she doesn't."

"I thought you'd be meaner." She squinted as she made her assessment.

"That's because Ivy's a frigid bitch."

Miri let out a girlish laugh. "Careful, Lex. Ivy's my best friend."

"Christ." I let out a defeated sigh. "What does someone like you want with someone like her?"

"What's that supposed to mean?"

"You're standing outside Buckingham Palace smoking pot with a guy you met an hour ago. Cameras could catch us. Paparazzi could catch us. You don't give a fuck."

She bit her bottom lip.

"Ivy would be pissing her pants," I said.

"Don't be so sure." Miri narrowed her eyes and a hint of a small smile ghosted over her lips before she hid it away. I seized on that like a dog with a bone, that grin saying so much without saying anything at all.

What could Ivy have done to put that look on Miri's face? What memories flickered through her mind when she thought about her old roommate?

Why did I care so much?

I didn't.

Miri and I stayed outside another hour, talking about people we knew from Mount Oberon—teachers we liked, teachers we hated, people we fucked. She eventually pulled out another joint, and we smoked that, too. The munchies drove us to the kitchen, where the staff shook their heads and sighed while we raided the pantry. Which begged the question—How many other royals had gotten high as a kite and absconded with the queen's secret stash of treats?

Then we went upstairs to the rooms reserved for her whenever she wanted to stay over, a modest-size space done in pastel lavenders and soft violets. We spread our bounty out on the floor and sat around it, tearing into the candies while we talked.

I texted my mother to say Miri and I had hit it off and not to wait up. Ecstatic I found a potential high society love match, my mother agreed and left me alone for the rest of the night.

Miri and I didn't fuck. Sure, she was hot, and I would have. But much in the same way I'd needed Carter to be a normal person for one night, I sensed Miri needed that from me. I didn't know what happened between her and Ivy before she left, only that she got a wistful look anytime she brought up the ginger. I had set out to be a better, healthier person, and maybe paying it forward could be a good start.

That didn't last long, though.

The next morning, we woke up passed out on the floor together. Miri said she planned to go to her country estate in Scotland and asked if I wanted to go with her.

"You just met me."

"So?" She shrugged. "You could have been a bastard to me last night and you weren't. Despite what Ivy says, I think there's a soul in there, Alexei Fairfax, and I'm determined to find it."

There was no arguing with Miriam Stuart when she made up her mind about someone. Especially me.

"Why do you care?" I asked.

"Because you remind me of her."

I balked. "Who?"

She smiled. "Ivy."

"What?" Ivy and I couldn't be more different. She was a stuck-up do-gooder, and I'd consumed every thing I got my hands on. I bet Ivy hadn't even been drunk. We were not the same. At all. "You're fucking with me."

"You're both made of fire," she added. "She burns hot. You burn cold. A prince of darkness."

How in the hell could Miri possibly know that about me?

She'd sized me up before she even met me. She'd learned about me through my archnemesis, who hadn't done me any favors.

I found myself packed in a car on the way to Scotland while I was still explaining to her why it was a bad idea.

Miri's family owned a three-bedroom cottage just outside Aberdeen. For someone who came from royalty, I expected it to be a castle or a four-mansion complex. What I found was a stone building half covered in ivy with a gray slat roof and two chimneys sticking out from either side.

"I know it doesn't look like much," she said, climbing out of the car, "but I love it here. I'd stay full time if I could."

Pink rose bushes lined the cobblestone entryway, an old-fash-ioned wooden fence on either side. It was like stepping back in time, like I'd suddenly reverted to the eighteenth century. The inside had an open floor concept, the living area off to the left with a couple of couches and a kitchen in the far corner. The dining area was next to that, and a set of stairs to the right went to the second level that had two tiny bedrooms, the bigger one containing another fireplace.

The old secondhand furniture seemed out of place. The antique pieces had been well taken care of, but none of them matched. The portraits on the walls were a mixture of oil paintings featuring her dead relatives and oversize canvas photographs—some of nature, others of people I didn't recognize. It was so *her,* so out of place, and yet, intimately fascinating and unique.

"Why can't you stay here?" I asked.

She sighed and dropped her purse on the table next to the door. "Gran says I need to keep up appearances. I can't vanish into the Highlands."

"Fuck." I fingered a ceramic trinket on her mantel. "We could vanish here together."

She arched a brown eyebrow and bit her bottom lip. "What does Alexei Fairfax have to escape from?"

I snorted. "Everything."

"I'll tell you what." She hummed a playful sigh and took a step closer to me, linking her arms behind her back. It made her arch forward and push her breasts out so I'd notice. And I did. "I'll let you vanish here whenever you want...for a price."

Something hot flushed through me, straight down my spine and into my balls.

At eighteen, I'd fuck anything, and even if I promised myself I'd be respectful, I wouldn't turn her down if *she* came onto *me.* Besides, she was a beautiful princess. I'd be an absolute moron if I didn't take her up on whatever she offered.

I raised an eyebrow, matching her playfulness with my own. "Oh? What could Her Royal Highness possibly want?"

She leaned in close, pressing her forehead to the side of my jaw, her hand on my shoulder. Overheated breath spilled down that side of my body when she whispered, "A kiss."

She tunneled her hands through the back of my thick locks, drawing me closer to her lips. When she pressed that perfect little mouth against mine, I moaned and collapsed into the touch, wrapping my arms around her waist.

Sure, less than forty-eight hours ago I'd been on a date with Karli that had ended with my mouth around Carter's cock, but literal eons had passed between then and now. The present seemed so immediate and the past so far away. No one knew me the way Miri did.

My dick pulsed and something fiery and wanton raced through my veins, and when I moved to unbutton her jeans, she pulled away from me.

It was there for just a second—the sadness, the heartbreak, the tender vulnerability buried deep inside her. Even when she forced a smile, shook her head, and looked down, avoiding my questioning gaze.

Had I done something?

No. I couldn't have.

"Come on." She nodded toward the back door. "I'll show you the best part."

I half expected her to take me to her bedroom to finish whatever we'd started, but she didn't. She took me out back and showed me her garden. The groundskeeper started it for her since she'd been away at school, but she liked to be the one to maintain it in the summer before she went back.

"It's soothing," she said, cupping a purple flower and bending at the waist to smell it, her wavy brown hair falling over her shoulder. "Being here. Tending to my plants."

I had to admit that the scenery was beautiful. Enormous emerald mountains surrounded us on either side, heather swaying and whistling in the wind. As much of a city dweller as I was, a sense of serenity fell over me, making me lighter. Free.

"One of my nannies used to say the trees know all." She smiled, her eyes drifting shut while she soaked up the memory. "Sometimes, when I'm alone here, I think I can hear them talking. Silly, I know, but I swear it's true."

I didn't know what to say to that, so I took it how she meant it and tried to listen for the trees myself. I didn't hear anything.

A few moments passed in silence until I finally said, "Why did you bring me here, Miri?"

She shrugged. "Maybe you could use some peace, too."

Turned out, I could.

We spent the rest of the night getting high and chain-smoking cigarettes, telling each other stories that made me laugh until my sides hurt. Occasionally, my thoughts went to Carter. Beautiful, radiant Carter. How was he doing? Did he think of me? I regretted not texting him, and now it seemed like too little, too late, especially after I didn't come to the show. I rectified that shame by indulging myself with Miri. We were kindred spirits, complementary contrasting colors painted next to each other. A bright pastel pink against the darkest obsidian.

It was easy between us, and even at the beginning, it felt like it would always be *easy* between us. I didn't have to hide around her. I could say whatever I wanted or whatever I meant, and she took it in stride. Where I held a certain level of competitiveness with Ivy, Miri didn't bring that out in me. She calmed me, just by being herself.

This was part of her enigma. The world labeled her a slut, a misguided youth who had survived the loss of her parents by partying and sleeping around. Who could blame her, right? The royal family's greatest blight. One so big, they hid her in the States for the better part of a year. But underneath that scrutiny, she wanted nothing more than to smoke pot at her cottage and tend to her garden. Such a simple creature.

One night, two weeks after we arrived, we were cooking dinner together. Or rather, Miri cooked, and I stood around with my hands in my pockets while she rambled.

"And then I told him, those are quite the same, isn't it?" She crinkled her nose and shook her head, stirring the sauce in the pot with a wooden spoon. She'd pulled her hair back into a ponytail and wore a cute pink apron I wanted to rip off.

We'd made out a few times since we'd been here, but nothing serious and definitely nothing below the belt. It didn't bother me, though. Which surprised the fuck out of me. The only other girl I'd ever spent any amount of time around without fucking was Ivy.

Not that I wanted to fuck Ivy the way I wanted to fuck Miri.

Definitely not.

If I had to guess, I'd say Miri was heartbroken about someone and was using me as a distraction. Honestly, I'd been doing the same to her.

"Why are you looking at me like that?" she asked, narrowing her eyes. "Like you're about to gobble me up."

I shrugged. "Maybe I am."

She raised an eyebrow and pursed her lips, returning to her sauce on the stove.

"Where did you learn to cook?"

"My nanny," she said. "One of them." A brief silence. "You know I'm going to TW, right? I don't know if I ever told you that."

Hot blooded excitement shot through me, but I played it cool. "Oh?"

"Ivy and I are going to room together again." Another long silence. "Are you still planning to go there?"

"Yep."

This time the pause was pregnant with the *what-ifs* and *what-could-bes* between us. It had accumulated over the course of these last few days, in the times we'd gotten close, only for her to pull away at the last second.

"I don't do relationships," she said. "You being here is the longest I've ever spent around someone alone." She laughed. "Except for Ivy. I suppose that's why it works, isn't it? Because sex isn't involved."

"I could say the same," I added.

"Do you despise me as much as you pretend to despise her?" Miri raised an eyebrow and grinned.

I took a step closer and brushed a piece of hair out of her face. "Never, Princess."

The sound of her laughter rattled through me, putting a smile on my face. She curled her body into mine, wrapping her arms around my waist so she could rest her head on my chest. "Would you want me, Alexei? I'm not saying forever. I get bored with people rather quickly."

I sighed, warmth settling in my stomach at the thought of having her all to myself, at least for a little while. "Me, too."

"But let's try, yes?" She looked up at me. "You and me? If we get bored, we'll tell each other. No hard feelings."

I let her kiss me, relishing in the warm embrace of her delicate lips. When she sagged into my touch, I wrapped my fingers around the back of her thighs and lifted her into my arms. She wrapped herself around me. She was so warm and inviting, and when my cock throbbed against her warm cunt, I thought I'd lose control and fuck her like I hadn't touched anyone in ages.

She reached in between us, unbuttoning my pants, grabbing me, and slipping me inside her while we were both still clothed. I fucked her right there on the kitchen counter, inhaling her exhales, kissing her anywhere I could get my mouth. When we came, we came together. She yanked at my legs, forcing me deeper inside her, our mouths inches apart. It hit me like a ton of bricks, right down my spine and exploding behind my eyes.

Pleasure and euphoria and something uniquely profound.

Like this moment was special, and I needed to pay attention to it.

After we came back down to Earth and salvaged what we could from the burned meal, Miri took me outside, and we made love again under the clear night sky.

6

IVY

FALL - FRESHMAN YEAR

"I have something to tell you," Miri said. She'd been back in town for two days, and even though I'd missed her, I hadn't realized how much until she was here, like a piece of me had safely found its way home.

We didn't talk about the last time we'd seen each other. We hadn't mentioned it when we'd spoken over the summer, and we didn't talk about it for the two whole days we'd spent catching up. This did not stop me from wanting her. Her mahogany eyes shimmered in the sunlight, her dark curls catching just right so the red undertone stood out. I ached to run my hands through it, pull her head back, and devour her lips. I wanted to pull her into my bed and spend days there making up for lost time. I had fallen tragically in love with her, and one summer apart didn't change that.

Still, I swallowed all that down for the sake of our platonic relationship. I'd rather have her in my life as my best friend than not at all, and given the fact that she'd moved on with someone else, I figured hope for the two of us had ended the same night it began.

Now, we sat at a four-top in the food court at TW, Miri directly across from me.

"Okay." I stuffed a fry in my mouth, wary of her ominous tone.

"I've been seeing someone," she said.

"You told me. Your mystery lover." I tried not to let my disappointment show, hiding my emotions behind deflection and forced happiness the way I'd always done. I hadn't exactly waited for her either, and if this new person had brought her some sort of peace, then I wanted to be happy for her.

Miri wrung her hands and clenched them into fists in front of her.

"Okay, out with it," I said. "Who is it? George Clooney? Brad Pitt? C'mon. Just tell me."

"Long time, X," came the voice from behind me.

I straightened. Every hair on my body stood on end.

Lex Fairfax.

My enemy. My archnemesis. The only boy to ever kiss me. He'd stolen my first and acted like it meant nothing. *The audacity.*

He took the seat next to Miri and wrapped an arm over the back of her chair. I'd admit, he looked good. Healthy. Happy. No deep, dark bags under his eyes. No perpetual smirk between his brows. His dark hair hung over his forehead, longer than I remembered, but still shiny and thick.

"Hello, darling." Miri gave him a kiss.

"Hello, Princess," Lex murmured against her mouth.

My heart dropped into my stomach as I caught up to reality. All the puzzle pieces locked into place. Miri had gone home for that fancy royal dinner with some US politicians, who I now knew must have been Lex's parents. Lex was already in London, and he had stayed there for the summer. In Scotland. With Miri.

All the stories she'd told me. It was all Lex. All of it.

God.

Venom raced through my veins, hot and fiery, and I set my glare on him, wishing not for the first time that I could shoot bullets out of my eyes. He didn't deserve her. He barely deserved the air she breathed. How dare he take my best friend from me?

"Him?" I snarled.

"Ivy," she tried.

"You're dating Lex Fairfax?" I kept my voice calm and level, even as it shook with jealous disbelief.

"Ivy, darling. Please, listen to me."

"You know he's the biggest jerk in the world, right?" My fingernails cut into my palms. I was sure I'd have half-moon imprints later.

"You realize he's sitting right here, right?" Lex cut in.

"Oh, please," I scoffed. "You've been nothing but a shit to me your whole life and you're upset I'm calling you on it in front of your shiny new girlfriend. That's called karma, Lucifer."

"That's not what karma means, X," he said. "That's called you being a frigid, stuck-up bitch."

A frigid bitch you kissed at your brother's funeral.

It was on the tip of my tongue, and I only managed to bite it back at the last second. He could see I was about to say it, his hazel eyes widening at the taunt and his lips preparing for an equally horrible retort.

But Miri didn't know Lex had been the one that who kissed me. I'd purposely kept that a secret because I didn't want to have to explain why I hated it so much. Or why I dreamed about it all the time. Or why I could still feel his mouth on mine even as we sat at that table.

Did he know about Miri and me? Would she have told him that?

No, I decided. We never talked about it, not to each other, and not to anyone else.

"Are you two quite finished?" Miri said.

I crossed my arms and squared my jaw, surprised by my reaction. Moments ago, I'd been desperate with unrequited yearning for my one true love, and now I burned with scalding fury at how Lex always ruined everything he touched. *He'll ruin her too, one day, if she let him.* I shouldn't care. I didn't.

"DC?"

A voice whipped our heads up.

There he was—six feet two, dirty-blond hair sticking out from under a backward Bears cap, amazing indigo eyes that looked like the sky at twilight, dark and shimmering, and pouty lips that curled into a boy-next-door grin. Even at eighteen, Carter Scott could bring me to my knees.

"Chicago?" There was a shimmy in Lex's voice as he said it. I doubted anyone else noticed it. Lex was good at hiding his emotions and always had been, but I'd known him my entire life. Something about this guy made him nervous and not in a bad way.

"Jesus Christ, it's you." Lex stood and wrapped his arms around his friend. "How have you been? It's good to see you."

"Good, good," Chicago said. "You look great."

"So do you. Did you get some sun? You're burned."

"Irish boy down south for the first time, you know," Chicago said.

"You never called," Lex said.

"Neither did you."

"I'm an idiot. You should have known better." Lex shook his head and gestured to us. "This is Miri and Ivy." Then, he returned to his friend. "And this is Carter. We met in London." Lex returned to his spot next to Miri. "Come. Sit."

"Actually," she cut in, "Ivy and I need to talk."

"No, it's okay, Miri," I said, suddenly intrigued by this Carter guy and specifically what about him made Lex anxious. I mean, he was gorgeous, sure, but something had gotten under Lex's skin. "I'm curious how you two know each other. You said you met in London?"

"Yeah, we were friends of friends," Lex said as Carter lowered into the seat next to me. He smelled like outside and clean clothes and sunshine, and he had this artsy frat boy vibe about him that drew me in like a child in a fairy tale who had discovered a house made of candy.

Carter told us the story about the pub and the girl with the ex-boyfriend, but I returned my attention to Lex, watching for his reaction. When Carter got to the part about going back to the girl's place and getting kicked out by her father, Lex licked his lips and one of his eyebrows twitched.

There. Right there.

X might have marked my lie, but Lex's eyes gave him away every damn time. Now, I was *very* curious. Still, I'd just met Carter, and I was lonely without Miri and fueled by hatred for Lex, so after Carter finished his tale, I gathered my books and stood.

"Well, I have an audition in an hour so…Nice to meet you, Carter," I said. "Miri, I'll talk to you back at our room. Lex, go fall off a cliff."

"Audition?" Carter asked. "You're trying out for the winter play?"

"Yeah, my mother says it'll help with my stage fright. I doubt they'll cast me. They usually don't want freshmen, but we'll see." I threw my bag over my shoulder to leave, but Carter stood, too.

"My audition's at 2:30. I'll walk with you."

"Wait," Lex cut in. "You're doing theater on top of poli-sci?"

"That's what double major means, himbo," I snarled.

Lex rubbed at the back of his head, looking between Carter and me, but I didn't wait around for any more of his commentary.

"I take it you and DC don't get along, huh?" Carter asked once we were outside, strolling across the courtyard toward the theater building.

"He's an ass."

"Oh, he's not so bad." Carter straightened and pulled his lips into a knowing grin.

"You've known him one night. I've known him eighteen years. Come talk to me then."

He smiled, and a wicked girlish lust shot through me at the hint of his dimples. He was incredibly attractive and so kind, all the alarms I had about not getting involved with anyone blared deep in the recesses of my mind. Carter would spell trouble with a capital T, and I didn't want any part of that. Still, I couldn't deny his appeal, and I desperately wanted to know the history between him and Lex.

"What monologue are you doing?" he asked, changing the subject.

We talked like drama nerds the rest of the way there. He told me about his time in the Royal Theater Company and how he'd wanted to act ever since he knew what it meant. He planned to go to LA after graduation to do it for real. TW had an amazing theater program and counted several award winners among its alumni. He talked about his younger sisters with a deep abiding affection, especially the youngest, Lizzie. It reminded me of how I felt about my sister, Abigail, and I bonded with him about being the oldest and feeling responsible for the rest.

"I try to protect them from my old man," he said.

"Me too. With my mom, I mean." We had so much in common, and I'd only known him twenty minutes.

"Yeah, I can imagine that might suck—being the president's kid."

"It's not fun." Even if I couldn't deny my privilege. I'd been afforded more than most because of it.

"My dad thinks me wanting to be an actor is a joke. Like I'm wasting my energy." Carter rolled those gorgeous dark blue eyes and shook his head. "Which only makes me want to do it more, you know? To prove him wrong."

I sighed. "My mother thinks doing this will get me more comfortable with my future role in politics. I didn't get much of a choice either way."

"I promise it's not too scary," he said. "Just imagine the audience naked."

My cheeks burned, and I widened my eyes at the mental image, nearly tripping over my own two feet. "That's—uh—that's not likely to help."

He laughed, and pride flooded the center of my chest, making me yearn for that sound again. For all that he joked about everything else, Carter took school seriously. He was here on a scholarship, so he couldn't mess it up. His look and his genuine personality initially attracted me to him, but when I found out he had goals and aspirations, I nearly wilted from how hard my knees trembled. Eighteen-year-old boys usually only had one thing on their minds, and it wasn't a career plan.

We auditioned together and even ran a few scenes at the request of the director. He thanked us for our time and dismissed us, but a natural, easy chemistry had blossomed between us on stage, almost as if it had been there all along. After it was over, we got milkshakes and figured out we were in a lot of the same classes. We even lived in the same dorm, two floors apart from each other. We agreed to study together and share notes so we could do half the work for all the grade. In a matter of a few hours, Carter Scott had weaseled his way into my life easier than anyone before him.

"If we get cast, we'll run lines together, too," he said.

"You're assuming I have all this time to spend with you, *Chicago*," I said, mocking Lex's nickname for him as I took a sip of my smoothie.

"I'm a straight-A student, and I don't dick around with my study partners. If I promise you something, I'll deliver."

I snorted. "Are we still talking about homework?" I said it before I could stop myself, realizing too late it sounded awkward and weird.

Carter wiped at my bottom lip with his thumb, coming away with a bit of milkshake. "Even if we weren't..." He winked, sucking his finger between his lips. "I'd deliver on that, too."

We locked eyes and the smile faded from my lips as his meaning settled somewhere between my thighs. How I must have looked to him—mouth open in surprise, cheeks bright red, the X on my neck burning against my windpipe. I put a hand over it to cover it up.

"What's the catch?" I asked.

"Catch?" He sucked on his straw.

"Yeah, the catch. Beautiful, smart, charming. No one has it all." I narrowed my eyes at him again. "There's got to be a catch."

"C'mon. It's the same as you, Miss Double Major." The knowing judgment in his indigo eyes rocked through me, making me tremble. "Ambition, Ivy. That's the catch."

Making up with Miri came easily, and even though I could see their mutual affection for each other in everything they did, it still bugged me she'd willingly spend her time with *Lex Fairfax*. Or touch him. Or kiss him. Or fuck him. I understood why we couldn't carry on the way we had at Mount Oberon, especially not now that she was seeing someone else, but it still chafed.

"He's different with me," she said. "I think I'm in love with him."

And that only made me more frustrated.

In love? With Lex?

"What happened to the Miri who wanted to stay single forever and retire to her country estate with fifteen dogs and a house full of plants?"

She laughed, making me want to pull her close just so I could feel its breathy weight on my skin. "That's still the fifty-year plan, but I want to live a little first and fall in love, over and over again. Right now, it's Lex." She grabbed my hand and squeezed. "Can you accept that?"

"Of course," I told her, softening at her touch. At the end of the day, I loved her. I'd always love her. I wanted her to be happy. If for some stupid reason that was with Lex, much good may it bring her.

But after a few months, it annoyed me to spend any length of time with them. They'd kiss or cuddle and wrap their arms around each other, and he'd be so sweet with her, like he wasn't the goddamned Anti-Christ. It made me burn with an unquenchable fury. What was so great about Lex that Miri would rather spend her time with him? What was so great about Miri that Lex could treat her with such gentleness?

If I didn't have Carter, I would have holed up in my dorm room and never come out. True to his word, he delivered on his study partner promises. We got bit parts in the winter show, and we ran our lines together every night before bed. We shared notes from lectures and went through each other's homework, and more than once, he'd fallen asleep in Miri's bed only to wake us up an hour before class so we could do it all over again.

On the weekends, he forced me out of my comfort zone.

"People are generally good, Weeds," he insisted. I loved the nickname he'd given me, a play on my first name, which he described as an invasive species that spread until it choked the life out of anything in its path. I suppose he saw a similarity.

"Not when all they want to do is take pictures of you and sell them to magazines," I said. "The longer you hang out with me, the worse it'll be for you."

He gave me a look that said he was unconvinced. "Dude, let them see. I don't give a shit."

"But I do," I said. "Everything I do now, it'll come back to haunt me someday."

"Who told you that?"

"My mother." I put on my jacket, even as I insisted I didn't want to go. "She's usually right about these sorts of things."

"So what if she is?" He shrugged. "One day, you'll be old and look back on your time in college and wish you'd done whatever made you happy."

"Who told you that?" I mocked his tone.

"*My* mother. You're only young once." He gave me that pantydropper grin and his eyes twinkled with mischief and innuendo, sending a tremble down my spine that I tried to hide. In the time we'd spent together, Carter and I had done nothing more than flirt. I wanted to think I was special to him, that we had something he didn't have with anyone else. But once I got to know him better, I realized that's just who he was. He flirted with *everyone*. I learned not to take anything he said or did personally.

Even in moments like this, where his eyes shimmered down at

me like I hung the stars in the sky, like I was the only girl in the universe. Then the moment passed and we went back to being friends.

Carter took off his baseball cap and put it on my head, brim forward.

"There," he said. "Completely unrecognizable. Almost as good as Clark Kent. Let's go."

The first time he went home with another girl, I pretended it didn't bother me. I even looked around the party for a suitable option for me to take back to my place, but no one wanted to fuck the daughter of a former president. At this point, I was too afraid to admit the only person I'd ever let in my pants had been Miri. At the end of each and every night, I went back to my dorm alone and watched *Golden Girls* until I passed out.

Carter went through girl after girl. Sometimes, they'd hang around for a week or two, but he dismissed them as soon as they started talking about getting serious. Carter meant what he said about being ambitious; he didn't plan on letting a relationship get in the way.

Once or twice, I'd even caught him flirting with Miri—hugging too long, laughing too loud, touching and talking in a way that made my skin itch. As much as the friendship between them bordered on inappropriate at times, it never went any further. Whether that was because she was with Lex or she suspected how I'd started to feel about him, I'd never know.

By the end of spring semester, I was certain I'd been friend-zoned, and Carter had no interest in me aside from our scholastic partnership. Even if an undercurrent of undeniable wanton adoration always simmered between us, neither of us acted on it.

"Hey, Weeds," he said on the morning of our Econ final. "Get up."

I cracked my eyes open and focused on him, standing in front of me wearing a towel and nothing else. Water dripped down the front of his body and over the curves of his abs in delicious rivulets, and my tongue damn near fell out of my head, aching to lick every last drop.

"Enjoying the view?"

God. Yes.

"You're the one prancing around a girl's room wearing only a towel." I stretched my arms high over my head. "How else should I react to the sight of a beautiful naked man first thing in the morning?" I blamed a blatant lack of caffeine for my uninhibited tongue.

"I can think of a few ways," he murmured.

"Name the one you want the most." Sure, that bordered on risqué, especially for me, but I gave him a Cheshire grin when his cheeks turned bright rosy pink and he hung his head between his shoulders. Only I got this reaction from him, this bashful, unfiltered Carter. Everyone else saw the confident lady killer. I could make him blush. A yearning twist of warmth radiated down the center of my torso at the thought, licking the space between my legs in the worst way.

He took a deep breath and let it out through his nose, biting his lips into a thin line. The tension shifted between us, and what once had been playful now turned stifling with all the months of saying *it wasn't like that* when sometimes it could never be anything but *that*.

I wanted to kiss him so bad it hurt, but I was afraid I'd lose him as a friend if it didn't work out. What if I made the first move, and he rejected me? He might only pretend to like me the way Marcus had, the way Lex teased me about. He might only want me once and never again.

"We have a final in an hour," Carter said. "Get up."

"Whoa," Lex shouted, walking into the room without knocking. The door banged off the wall behind it and sprung back on him. "Did you two finally blow up that friend zone?"

"Ignore him, darling. We're only here for my biology book." Miri came in behind him and ran her eyes over Carter before looking at me and raising an eyebrow. "Unless he's correct?"

"Shut up, Lex," I said. "Carter and I have a final. That's all."

"Is that what the kids are calling it these days?" Lex said.

"Har har." I sneered at him and ran my hands over my face to more fully wake up. Lex and Carter talked about a party they wanted to go tonight, the last party of the year, and Miri searched around her desk for her book while I pushed myself upright.

"Layla's coming, too," Carter said.

"Layla?" My stomach dropped.

"Yeah, Layla McIntire. Junior. Brunette," he said.

I knew who Layla McIntire was. I just didn't know *Carter* knew who she was. "Why is she coming with you?"

"Because Carter's hoping she'll put his penis in her mouth." Lex used a patronizing tone that made my fingers curl into a fist, the one that sounded like he was talking to a child. "Unlike you, X, some of us want to get laid."

I glared at him, a million comebacks bubbling through my mind, but I'd promised Miri I'd make an attempt to be nicer to him. She hated when we fought.

"Hey," Miri cut in, pointing at him. "You said you'd behave, Alexei."

"Yeah, back off, dude. Ivy gets laid." Sweet, sweet Carter. Always jumping to my defense.

"No, it's okay, Carter," I said, "let the Neanderthal think the only reason to be nice to someone is because you want to fuck them."

"Which gives you enough reason not to be nice to anyone, right?" Lex said. "No one is good enough for Ivy Washington."

"That sounds like jealousy," Carter cut in.

"That's not what it's about, Lex." I ignored Carter's attempt at dissipating the tension between us. "No one can make me come as hard as my vibrator, so why waste my time?"

I regretted it as soon as I said it. Miri shot me a look, a momentary wince behind her eyes that she quickly pushed away.

Fuck.

I didn't mean it like that, but now that I'd said it, I couldn't take it back without making it more awkward.

"And that," Carter said, pointing to me, "sounds like a challenge."

My cheeks flamed harder, but Lex barked out a laugh, and Miri giggled to herself, pushing another set of papers out of the way.

"But we've got a final, and I gotta get dressed. Not necessarily in that order." Carter backed toward the door and waved goodbye to Lex and Miri before shooting me one last look full of the heat. "Meet me downstairs in thirty, okay?"

7

LEX

I wished Carter Scott had gone to any other school in the world. I wished he'd stayed in London. I wished he'd gone home to Chicago or maybe dropped off the face of the Earth. Because then I wouldn't have to watch him strut through Ivy's room in a towel and act like the sight didn't make me want to drop to my knees and claw at the fabric until it fell away. I loved Miri, I did, but my draw to Carter had not gone away. And by the end of spring semester, it had started to drive me wild.

He and I never talked about it. We pretended we were friends, college dudes, drinking and partying and acting like assholes together. But sometimes when I was alone at night, I remembered the way he growled as he came, and I fucked my fist thinking about his hands in my hair.

It didn't make me love Miri any less. It just *was*. And it wasn't a problem, so long as I kept my shit together when I was around him. That became increasingly harder to do the closer he got to Ivy. She and I hated each other. That was our schtick.

But in some dark, twisted part of my heart, I was protective of her. I'd known her my whole life, and in a way, we were sort of family. Someone like Carter would chew her up and spit her out. On the other hand, that could have been fun to watch.

We sat around the bonfire out behind the frat house in Hyde's Square. It wasn't the best part of town, but who gave a shit when the taste of bad decisions hung in the air like an aphrodisiac? Miri was on my left with Carter and Ivy across the flames in seats by the pool. They were playing the slap game, where you hold your hands out and a person puts theirs on top and you try to slap the top of their hands before they can pull away. He was quicker than her, but she hit harder. (I knew that from personal experience.)

"You're staring again, darling," Miri whispered in my ear.

At the time, I didn't know why I hated it so much. Maybe because I wanted to make him laugh like that. Maybe because he showered her with the affection he couldn't, or wouldn't, show me. Or maybe because Ivy would never look at me the way she stared at him...the way she sometimes stared at Miri. Up until recently, I wasn't sure she was capable of such adoration, but that was another bag of cats I didn't want to deal with tonight. I took a drink of my beer.

"Why don't you tell him how you feel?" she said. "Either you're jealous of Carter or you're jealous of Ivy. I don't think it's the former."

"I don't feel any way about Carter."

"You're a good liar, but you can't trick me, Alexei."

I loved it when she called me Alexei. I'd hated my full name most of my life, but to hear it fall from her lips in that glorious accent made me shiver.

"She's not right for him." I cleared my throat as the lie poured over my tongue.

"You don't know that. He cares for her."

I adjusted my hips in my seat, suddenly uncomfortable with her line of inquiry. When had it gotten so hot out here?

"Only until he's had her." I took another sip of my beer and my throat ached. "Trust me. I know his type. I *was* his type." *Not true.* "I'm still his type."

"You think so low of your friend?" Miri brushed a piece of hair back behind my ear. "What if he makes her happy?"

"I don't give a shit if she's happy." That also didn't sit right in my gut, but I pretended it was the beer and not the subject of conversation.

Miri chuckled and leaned in to kiss me on the cheek. "You can like her, you know. It's okay."

"Ivy and I will never say we like each other." I gave her a quick peck on the lips, pretending the ache in my chest had nothing to do with my shame. I didn't want Ivy to like me, and frankly, I hoped she never did. "I mean that."

"Of course you do, darling."

It was with Miri's taunts and a heavy inferno brewing inside my chest that I made a reckless decision. I'd been trying to sever this stifling, entangled thing between Carter, Ivy, and myself, but even at the time, I knew I'd only been acting like a spoiled, selfish prick.

"Did you decide to go back to Chicago, Carter?" Miri asked, refocusing her attention across the flames. "For the summer?"

"No. I'm, uh..." He met my eyes for a brief second before shifting them to Ivy. "I'm staying here."

That vile sensation writhed in my gut, growing more desperate the longer I acted like it wasn't there.

"Really?" Ivy's face lit up.

"Yeah," he said. "I'm taking some summer classes, trying to catch up to you, Weeds."

"Good luck," Miri said. "The girl's a savant. No one will ever touch her."

Except for me. No one knew it, but I was neck and neck with her. After Ivy announced her double major, I'd decided to do the same thing. By graduation, I'd be poli-sci/theater right alongside her.

"So you'll be here?" Ivy asked Carter with that hopeful lilt in her voice. "All summer?"

The *with me* went unsaid, but it glittered in those steel-gray eyes all the same. Ivy had it bad for him. He had started to reciprocate. I didn't like that shit one fucking bit.

"Yeah, Weeds. All summer." My heart clenched when he smiled at her like he had the same whimsical summertime thoughts floating through his mind.

Time for me to do something horrible.

"What about you, X? Any big plans?" I said. "Are you finally going to remove that enormous stick from your ass?"

The few people sitting around us reacted with laughter or ominous *ohhhhs.*

"Alexei," Miri said. "Don't."

It was too late. Ivy recognized the taunt in my voice, and the beast inside of her blinked awake, staring out at me with vengeance on its teeth.

"Yeah, and maybe I'll shove it down your throat," she said.

"Don't threaten me with a good time." I huffed out a laugh, narrowing my sneer on her. "Of course, what do you know about deep-throating anything?" I tilted my head as she tightened her hands around the armrests, evidently knowing where I was going next. Fear replaced the thrill in her wide eyes. I should have pumped the brakes, but my temper had already slammed on the gas. "You *are* still a virgin, right, X?"

The crowd gasped. Everyone. Even Miri.

"Lex, shut the bloody fuck up." Miri smacked my arm, but I glared at my adversary. She glared right back, her jaw clenched, and I knew I'd hit my mark. But Ivy...oh, wonderful, competitive Ivy. She never backed down from me, and that's what anchored me to her like a splinter in my cold, dead heart.

"No, Lex." She launched out of her seat. "Ask your girlfriend about that." She gave me the finger and stormed away.

Most of the crowd laughed, evidently thinking she was giving me shit, that it was a joke between us like the way frat brothers teased about screwing each other's moms. But my brain stumbled to a halt, all thoughts skidding to a gory demise on my mental asphalt like a bad motorcycle wreck.

Uh…What. The Fuck.

When I snapped my attention to Miri, she clenched the seat so hard her knuckles had turned white. She hung her jaw open and her wide-eyed stare burned shame and anger.

It's true.

I thought about the first time I met her, when she'd taken me to her cottage in Scotland. The way she sighed when she talked about Ivy. The twinkle in her eye and the ghost of something personal in her smile. Now it made sense.

My heart raced at the thought of them together. Most guys probably would have reacted like cavemen about their girlfriend hooking up with her roommate, especially if that roommate was Ivy Washington.

But me?

I seethed with something icy and rotten. Not only had Ivy stolen Carter, but she'd lain claim to Miri before I could. Why did she get to have everything? Why did she get the big family and the brother who didn't die and the presidential burden of history? Why did people love her so damned much when I was just as good, just as smart?

Carter ran a hand over his mouth, his indigo eyes scouring me with rancid incredulity. "Nice, Lex," he said, standing. "Real fucking smooth."

He followed Ivy around the front of the house, and all eyes shot to us, waiting for my reaction, waiting for Miri's. When she couldn't stand it any longer, she stood and stalked away to the jeers of the onlookers. I followed her like my ass was on fire.

"Why did you say that?" Miri whispered after I caught up. "Why do you always start this shit with her?"

"I was just fucking around," I tried. "She took it too far."

"You know how she is about her personal life." Miri crossed her arms over her chest. "Telling all those people about that? What if it ends up in *The Puck*?"

"No one gives a shit who Ivy's fucking."

"It's different for you, Lex." She stopped so she could look me in the face. "The public looks at you and marvels at how many women coast through your bed. They look at me and Ivy, and we're the whores who can't keep our legs closed."

"I know."

"No, you don't," Miri said. "If you did, you wouldn't have teased her about it, and if you want to keep doing this thing between us? You'll never tease her about it again."

"What?" I said with a laugh. She couldn't be saying what I thought she was saying.

"I'm serious, Lex," Miri said. "I don't know what your obsession is with needling her, but it has to stop. She's my best friend. I love her."

"Yeah, a little too much, evidently. You and I need to have a long talk about that shit."

She raised an eyebrow. "What happened between you and Carter in London?"

I opened my mouth, but nothing came out. I didn't know what to say. Carter and I had agreed to keep it between us. I wouldn't lie, but I also couldn't tell her the truth.

"Exactly," she said. "We're entitled to our secrets, but the minute you start being cruel about the ones you know is the minute I stop sharing any of mine with you. Don't follow me home and don't call me for a few days. I want to be mad at you."

She left me there, confused and drunk and pissed off at the world.

8

IVY

I didn't think it was possible to hate Lex more than I did, but he'd found a way to make me. I burned with fury. I wanted to launch myself across that fire and tear into his face with my bare hands. I wanted to wrap my fingers around his throat and watch as the life drained from his eyes.

I *hated* him.

"Weeds," Carter called after me. "Wait up."

"Go away, Carter," I said, walking faster.

I didn't know where I was going. It was midnight, and I was drunk. I'd managed to avoid the paparazzi thus far, but I didn't know how long that would last. I should've called a driver to come get me, but the cool air in my lungs kept me from doing whatever I could to get Lex thrown in supermax. So I kept walking.

"Weeds, c'mon. Lex was being a dick." Carter grabbed my elbow to stop me, and I whipped around, centering my wrath on him.

"Lex is always a dick. I'm tired of putting up with it."

"If it's any consolation"—Carter's mouth cracked into a huge grin—"I think you won that round."

"I don't care if I won."

Lies. I absolutely cared. It was the only reason I said it. A small ashamed part of me flushed because not only had everyone heard Lex call me a virgin, but I'd also insinuated that I liked to fuck other girls. While I'd said it in a way that could be interpreted as a burn, I should have been worried about the headlines on *The Puck* tomorrow.

Ivy Washington a lesbian? Sources say she's been sleeping with Princess Miriam for years. Quite the scandal. No comment from the royal family regarding these allegations.

My cheeks flamed as I imagined how my mother would react. I doubted I was the first bisexual Washington, that was a statistical improbability, but I'd certainly be the first publicly out one. That simply would not do for Evelyn Washington. Nope, nope, nope.

"You should have told me," Carter said.

"Why does it matter?" I barked. Carter had given me no indication he was interested in anything more than friendship. Even if I wanted to climb him like a tree, all the reasons I couldn't were still there—my dreams and his promiscuity and the public and the media and my mother.

We don't belong to us, her voice said at the back of my mind. *We belong to the public. That's the price we pay to live the life we do.*

Carter opened his mouth and rubbed at the back of his head.

"I don't know. I would have—" He stopped and looked down at me with playfulness in his eyes.

"What? Pity fucked me?" When he didn't answer, I rolled my eyes and started walking again. "You and Lex deserve each other."

"Weeds, that's not what I meant. Look." He put his hands on my shoulders, forcing me to stop and face him, his masculine sandalwood scent pluming up around me, unfurling this aching throb in my chest. "I don't pity you. I'd never pity you."

"So? You'd fuck me and get rid of me like you do all your other flings? No, thank you."

"I wouldn't do that to you."

I waited for him to continue, my pulse thundering through my

veins, but the longer the silence went on between us, the more infu-
riated I became. With both of them. With *all* of them. Lex. Carter.
Miri. I was so confused, and I didn't know who to trust. I started
walking again.

"I've wanted you since the day I met you," he called.

That stopped me. I turned to face him.

"But *c'mon*, you're Ivy Washington." He cleared his throat.
"Someone like me *does not* put his hands on someone like you unless
you make it obvious that's what you want."

My heart thundered against my ribcage, and I took a deep breath
to try to steady myself so I didn't show him how much hearing that
delighted me. My skin burned and grew tight, suddenly too small to
hold all of me in. I thought I might burst with how hard my muscles
trembled.

Was he messing with me? Was this a trick? It had to be. Any
second, Lex would jump out of the shadows and tell me he'd set up
the whole thing, but that never happened.

"You—you want *me*?"

"Yeah," he said. "You think I wake anyone else up for class every
day? You think I give a shit whether they pass their Econ finals? No,
Weeds. You're my favorite girl."

You're my favorite girl.

With a few hurried steps, I propelled myself into his arms and
wrapped my fingers around the back of his neck with my legs circling
his waist. Our lips collided, my nerves exploding as a rush of lust
surged through my entire body.

I kissed him.

As much as I devoured his mouth, he explored the depths of
mine. He felt so good—warm and demanding and sensual. All the
months of tension between us slid away, revealing a deep wanton
affection so profound that it made me shake, and I rubbed myself
against the thickening length pressed between us.

A chuckle echoed from deep in his chest, and he slid his hands up
my back while he put me back on my feet.

"I should have done that months ago," I said.

"Come back to my room with me." He pressed his forehead to mine, his hot breath pouring down the front of my shirt. "My roommate already went home for the summer. It'll just be us." He rubbed the tip of his nose against mine. "Let's see if I can make you come harder than your vibrator."

I grinned like a fool and carried that with me while he walked me back to his place. Our lips locked the minute the door closed behind us, and he took his time slowly peeling the clothes off me like I was a present. Then, he laid me on his bed and worshipped my body, kissing and devouring each part of me like he was memorizing how his touch made me moan.

He settled his weight between my knees, his legs outstretched behind him, and when he trailed his lips down the inside of my left leg with small, needy pecks, sparks flew up that entire side of my body. He teased and sucked and licked me, bringing me right to the edge of orgasm before working me back down again. He did this twice. He made me moan and beg and plead, my hands fisting in the sheets and sweat beading on my forehead, only to leave me panting and anxious for more. When he finally let me come, it was earth-shattering. Absolutely astounding. I arched into him and moaned, every muscle clenching with the intensity of my climax.

He kept going, probing and licking me, even after I became too sensitive. I pushed his forehead away, and he laughed, fighting me and wrapping his hands around my knees to hold them apart.

"No, no, no. Stop, stop, stop," I panted, trying to get away, trying to sit up and close my legs around his head.

Carter smiled up at me from between my thighs with a huge grin that stole my heart. "Say I made you come harder than your vibrator." Another greedy lick, and I let out some defeated laugh that came from my postcoital bliss.

"Carter—"

"Say it."

"Okay, okay." I struggled to get the words out between giggles and heavy pants. "You made me come harder than my vibrator."

"Challenge completed, Miss Washington." He crawled back up my body and kissed me, tasting like me and him and sex, and it turned me on again, my aching cunt already wanting more of him. Pride swelled up in him, making him impossibly more beautiful with the added confidence.

"Now it's my turn," I said, pushing him so he was on his back. I climbed on top of him, positioning myself between his knees and dancing my hands down the front of his body. I kissed him once… twice…and trailed my tongue down the center of his chest, loving the way he groaned and rolled into my touch, brushing the hair out of my eyes. "I've been dreaming about doing this for so long."

"You have dreams about sucking my dick?"

"I have dreams about doing a lot worse to you, Mr. Scott."

I gave his cock a lick, and it bobbed in response.

"Jesus Christ." He crossed his arms under his head to prop himself up and watch me, the undivided attention urging me on. I sucked him deep, swallowing him and making him grip my hair. He tasted salty and sweet, and when I cupped his balls and propped him up so I could really focus on his sensitive tip, he fisted his fingers in my hair and he let out a guttural noise. "Keep doing that. Just like that. Fuck, that feels so good."

I relaxed my throat and focused on my breathing, taking him all the way back and letting him buck into me however he wanted. I gagged around him, my eyes burning and tears streaming down my face, his grip on my hair punishing. This was so dirty, and breaking him down like this, knowing I'd been the one to make him so disheveled, turned me on in ways I couldn't understand.

"Stop," he said, pulling my head off him. "I'm gonna come. Stop."

Something had been unleashed in Carter, some kind of hunger that he'd finally let himself satisfy. He yanked me up his body, twisted us around so he was on top of me and positioned his cock at my entrance. When he pushed inside me, the connection between us sparked to life like a scalding flame. He paused, letting me adjust, but I didn't want him to be careful. I was *done* with being careful.

I won't lie and say it didn't hurt. It did. Even though Miri had fucked me hard. Even though I fucked myself with vibrators. But it mixed with a pleasant euphoria that overpowered all my other senses. He took me carefully, lovingly, and the indigo in his eyes glittered with all the adoration he had for me.

Finally, my climax burst behind my eyes, a moan barreling out of the abyss inside me. He surged inside me, his cock kicking as he found his own release. Then he collapsed on top of me, and we breathed down the serotonin high together.

In the afterglow of all the things we'd done, I lay pressed up against Carter's body, my head on his chest and my arm draped over his stomach as he played with my hair.

"You have to make me a promise," he said.

I glanced up at him.

"I want this, Ivy. I do, but I still want Hollywood. I still want my dreams."

"Me too," I said. "I don't want this to hold us back from anything."

He kissed me, and the sensation rattled down my body, making me curl my toes.

"That's why I kept my distance from you," he said. "I can't afford to get distracted."

"Me, neither," I told him.

He took a deep breath.

"We have a deal, then. If we make it to the end of college, we let the chips fall where they may. We go into this knowing how it will end."

I sighed and trailed my fingers over his naked chest. "Do you think that will make it any easier when the time comes?"

"No. But I can't stay away from you any longer, and I'm tired of trying."

Carter had never been a part of my ten-year plan. No, that solely included graduation, Harvard Law school, and election to Congress. I wanted to be the youngest representative ever elected, even younger than my mother. Carter would never—could never—play a part in that, especially if he wanted to go to Hollywood. Our lives went in opposite directions after this, but I couldn't find it in me to stop the relationship from happening. It seemed fated, perhaps, even if completely doomed from the start.

"Thank you for taking care of me tonight," I told him. "Thank you for being so awesome about all of it."

"Ivy," he said. "I'd do anything for you."

My heart overflowed with contentment, like nothing or no one could burst my bubble.

ACT II

I know a bank where the wild thyme blows,
Where oxlips and the nodding violet grows,
Quite over-canopied with luscious woodbine,
With sweet musk-roses and with eglantine:
There sleeps Titania sometime of the night,
Lulled in these flowers with dances and delight.
-Oberon, Act 2, Scene 1

9

IVY

SPRING - SENIOR YEAR

Time had a way of spinning out of control. An hour passed in a heartbeat. A year in the blink of an eye. Four in the space of a breath.

Miri and I made up the way we always had, brushing things under the rug and forgiving the worst in each other. In four years, we'd proven our devotion to our friendship so much so that we moved into a two-bedroom apartment a few minutes north of campus. Lex and Carter rented the space across the hall, and for the last twelve months, we lived that *Friends* life. Perhaps most surprising, Lex and I had called a truce on behalf of our proximity. No more public outbursts, no more accidentally disclosed secrets.

As for Carter and me, we promised to love each other as long as we could and kept that up the entire four years. This seemed so easy through the eyes of eighteen-year-old Ivy Washington — young, naive, and ignorant of the cruel ways of fate. We were inseparable. I fell hard for him. Fast. I might have even loved him after that first night. He awoke a side of me only stirred once before by Miri, a sexual deviant, and once she was awakened, we both had a hard time calming her down again.

But like most good things, it couldn't last forever. Eventually, the rose-colored make-believe reality I'd created within the safety of TW's comfortable walls crumbled to my feet.

On the day before I was supposed to leave for a class theater trip to Ireland, my parents invited me to brunch at the ancestral family estate in Mount Vernon. I arrived twenty minutes late, so when the driver pulled up to a stop in front of the mansion, I frowned at the Audi A8 sitting next to my mother's Land Rover. But I didn't stop to think more about it. It was Lex's car, and he didn't mention that he'd be at brunch today when I saw him earlier this morning. That should have been my first clue that all was *not* well in the state of Denmark, and like Hamlet, our parents were up to something shady.

Apprehension growing in the pit of my gut, I climbed the marble stairs to the front door and greeted the man who opened it for me, the butler who had been working for my family for twenty years.

"Your parents are waiting for you on the terrace," William said.

I smoothed my hands over my hair, brushing it away from my face, and pulled up the political shield around my emotions as I walked through the foyer to the dining room and out the open French doors at the back to the patio.

I froze at the sight.

My parents sat at opposite ends of the table, former Vice President Kellan Fairfax and the Grand Duchess Anna on one side and Lex on the other.

The wide-eyed look he gave me screamed, *"Run."*

I took another step closer.

"Ivette, happy you could make it." My mother gestured to the open spot next to my nemesis.

Except he wasn't my nemesis anymore. No, in the last four years, Lex and I had formed an uneasy alliance. We didn't argue, at least not in front of Carter and Miri, and we didn't poke at each other for the sake of poking. We kept it civil for our friends, and so far, that had worked.

"Apologies for being late." I forced a smile and sat, wincing at the tension rolling off him in suffocating waves. "Traffic."

"Well, you're here now." My father smiled and picked up his silverware, an obvious attempt at keeping the peace. "Let's eat."

His parents flashed their fake grins and placated my father by also starting to dine. Meanwhile, my mother shot me a terse look, which I interpreted as frustration for my tardiness. There and gone in a blink, she refocused her attention on our guests and turned on the political animal, trading old White House stories with Kellan while they ate gourmet eggs and drank mimosas.

Lex avoided looking at me altogether. He sat stone-faced and slouched in his chair, head propped up on his thumb with his tie loosened around his neck. He reminded me of the seventeen-year-old version of himself, the guy with the chip on his shoulder who couldn't wait to find my buttons and push.

The last time he didn't have anything to say to me, his older brother had just died. That made my hackles rise even higher.

Whatever this is, it isn't good.

I opened my mouth to ask what was wrong, but his mother prompted me about the upcoming theater trip and drew my attention back to the conversation.

"We leave tomorrow," I explained. "It's a three-week theater intensive in Killwater, Ireland, as part of a sister school exchange program with the local college. We'll put on a play from scratch for the summer residents, and likewise, they send students here to do the same."

"Oh," Anna said, pulling a deep gulp from her champagne. "How lovely. Do you know what play you'll be performing?"

I shook my head. "We won't know until we get there."

Even with the uneasiness in the air, things went on as normal, and by the time we got to the fruity dessert, I had let my guard down. *Maybe something happened with Miri. Maybe that's why Lex is in such a shitty mood.*

"So," my father said. "Shall we talk business?"

I took that as my cue to leave, pushing my chair back from the table.

"Ivette," my mother snapped. "Sit."

Confused, I did, dropping my rump into the seat.

"Now that you're graduating college," she said, her ice-cold eyes freezing me to my spot, "it's time we start mapping the rest of your career."

"I haven't gone to law school yet." I flicked my nervous gaze to Lex again.

"Yes, about that." Mother drummed her nails against the table, the speculative tone in her voice turning my breakfast to cement. "Harvard is a great option. Georgetown is better."

"Closer," my father added.

"Keeps you in the heart of the capital." Kellan pursed his lips and gave me a reassuring nod.

Lex took a giant gulp of his water.

"I'm sorry, but I'm missing something. I've already accepted admission to Harvard." I pleaded with my eyes for an explanation, my heart beating so hard, my stomach churned as eggs crept up the back of my esophagus. "Mother?"

"This is what's best for the family," she said, narrowing her gaze on me. "You'll go to Georgetown. It's better if you're closer. We can appear more united."

"Why do we need to appear more united?" I swallowed against a parched throat, praying I didn't embarrass myself when I opened my mouth again. My anxiety warped into full-blown panic when Lex still said nothing, cleared his throat, and glanced out over the perfectly manicured backyard, avoiding my stare.

"I'm running for president this year," Kellan said, bringing my focus back to him. "Beating an incumbent is more difficult than another primary candidate. You know this."

"We're not doing great in the polls," my mother said. "He's got the Washington support, but we've been out of the game for a while. People have lost interest."

I'd noticed. Mother's second term had ended three years ago, shortly after we graduated from high school and went to college. At the time, Kellan and Anna were still picking up the pieces from Marcus's death, so they hadn't tried for the White House. In the absence of headlines, the paparazzi had stopped following us around. They'd left Lex and Miri alone. Things were finally almost normal. Which meant they were about to blow up in my face because now that enough time had passed, Kellan wanted the presidency, and my parents would help him get it.

"We need to get the public talking about the Washingtons and the Fairfaxes again," Mother continued, her icy-blue eyes imploring me to be reasonable about what was coming next. "You and Alexei—"

"Alexei and I are friends," I interrupted.

"Ivette," my father snapped. "Your mother is speaking."

Evelyn made a show of taking another long sip of her mimosa, drawing it out, letting me sit in silence with my shame.

"You and Alexei are the same age," she finally continued. "You're similarly matched in terms of background, and you've been friends since you were children. People have photographed you together your entire lives."

My heart raced. My hands grew sweaty. My gut churned, the acid from the mimosas mixing with the impending doom I saw on the horizon. I knew where this was going.

No.

I wouldn't do this. I wouldn't do this to Carter or Miri. I wouldn't do this to myself.

"A marriage between you would form a perfect political dynasty," my mother continued. "Not at first, of course. You'll have to get through law school, but by the time you're twenty-four—"

"Yes," Kellan agreed, cutting Mother off. "Twenty-four. That'll give you three years to get used to the idea, just in time for re-election."

"No." I shook my head, chuckling at the audacity. "No, I won't do that."

"What do you mean?" My mother furrowed her brows, and I squirmed, forcing myself to hold her gaze lest she see my weakness. I wouldn't back down from this. She'd had control over my entire life and now that I had my first taste of freedom, she wanted to take that, too. "Do you think you have a choice?"

I scrambled for an excuse, anything I could think of as to why this would be terrible. "What do you think will happen to Lex's reputation when he breaks Princess Miriam's heart?"

"From what I understand, she's been slumming her way through England most of her life," Kellan said. "She'll move on."

I set my gaze on him, a thousand retorts on the tip of my tongue, each more stinging and horrible than the last. Did this guy know how messed-up Lex had been after Marcus died? Did he care? No, he'd shipped his surviving son off to London and hoped for the best. Now he wanted to rip apart the one person who had reached inside Lex and pulled him back to life?

My friend? My best friend?

No, I'd tell this portly asshole *exactly*—

Lex placed his hand on top of mine. "Stop."

Stop?

Appalled, I whipped my attention to him. "You're okay with this?"

"There are worse people I could marry." Eyes brimming with unshed tears, he cleared his throat and swallowed.

Shock hit me like a cold, hard slap, and words choked in my throat. I didn't know what to say. I didn't know what to think. Marry him? Marry Lex? My archnemesis. The one person I hated the most in the world.

Marry him?

Carter's devastating smile echoed through my mind. We'd promised we wouldn't let our relationship stand in the way of our dreams, but how would he feel if he knew that after we broke up, I'd married his best friend? And not even because I loved the guy, but because my parents told me I had to.

"I'm already with someone," I said.

"Oh, what? That silly boy from Chicago?" Mother scoffed. "Alexei is worthy of a Washington."

"So is Carter."

"Don't push your luck, Ivette." She narrowed her cold eyes.

I cleared my throat, choking back the rising bile. "And if I refuse?"

"You're either a part of this family or you're not," Father said, and I recognized the look in his eyes. The one that reminded me who I was. What I represented.

Exitus acta probat. The Washington family motto. *The outcome is the test of the act.* You do big things, you get big rewards. Lex's parents needed to win an election, and they were willing to screw over their child to do it. We'd never had a choice, not as children, not as adults. This train never slowed down, never stopped, and it wouldn't matter what ten-year plan I'd drawn for myself, my mother had her own.

I shoved my chair back from the table and stood, slamming my napkin down on my plate.

"If you'll please excuse me." I barely got that out before I stormed around the table and over the patio, back through the French doors to the dining room inside, my mother following close on my heels.

"Ivette," she called.

Somewhere around the entrance to the kitchen, I stopped and turned to her.

"You can't do this to me," I said, eyes burning, vision blurring. "Please don't make me do this."

I was so close to freedom. I had law school and my entire future, one *without* Lex, one that I chose, one that got me into Congress.

"Ivette," she said again. "Think about this. Think about the things you want for yourself."

"I can get that on my own," I said. "They don't need us. We don't need them."

I don't need Lex.

"Yes, we do," she said. "The Fairfaxes and the Washingtons have been allies for hundreds of years. The boy has the right name and the right background. This is what you must do."

"This isn't the Middle Ages, Mother," I said. "You can't sell me to the neighbors like a broodmare."

"Is that what you think this is?" she said. "Do you think your life is your own? Do you think any of our lives are our own?" She took another step closer to me, tsking her teeth and shaking her head with that disapproving expression that used to terrify me as a child. "Do you think I wanted to marry your father?" She whispered it like it was a sin for her to speak out loud. "These are the sacrifices we make for the good of the country."

"I fail to see how my marrying Lex Fairfax has *anything* to do with the good—"

"If the idiot currently in office stays in office, he may never leave it. He's a fascist, and he needs to be stopped. The only way to do that is to unify our party again." She pushed my hair behind my ear like she used to do when I was a child. "Trust me, my dear. If there were any other way, I would have taken it." She kissed my temple, like that was supposed to smooth over the wound she'd carved so cleanly inside my soul. "But we don't always get what we want."

I sat silently in the passenger seat of Lex's Audi, staring out the window at the bustling downtown city below the parking garage at our apartment complex. People carried on with their lives without a care in the world, without the knowledge that right now, a group of maniacal, power-hungry monsters sat around morning bunch, drinking champagne and plotting to manipulate them into voting blue for the upcoming election.

I didn't know which was worse—being willfully ignorant or an involuntary party to the plot.

"Are you going to tell her?" Lex rubbed his hand over his eyes and pulled on his cigarette, flicking ash out the window.

I clenched my jaw and balled my hands into fists. "I thought maybe you should. Seeing as there are worse people you could marry."

Lex snapped his eyes to me, recognizing the challenge. We hadn't talked to each other like this in months. But damn it, my skin felt too tight and my heart raced and all I could see was his stupid silent face as my mother explained why this was going to happen.

Why didn't he say anything?

Why didn't he fight it?

"Don't blame me for this." He squared his jaw and shook his head. "I didn't want this."

I clenched my fists tighter, frustration boiling my blood. "You just sat there and let it happen."

"I've been fighting this for months." His wide eyes turned pleading, like he was desperate for me to understand and forgive him.

My heart dropped. "You've known about this for months?" *This asshole.* "And you didn't tell me?"

"What was I going to say?" He stabbed out his smoke in the ashtray he kept in the cupholder. "Hey, Ivy. I know we hate each other, but my father needs better polling numbers. Let's get hitched."

I wanted to strangle him.

"You could have warned me. Goddamn it, Lex." I dug my palms into my eyes so I didn't cry. They stung, the rage nearly boiling over.

"Listen to me." He yanked my hands away so I had to look at him. "Stop it, X. Listen."

I glared at him, my lungs desperate to get air in my body, my molars grinding so hard together, they might crack.

"I know you love Carter. You know I love Miri. There's no reason to think we can't go on doing that if we're together."

His meaning hit me like a sledgehammer, a consideration I'd never factored into any ten-year plan. "A sham marriage."

"It was always going to be a sham marriage." He sat back in his seat and lit up another cigarette. "At least with you, I don't have to hide anything." He met my gaze with a tormented one of his own, the hazel of his irises almost completely black now. Lex's tell had always been in his eyes. "You've always known who I am, and I know who you are."

Yep. We sure did, and we hated everything about each other.

"What happens when our parents expect us to have children?"

He returned that wild stare to the front window. "We've got a while to figure that out. They won't expect it until we're married."

"Jesus, Lex," I said. "You're going along with this?"

"I don't have a choice, Ivy," he said. "Neither do you. We never did. Now we're in it together, just like we always have been."

"No," I said, crossing my arms, refusing to give in. "No, I won't do this."

"What else are you going to do about it?"

"Fight it. Fight *them*." I pleaded with him to help me, to see my side in this. We could take them down. We could figure out a way, we had to.

He scoffed and rolled his eyes. "And how are we going to do that? They're the most powerful people in the world."

I dropped my jaw open, willing the words to come out, but what could I say? I had no plan, no idea how to get out of this, only that I had to. "I don't know, Lex. But we'll find a way."

"We're going to Ireland tomorrow," he said, raising his eyebrows. "We'll be there for three weeks and when we get back, it's all over. Miri is going home. Carter is going to California."

I scrabbled for a plan, for some idea, anything. "They said we didn't have to get married until the re-election. That's four years to figure it out."

Lex narrowed his eyes, ice-cold hazel assessing my idea. "Are you, Ivy Washington, suggesting we *defy* our parents?" He snorted out a laugh. "Wow, I thought I'd never see the day."

"Are you in or out?" This would go much easier if I had him as a partner, but knowing him, he'd act like a petulant snob about it.

"Of course I'm in," he said. "I just can't believe you'd have the balls."

"Aren't you tired of this? Aren't you tired of the great game?" The whole thing made me so angry, I could burst into flames. I didn't know how I'd get out of this, I didn't know when, but as I sat there in that sports car with my archnemesis turned frenemy turned fiancé, I swore to myself that I would. My mother may have thought she had a collar around my neck, but I was *her* daughter. I had never gone down without a fight, and I wouldn't start now.

"The game never stops, Ivy," Lex murmured, "it doesn't matter if we're exhausted."

I took a deep breath and let it out through my nose, determined to fight for both of us until he had the courage to defend himself. "What are we going to tell the others?"

"I promised Miri no more secrets." He shifted in his seat, clearing his throat as if the thought made him uncomfortable.

"I've never kept anything from Carter." I didn't like the idea, either.

"But this?" Lex blew out a dramatic breath. "This is a fucking bombshell."

I didn't trust him, I never had, except for maybe one grief-filled night in my room at the White House residence. Maybe just like that night—we were in this together. If there were anyone I could do this with, it would be him.

"I wanted Ireland to be amazing." My soul lamented the versions of us that got to go on an incredible trip without this baggage hanging over our heads. "I wanted it to be our last hurrah."

He grabbed my hand in that gentle, loving way he did the night Marcus died. One simple act of solidarity.

"Me, too." He gave it a squeeze.

"What if we hold off until I can think of something?" I grasped for straws at this point. "I mean, we're *going* to law school. If there were ever an opportune time for us to twist things in our favor, this is it. I'll find a way to get us out of this, I swear I will."

He sighed and took a long drag on his cigarette, stabbing it out in the ashtray. "I believe you, X...I just don't like the thought of keeping secrets."

I didn't either. I didn't like any of this. I wanted to run away with Carter. I wanted Miri to marry Lex and have a million royal babies at their cottage in Scotland. I wanted a world and a life that seemed even further out of my grasp than it ever did. But God help me, I would resist this. I had to. I'd find another way.

He stayed quiet for a moment as he considered, and I watched the change in his eyes when he accepted it. "Okay, Ivy. It'll be our little secret...for now."

IO

LEX

IRELAND

Four years was a long time to pine for someone, to watch as they laughed and preened with the wrong person.

I couldn't explain the way I felt about Carter, even as I continued to love Miri as fiercely as I ever had. Once he and Ivy went exclusive, whatever happened between us in London had to stay in London. Perhaps that made it easier for me to be friends with him. It certainly made it easier to be around him every morning, when he'd stumble out of his room with a sleepy, rumpled look on his face, wearing only his boxers, and I would smell *her*.

Vanilla. Sugar. Girl. *Ivy.* The mixture of their scents did something to me I was deeply ashamed to admit, so I kept it to myself. Did he think about what happened in London? Did he imagine it over and over the way I did?

For four years, I watched them get closer. I watched him light up her world the same way I once longed for him to brighten mine. I watched her meet his enthusiasm for the stage with equal intensity, her performance anxiety dissipating the minute he grabbed her hand. They loved each other, truly and always. That much was apparent to anyone who spent time around them.

Four years was also a long time to date the same person. Especially someone who swore at the beginning they got tired of people after a few months, someone who craved freedom like everyone else craved air. Miri and I made it through to senior year. It wasn't easy. We were broken up almost as much as we were together. She didn't want to do monogamy, especially when she was in the UK and I was in the States. Her gran would never allow a public relationship between us, and now that things had taken a huge plot twist with Ivy, that might have been for the best.

By the time my parents told me their plans, I had almost forgotten who and what the fuck I was: Alexei Fairfax, great-great-grandson of Tsarina Anastasia Romanov, son of a grand duchess of Russia, son of a former vice president, son of a future president, likely a future president himself. If I went to law school and married Ivy. If I followed the track my father outlined for me. I protested. I swear I did. I fought it as hard and as long as I could.

And I lost.

I hated keeping the secret from Miri. The entire flight to Ireland, it weighed like a boulder on my chest. Every time she opened her phone, I winced, thinking our parents might have jumped the gun and announced the engagement early. I should have told her. Ivy and I should have told them together, but we didn't. We let it fester between us until it was an itchy, putrid thing that needed to be lanced. I believed Ivy when she said she'd find a way out of it, some loophole or desperate measure that would ensure our freedom, but I'd been searching for weeks and hadn't turned anything up.

They controlled our money, and if wanted to have any chance at our inheritance, we had to fall in line.

"Are you sure you're all right, darling?" Miri wrapped her arms around my bicep and leaned her head on my shoulder. I unclenched my jaw and forced a smile.

"Yes, of course. Just jet-lagged." I could only use that excuse for so long. Ignoring the hundredth call from my mother, I turned my phone off and tucked it in my back pocket, resolving not to look at it until the trip was over. I couldn't face her, not yet.

She owed me a hell of an apology, and the only thing I'd get from her were excuses. She made a promise, and she broke it. End of story. Not that I cared anyway. I had more important shit to deal with, like how to tell my lover I had to marry her best friend or how to tell my best friend I had to marry his girlfriend.

But it's okay, I'd say. *We can still keep fucking whoever we want.*

Jesus Christ.

We were on the bus, driving down some back-country road in the middle of Nowhere, Northern Ireland. Carter and Ivy slept in the seats across the aisle from Miri and me, Ivy's head on his shoulder and his Bears hat over his eyes. I licked my lips and bounced my knee, every molecule in my body itching for nicotine. The urge to smoke thrummed through me, and if we'd arranged our own escort like I'd wanted, I would have devoured an entire carton by now.

But no, we needed to blend in, appear normal, and Ivy wanted to spend every moment she could with Carter. Not that I blamed her. I wanted to spend every moment I could with Carter, too.

"Talk to me," Miri whispered. "You've been on edge since that brunch with your parents."

"It's nothing." I rubbed my fingers over my eyes again just to give them something to do. "I just need a cigarette."

After driving for eons through the woods, the bus finally stopped outside a Gothic monstrosity. I'd been looking at trees for so long I assumed the driver planned to kill us where no one would find us. Then Killwater College loomed out of the fog like a villain from a horror story, reminding me of the college from every secret society movie ever made. Turrets and gargoyles gave it a dark academia vibe that made it seem ancient and mysterious.

I was the first one out of my seat and down the aisle, clawing at my smokes with shaking hands as I climbed off the bus. God bless that first inhale. It made my knees weak.

"You should really quit that, DC," Carter said, climbing down the stairs. He had his hat on backward, dirty-blond hair sticking out the front of it. "It'll kill you one day."

"Are you my mother now, Chicago?" I asked. Miri and Ivy followed behind him, yawning and stretching and hugging each other.

"If I were your mother," Carter murmured, "I'd put you over my knee and belt you until you swore never to touch them again."

"Ohhh," I teased. "Is that a threat or a promise?"

Carter's dimpled grin made adoration swell in my gut, a warm mushy feeling I quickly ignored. He meant nothing by it. It was just Carter being Carter.

"All right," Stephens said. He was the director of the theater project this year and the staff sponsor of the trip. If one of us fucked up, his ass was on the line. "Everyone stay here. I'll get us our rooms. I know we're jet-lagged, but don't forget we have orientation tomorrow morning at eight a.m. I'll read the cast listing right after. Don't be late." He turned around to walk inside.

"I still can't believe they're doing *Romeo & Juliet*," Ivy said with a groan.

Yeah, this year's play sucked, but I'd been forced to read it a few times, so I knew most of the lines already.

"You're just pissed because there's only one good lead, and it's a thirteen-year-old girl," I teased, curling my lips into a grin.

Ivy rolled her eyes and hugged Miri harder, her head on my girlfriend's shoulder. "I'm not going to get the lead, Lucifer." Miri squirmed and pulled away, giggling as Ivy tickled her sides. "Princess is."

"Stop it." Miri laughed and wrapped her arms around Ivy's shoulders, tugging her close again. "You have as much of a chance as I do. Your audition was fantastic, darling."

When Stephens came out, he read through everyone's names and their dorm assignments. Carter and I were together, and Miri and Ivy were on the same floor but at the opposite end of the hall.

Despite its looming exterior, the inside of Killwater had been kept relatively modern. I expected tapestries hanging from stone walls and wax candles dripping from the mantel. Instead, bulletin boards hung from white plaster and my shoes echoed off shiny laminate floors as we made our way down the corridor to our rooms. The entire college had that millennia-old patina that had built up in the five hundred years the college had been standing.

Sure, they'd slapped some new paint over it, but I stood in hallways that had been occupied by people longer than the US had been a country. Nothing could fake that smell. Carter opened the door to our room, and a wave of stale humidity hit me in the face.

"Fucking hell." I walked through the small space to open the window on the other side.

"That's our luck, isn't it?" Carter said with a small chuckle. "To come to the land of no AC when it's having the worst heat wave in history?"

Too true. With record highs near a hundred degrees in the day, with the nights only dropping down to the mideighties, Ireland was literally melting. These old buildings didn't have air conditioning because it never got this warm so far north. But climate change put a damper on everyone's party.

"Can you imagine how hot it's going to be under the spots with all that shit on our face?" I dropped my bags next to the twin-size bed against the far wall. Being on stage and trying to keep my energy up for hours on end was exhausting enough. The spotlight eventually became like bathing on the sun, and with the stage makeup, I'd be lucky not to have heatstroke by the end of performance week.

"Dude," Carter said. "I'm trying not to think about it."

I snorted a laugh as he unpacked his jeans and shoved them into the waist-high dresser next to the tiny study desk. He'd started working out recently in preparation for his move to LA, and the extra muscle suited him.

How many times had I done this to myself? Stared at him while he did the most mundane shit? Wanting something I'd never get?

Almost like he felt me looking at him, he stopped and glanced up, hunger and desire passing behind his eyes. I swear I saw it before he locked it down and shot me a genuine smile.

Nope. Nothing to see here.

Just two bros doing college bro shit.

"I bet you get cast as Mercutio," he said. "You both have that devil may care thing."

I smiled and ran my hands over my hair. "Yeah, maybe."

"Hey, I've been meaning to ask you about something," he said. "You never told Miri about London, right? The two of us?"

"Uh...No." I ignored the drop in my stomach from the fact that this was the first time he and I had talked about it in years. "Why?"

He shook his head and sighed. "I hate keeping secrets from Ivy. It's become a bit of a sore spot. I need to tell her."

Fuck.

"It's been four years," I said. "Aren't you guys breaking up in three weeks, anyway?"

"I don't know." He sighed and hung his head, rubbing at the back of his neck. "Even if we agree to see other people, Ivy and I will never be over. Not really. I love her, Lex. I love her more than I've ever loved anyone. It's terrifying."

I'd never admit to actually having a heart, but if I did, it would have shattered for him. He was in love with someone he'd never be able to have, and so was I. Weren't we a pair?

I waited to see if he'd add anything else, and when he didn't, I rummaged through my shit, looking for nothing in particular. If I didn't do something with my hands, I'd be tempted to twist them in his shirt and yank his lips to mine.

"You're okay with it?" he asked, his tone hopeful and optimistic. "If I tell her?"

I swallowed, hating how dry my throat felt, despising I'd have to tell Miri, and surprisingly relishing Ivy might finally learn I'd fucked her boyfriend before she ever came into the picture, something I could have used against her but hadn't.

"Yeah." It was bound to come out anyway. "If you must."

"Great." He smiled, pinching my chest with the appearance of his dimples. "Thanks, man." An awkward silence fell between us before he cleared his throat and asked, "How did that thing with your parents go?"

I furrowed my brows. "What thing?"

"Didn't you have a thing with your parents before we left? Brunch or something?"

A silly proposal. The rest of my life planned out for me. Nothing worthwhile.

"Oh...Yeah...Fine."

He looked up from his luggage, narrowing his eyes as he seemingly tried to read me and figure out my damage. "Are you sure you're okay?"

"Yeah." I shrugged it off. "Totally fine. Are you okay?"

"Yeah." He sighed and shook his head. "I found out my dad got remarried a few days ago. He knocked up the nurse that saved his life in a car accident a few years ago. I've got a little brother I've never met."

I didn't know what to say. Carter didn't get along with his father because they didn't agree on Carter's chosen career path. Because of that, he never talked about him. Carter had three younger sisters that his mother raised on her own since her sleazy ex had taken off with his mistress.

"I'm sorry, Chicago." I took a step closer to him. "Want me to have him murdered?"

He threw his head back to bark out a deep belly guffaw before shaking his head and flashing his grin in my direction. "No. He wouldn't be worth the hit money."

Damn. Ice cold.

But honestly, I had the same opinion about my old man. It was probably these shared daddy issues that had driven Carter and me together in the first place. Two knocks at our door broke the camaraderie between us, and Miri poked her head in after cracking it open.

"Just wanted to see what you guys ended up with." She took a few steps inside and spun around, taking in the meager surroundings. It was the shittiest room I'd ever stayed in, but that wasn't the point of the intensive. We wouldn't be in here very much.

"Wow." Ivy came in after her and wrapped her arms around Carter's waist to stare up at him. "Your room sucks."

"It really does, darling." Miri perched herself on my bed. "Our room is at least three times this size."

"And our beds are bigger."

Miri nodded.

Carter raised his eyebrows and gave her a goofy grin. "How much bigger?"

A lot, it turned out. After we went to inspect their living space, I wondered what in the hell they'd done to get such an upgrade.

"Well, I guess I know where we're sleeping." Carter grabbed Ivy around the waist before tumbling into her full-size mattress, pulling her down with him.

"No fucking way," I said. "I need my beauty rest, and I'm not interested in listening to you two fuck all night. I get enough of that through the walls of our apartments."

"Don't be jealous, Lucifer," Ivy said. "You're welcome to cuddle with Carter any time you want."

"What makes you think I don't already?" I meant it as a joke, but Carter met my eyes, echoes from our earlier conversation behind them, and he sat up, twisting his hat around so the brim was on the front.

Well, now it's weird.

"We should all stay in here," Miri said, draping a blouse on a hanger in the closet. "It's our last few weeks together. It's better when it's the four of us. Isn't it?" The words simply rolled off her tongue, as if summoned from somewhere deep inside her subconscious. I couldn't argue with her logic. It did feel better. And worse. And so incredibly depraved.

My focus went to Ivy, recognizing the same signs of panic in her glare, before I resettled on Miri. "I'm sure the lovebirds want their alone time before the blond one flees the nest."

Miri rolled her eyes. "Like we haven't spent the last four years basically living together. I just...I want to be close to all of you, and it'll be easier to run lines."

"Okay, Miri." Ivy gave me a nod. "Let's stay in here."

It was settled, and despite as much baggage as I had with everyone in this room, that arrangement was somehow perfect.

The next morning, we gathered around a dining table in the lounge, waiting for the mandatory orientation to start. Carter and Ivy sat across from me, their heads huddled together as they whispered salacious and revolting nothings to each other. Next to me, Miri leaned on my shoulder, her arm wrapped around my bicep as she nursed her tea. I did the same to a black coffee.

"All right, all right," Stephens said, brushing his chin-length hair over his head. Everyone in the room, all twenty US theater kids, quieted to hear what he had to say. "Thank you for showing up on time this morning. I know you're anxious to hear the cast assignments, but we need to take care of some housekeeping things first. I want to introduce you to a few people." He gestured to a table. "Ashley Murphy, our coordinator this year. She'll go through the etiquette and folklore in Killwater, so you don't accidentally piss off a townie and get us banned from Ireland. Yes, I'm talking to you, Greenburg."

Everyone laughed, and Greenburg had the nerve to blush.

"We also have Sheila Fitzgerald, the head of the liberal arts college. She'll make sure we have everything we need. Finally, we have Peter Smythe, an associate professor of theater and an old colleague of mine from my younger days. He is the reason we have this partnership, so try not to embarrass me."

The students laughed again, and I shook my head. Stephens had that *I'm-not-like-other-professors-just-call-me-Stephens* persona he thought made him more likable and approachable. If anyone took a closer look, they'd see that his relationship with his TA, Caroline, was a little too close for comfort. But that shit was none of my business, so I took another sip of coffee and sighed.

"All right, I'll hand it over to Ashley."

"Thank you, thank you." She waved as she stood and walked next to Stephens. "Welcome to Killwater. We're so pleased to have you." She was a small woman, brunette and pale-skinned, with impish features that made her seem younger than she probably was. The thing I noticed about her was the tattoo snaking up her arm and twisting under the cuff of her tank top. It looked like vines of ivy, but the detail was incredible. Fine lines and amazing shadows accented each leaf as it twirled and shimmered on her body.

"Killwater College has been standing for over five hundred years," she said, "and the town is proud of this tradition. Because we are so far north, our community was sheltered from a lot of the political strife that plagued the rest of the country. Our superstitions are engrained in everything we do, from the way we cheers before a drink to the way we plan our infrastructure. All of it has to do with these myths and legends." She clamped her hands in front of her. "Now, has anyone heard of fairies?"

The students snickered, and to be fair, taking her seriously took a bit of work. *Fairies? I mean...c'mon.*

Someone shouted, "What? Like Tinker—"

"No, no, mate." Ashley shook a finger. "I'm not talking about some sparkly Disney princess. I'm talking about *old* fairies."

"You mean like Oberon and Titania," Carter said.

"Exactly." Ashley pointed to our table and smiled. "What's your name?"

"Carter," he said.

"Carter what?"

"Oh, I know better than that." Carter grinned and drank his coffee.

Again, Ashley smiled. "Smart lad. It's believed that if a fairy knew your full name, they could bewitch you, which is why so many of us have three or sometimes four middle names. In fact, that's why middle names exist in the first place." Ashley's eyes lingered on our table for a moment more, and a shiver raced down my spine, some kind of instinct telling me that look had to do with more than interest. I probably needed a smoke, so I ignored it.

"The fairies lived in Ireland before humans, and once mankind came, a great war ensued, one that pushed the fairies farther and farther north until they had to leave this realm altogether." Ashley cleared her throat and straightened her spine. "Killwater is the last surviving vestige of the fae in this realm."

This realm? This was all just mythology and lore, right? Like the Greek gods? None of it was real. Why the fuck we were listening to this shit again?

"The forest around us is sacred," Ashley went on. "As is the town to the west. Old magic runs through the ground on which you stand. It demands your respect. What do I mean by that? It's simple." Ashley gave us another one of her impish pixie smiles. "Should you choose to go into the woods, be mindful of where you walk and what you do. Leave your area cleaner than when you found it. Do no harm to the natural landscape. And should you come across a fairy, don't piss it off."

Everyone laughed.

"You think I'm kidding." Ashley shook her head and waved a finger. "But fairies have been known to curse humans in cruel, horrible ways. Especially those who insult them. A fairy curse is no laughing matter. Of course, fairies have also been known to bestow the most generous gifts."

"Uh-oh," someone said.

"Uh-oh's right," Ashley agreed. "Be wary. Not all gifts are what they seem. They might offer you endless youth, but at the expense of having to eat human flesh for the rest of eternity. They might offer you true love, but that love becomes suffocating. Should you happen to make a deal with a fairy, be very specific. Otherwise, they are free to interpret it as they please. I would suggest you never enter into such a reckless arrangement."

"You talk about them like they're real, like they actually exist," Greenburg said.

Thank God I wasn't the only one thinking it.

"We don't have any proof that they do," Ashley said, "but we don't have any proof that they do not. Students have been known to go wandering in the woods and never return." She shrugged. "Nowadays, we'd say they got lost or maybe murdered by a jealous lover. But two or three hundred years ago? The locals imagined them wandering into the fairy realm, a world of endless daytime where no one ages and the rules of this life don't matter." Ashley paused to let that sink in. "Why should one be any less true? A missing person is a missing person, and a fairy curse is forever. So be careful. Be mindful. Use the buddy system."

Again, Ashley looked at our table, her shifty gaze circling between the four of us.

"Now let's talk locals." She carried on with her presentation, explaining that everyone in Killwater was hospitable and willing to help if needed. Most of the professors and college staff lived in the town, if not on campus. It had a few clothing shops, a bakery, a grocer, and a hardware store. There were some touristy things and several restaurants, at which we should seat ourselves if we visited.

"And c'mon out to the pub for live music," she said, giving us all a cheery grin.

"You'd better be studying your lines instead of going to the pub." Stephens turned to look at us while he spoke, which made Ashley chuckle in a tinny nails-on-chalkboard way.

"That's all I've got," Ashley said. "I'll end on this. Believe me or don't believe me. That's up to you. But there's a section of the library devoted to local folklore and fairy curses. I assure you, that's not for nothing."

We clapped, thanking her for her presentation, and then Stephens stood again.

"Thank you, Ashley. That was fascinating. Truly fascinating." He bit his bottom lip, his eyes lingering a tad too long before refocusing on us. "Okay, I know some of you were disappointed in the choice this year. *Romeo & Juliet* has been done a thousand times. But we're giving it a Tarantino spin, subverting a few expectations, and maybe playing around a bit. So, keep that in mind as I read the casting announcements. Now, you all did well, and believe me when I say this was a tough call." Stephens walked toward us and held his hand out to Carter. "This year's Romeo."

Everyone clapped and erupted into applause, and Carter's cheeks flamed in that stupid humble way of his, genuinely surprised he'd gotten the part. Like it would have been anyone else. Everybody knew Carter and Miri were the most talented among us, so it also surprised no one when Stephens turned to Miri to say, "And our Juliet."

Another sound of applause. Fuck, they'd do a great job together.

"Mercutio," Stephens said, pointing to me.

Again, that made sense. I shared with Mercutio the same intolerance for the political bullshit of our powerful families.

Stephens gestured to Ivy. "And our Tybalt."

Even more perfect. A stuck-up bitch to play the stuck-up prince of cats.

A stuck-up bitch who's also your fiancée.

I pushed that thought away.

He went around the room, naming the rest of the cast, but my gaze landed on Ivy. She held her fingers up in the shape of a gun, pointing it and playfully pulling the trigger.

"Okay, okay," Stephens said. "Now that you have your parts, finish your breakfasts. We'll do a read-through this morning and start blocking this afternoon."

"Aww, I have to kill you, Weeds," Carter groaned, leaning to kiss her temple.

"Are you sure you're going to be able to do that?"

"For the sake of art "—he pretended to sigh—"it's a sacrifice I'll have to make."

"Well, at least you don't have to kiss your best friend's boyfriend," Miri said, flipping through her script.

The stab in the center of my chest meant nothing, even as it throbbed harder when Ivy and I met stares across the table.

"Oh, c'mon." Carter leaned toward Miri, making kissy noises and flirtatiously attacking her cheek. "I'm downright adorable."

"Yeah, yeah." She shook her head. "Goodness, could you imagine if it were Ivy and Lex?" She bit the cap off a highlighter and went through her lines, turning them a bright shade of violet. "Talk about subverting expectations. The audience would shit themselves when Romeo and Juliet killed each other at the end instead of themselves."

Yeah. Wouldn't that be a fucking sight.

My heart pounded harder as Ivy's stare bored into me, and I ignored it. The best way to keep a secret was to act like there wasn't one.

"That sounds like a missed opportunity," Carter said. "Someone should tell Stephens."

"I'm not giving up the starring role in the last intensive I'll ever do." Miri looked at him like he'd grown four heads.

Ivy winced, as if the thought of this being the last one twisted her heart as painfully as it twisted mine.

One last hurrah. One last time.

"I love that you're Romeo." Miri reached across the table to grab his hand in reassurance. "We're going to nail this thing."

"You bet your royal ass we are." Carter looked at Ivy and turned his hat around so the brim sat on the back of his head. "Hey, you okay?"

She cleared her throat and plastered that fake politician smile on her face, the one in every photo ever printed of her.

"Yeah, of course," she said.

"Tybalt's not the lead"—he gave her hand a squeeze—"but it's still a great part."

"It's not about that." She pushed to her feet, shoving her script in her bag. "I'll see you guys at rehearsal."

"Wait," Carter said. "Where are you going?"

"I've gotta go to the bathroom," she called over her shoulder.

Carter was already stuffing his phone in his pants so he could go after her, but Miri held up her hand and slung her purse over her shoulder. "I'll go. She's been weird since we got here." She gave me a kiss before taking off after her friend, leaving me alone with mine.

II

IVY

I needed air and an escape from that stifling room. All that talk of fairy curses had me feeling like I might throw up. With the play about the star-crossed lovers and the fact I was in an arranged marriage with my worst enemy, I might as well have been stuck in a nightmare worthy of the Brothers Grimm. I pushed through the doors at the end of the hall, the oxygen outside less heavy than inside, but more humid and sticky.

Fuck.

I ran my hands through my hair and tried to get a hold of myself.

It'll be okay, I said. *I'll review past litigation and...and...what?* It was definitely illegal for our parents to force us into an arranged marriage, and since we were both over the age of eighteen, we could refuse. But that would come at the expense of my family allegiance. If I didn't do this, if *we* didn't do this, we would be cast out—destitute—completely on our own. Maybe that shouldn't have scared me as much as it did, but so much of my identity and self worth had always been tied up in being a Washington. I didn't know who I was if I wasn't in this family. I couldn't give it all up for the sake of love, especially when distribution of power sat at such an imbalance.

Between my parents, both former presidents, and Kellan, soon-to-be president-elect, they could bury us. They could destroy our lives and hide us away forever without the public ever questioning what happened. Money had a lot to do with it, but I didn't know what would happen if I did find a way out of this, much less if we put it into action.

The logical part of me urged caution. Evelyn and Kellan were pathological in their quest for power. They wouldn't stop just because I protested. This would have to be methodical and precise. The more I told myself that, the more I'd believe it. I had to believe it.

But sleeping next to Carter last night had been a challenge. Every time he rolled over and wrapped his arm around my waist, it weighed a thousand pounds. Whenever he told me he loved me and whispered filthy things, I remembered I was going to have to break his heart sometime soon, and I didn't know how to do it. I didn't want to do it.

I bent over at the waist, my hands on my knees and black spots in my vision. *Am I having a panic attack? Oh my God. I am.*

"Hey, you okay?" came an Irish accent from my right.

I jumped and stood up straight, taking in the woman leaning against the stone wall and smoking a cigarette. She had dark, shiny hair and kind brown eyes, tattoos of ivy winding from her wrists up her arms and under the sleeves of her black T-shirt.

She terrified me instantly...and yet, I wanted to know everything about her.

"Yeah, I'm okay," I said. "I think so."

"You look a little anxious." She took another long inhale, the cherry of her cigarette glowing around her face.

"It's just...uh..." What was I going to say? *I'm just freaking out because I have to marry my boyfriend's best friend. You know that old pity party. No big deal.* No doubt, this stranger had better things to do than listen to me whine.

"Nothing," I finally said. "Never mind."

She raked her curious gaze over me, the scan caressing my skin like fingertips. I wore shorts and a tank top, nothing too revealing, but I suddenly felt like I'd been stripped bare and not in a good way. She held out her hand.

"Siobhan Murphy. You have really pretty eyes."

"Ivy Washington," I replied, taking her hand and the compliment. "And thank you. Washington Blue, it's called. Though it's more like silver, I guess."

"Ohhhh, it's you." She raised an eyebrow. "I've heard about you."

"Yeah? All good things, I hope."

"What would be the fun in that?" Siobhan grinned, her eyes glittering in an entrancing way, like I could peer into them forever and all my issues would disappear. *How is she doing that?*

I snorted out a laugh.

"Your mother's someone important back in the States, yeah?" She stabbed out her cigarette in the ashtray on top of the garbage can and immediately lit another one. She offered one to me. Normally I declined unless it was Lex, but I needed something for my nerves, so I took it, lit it, and inhaled.

"President Evelyn Washington," I said, letting the head rush soothe me.

"Okay," she muttered, and that was the most thought she gave it. I expected a barrage of questions. Most people wanted to know what it was like to live in the White House or if I'd ever seen Lincoln's ghost, but Siobhan only pursed her lips and took a step closer. She genuinely didn't give a shit who my parents were, and that sort of freedom was liberating. "I run the pub in town. I'm here helping my sister, Ashley."

"I saw her presentation." I inhaled deep on the cigarette.

"Don't believe a word of it," she said.

I furrowed my eyebrows. "About the fairies or about the people being nice and hospitable."

"The people, obviously," she said with another laugh.

I paused, my cigarette halfway to my lips, but when she winked at me, I huffed out a small chuckle at the tease.

"Lighten up, Ivy. Whatever's bothering you will pass."

For some strange reason, I *wanted* to tell her my secret. Maybe I just needed to get it off my chest. But what could she do about it? My troubles would become her troubles, and if she knew who I was, she could break it to the press before I wanted anyone else to know.

No. Best keep it to myself.

"Thank you for the cigarette."

"You're welcome," she said.

"Ivy?" Miri's voice echoed from around the corner and my best friend came into view. "There you are! I've been looking for you."

"I'm here," I said. "I was just talking to—" But when I turned around, Siobhan had walked away, her hands in the pockets of her jeans.

"Hey, are you all right?" Miri put a hand on my shoulder.

"Yeah, just...tired," I said. "No big deal."

"Okay." She seemed unconvinced and grabbed my free hand the way she used to do when we were at Mount Oberon together. She pulled me over to a concrete bench near the fountain, wrapping an arm over my shoulders, enveloping me in her flowery scent. "You're my best friend, Ivy. I love you dearly. You can tell me anything."

Anything except this.

My heart hurt, aching painfully in my chest. I wanted to spill my guts, but once I did, things would change. Once they knew, they could never *not* know. I wished I didn't know.

"I don't want this to be over," I lied. "I don't want you to leave. I don't want—" I cut myself off before I confessed too much.

"It's not forever, darling. I'll visit. Carter will visit. It'll be okay."

I took a deep breath and nodded, and even though the emotion of the moment nearly overwhelmed me, the unnamed tension between us blared to life. Her pouty lips stole my attention, and I wished I could have married her instead. Maybe, in a different life, we could have run away together after that night at Mount Oberon. We could have changed our names and lived in secret, loving each other until the end of time. Her gaze dropped to my mouth and a flicker danced behind her eyes, almost like she had the same thoughts.

So much went unsaid in those few heartbeats, so much longing and yearning.

Then she glanced away, and pulled me further into a hug, breaking the moment. I sank into that springtime, flowery scent that had always driven me wild. Being in Miri's arms was always like coming home. I wrapped mine around her waist and fought back the tears, wishing I could tell her the whole truth and wishing she could give me some of that old-soul wisdom. Even though I didn't ask, she must have sensed I needed it. Because she kissed my temple and said, "My nanny used to tell me good things never last. That's what makes them so good."

And I didn't know if she meant Carter or that disastrous desire in our relationship.

This experience was called an intensive for a reason.

Now that we knew which parts we were playing, we had a week to memorize our lines. Carter and Miri were beside themselves with study. We rehearsed for eight hours a day, four hours in the morning and four hours in the afternoon, with a two-hour break in the middle.

After three days, the heat had gotten to even those of us used to a Virginian summer.

"No, put it over there," Stephens snapped at one of the stage-hands. "Over there. Over there."

"Jesus." I fanned myself with my script. We'd stopped at the part where Romeo and Mercutio crashed the Capulet party because Stephens wasn't sure if he wanted Juliet to be hiding behind the stairwell the first time she sees Romeo or if he wanted her behind the enormous fake spider plant.

"It's like I'm talking to myself," Stephens murmured, returning his attention to Miri when the stagehand stalked off. He was sweaty and disheveled. We all were. The auditorium was the coolest place on campus, but even that would be putting it mildly. I hadn't felt cool since I landed on this side of the Atlantic.

Carter raised his eyebrows and grimaced at Stephens's outburst.

"Where were we?" Stephens said. "Okay, Miri. Come over here. Carter, stand this way. Now take it from the top, and when he says the line, you move over there."

I pretended to talk to Piper, who played Juliet's father, and watched the two of them work. Even though I'd applied to be here, the heat and Stephens's pissy attitude made me wish I were anywhere else. The afternoon dragged, and by the time we finally reached the end, I could barely stand. I needed an ice bath and a weeklong nap.

"That was brutal." Carter slung an arm over my shoulder as we walked back to the dorms.

"Stephens needs to get laid," Lex said.

"Jesus, Lex," I said. "Not everything is about getting laid."

"It's just hot," Miri cut in. "Everyone's temperamental when they're uncomfortable."

I was about to mention Stephens was a dick most of the time anyway, but my phone rang with an incoming FaceTime from Kit and Jon. I told Carter I'd see him back at the dorm and headed outside for privacy.

"Hey loser," Kit said after I accepted. "How's Ireland? See a leprechaun yet?"

"Har har." The tension in my chest eased at the sight of my siblings. We didn't always get along, but they had survived the same shitty upbringing as me, so we were trauma-bonded for life. "Ireland is hotter than the sun."

"Yeah, you look melted," Jon said. Like me, he had the fairer coloring of our father — the strawberry-blond hair and the gray eyes. When we were little, Jon and I used to be mistaken for each other. It didn't help that we were only eighteen months apart. Now, the only people who could tell who was who in baby pictures were him and me.

"I need your advice," Kit said. "Mother is urging me to consider majoring in cybersecurity, but we all know that's a boring-ass way to rot in corporate hell."

I snorted a laugh. My dear little sister never minced words.

"I'm thinking about doing the hacking thing and not telling her. What do you think?"

"I told her," Jon said, "that she should just do what she wants. She's an adult now, right? Evelyn has to cut the umbilical cord at some point."

Kit scratched her fingers over her forehead. "You'd think that having five children would mean the ones in the middle sort of blurred together. I should have freedom through anonymity."

"Not with Evelyn Washington," Jon said.

They had a laugh together, but then focused their attention on me.

"Well?" Kit said. "What do you think?"

A month ago, I would have told her she had to toe the family line. *A Washington is a Washington.* This was the price we paid to live the life we did, and all that other cliché nonsense my mother had spoon-fed me since I was a child. But now?

I needed to protect Kit and Jon from falling into this trap the way I had. I'd done everything that woman had ever asked me. I did the poli-sci/theater double major. I'd gotten into law school. I was going to be the next Washington president. None of it mattered. She still had me by the throat.

If they could assert some level of independence now, they should.

"I think Jon's right," I said. "Do what you want."

"Wait, what?" Jon said.

"Are you high?" Kit raised her dark eyebrows. "I called you to be the voice of reason."

"What happened to everything you do now reflects on your future self?" Jon lit a cigarette and took a deep inhale.

I didn't have a good answer, short of telling them what was really going on, and I didn't know if I wanted to do that. If I kept it to myself, it was almost like it wasn't happening. If I didn't speak it out loud, it wasn't true, right? I'd pressed pause. Lex and I had both pressed pause.

Then again, they were the only ones who could commiserate. They were the only ones, aside from Lex, who would understand. Better to tell them than some random stranger. So I did. I spilled the beans about brunch and how Kellan Fairfax was running for election now that sufficient time had passed since Marcus's death.

"They did it to me; they'll do it to you," I said. "To you both. So if you can get some measure of freedom now, take it."

Kit's mouth hung open, the messy bun on the top of her head messier from having run her hands through it while I talked. Jon had stabbed out his smoke and lit another. Neither had spoken since I started my story.

"They can't do that," Kit finally said. "Ivy, they can't do that."

"I know. When I get home from Ireland, I'm going to figure something out. There has to be a way out of this." I shook my head and sighed. "They control our trust. They can cut me off. They can do a lot worse...but it's the twenty-first century. I'm not their political pawn."

"Let me do some research," Kit ran her hand over her face, giving me a look of pure sympathy, a rare thing for her stoic personality. "I'll see if I can dig anything up."

"Jesus, you and Lex?" Jon sighed, but then started laughing, and once he started, Kit joined in.

"Stop it," I whined, clenching my eyes shut at the humiliation burning through my throat and into my chest. "It's not funny."

"Oh, come on," Jon said. "It's hilarious. The only two people who hate each other more than our parents are you and Lex. Now you have to get *married?*"

"Fifty says she kills him first," Kit said.

"Oh, I'll take that action," Jon said. "Lex has been plotting her demise since he was twelve."

"Not helpful." I rubbed my forehead, the onset of a migraine brewing behind my eyes. "Do you two idiots need anything else?"

Kit shook her head and wiped at her eyes while Jon clutched at his chest, throwing his head back to chortle to himself.

"I'm hanging up now. I hate you both."

"Hate you more," Kit managed to say before I hung up.

Pissed at almost everyone in my family, I shoved my phone in my back pocket and turned to go find my friends. At least Kit had offered to help before razzing me about it, and I'd never be able to repay her for that. When I glanced up, I saw Siobhan standing a few yards away, leaning against the wall and smoking a cigarette. Panic sliced through me, nearly stealing my breath, and I paused. She was close enough for me to recognize her...did that mean she could hear me, too?

Oh shit.

She wiggled her fingers in a friendly wave before her sister, Ashley, got her attention and she walked back inside the school.

12

LEX

I hated it in Ireland.

It was so damn hot and miserable that my insides were boiling. There was no cool place to go except for the creek, and we couldn't spend all day there when we had rehearsal to slog through. Ivy and I weren't in the second half of the play, so somewhere around day five, we weren't needed on set in the afternoon, giving us ample time to get off-book in the water.

"Any but one word with one of us? Couple it with something; make it a word and a blow," I recited, lounging on my towel in the grass.

"You shall find me apt enough to that, sir, and you will give me occasion." Ivy stood in the water and ducked her shimmering tangerine hair back to get it wet, letting out a moan that echoed through my torso down to my cock. I zeroed in on her long neck, the curve of her breasts, and the way her stomach dipped into her belly button and disappeared under that string bikini.

She made that moan when she came. I'd heard it through the walls a thousand times in four years, always the result of Carter's handiwork. Lord knew he had a talented mouth, but I wondered what Ivy's felt like. I thought about more illicit topics, like how soft her skin might be under that bikini and how tight her pussy—*Wait... What? Where the fuck is that coming from?*

"Could you not take some occasion without giving?" I replied, inhaling deep on my cigarette and readjusting my hips so my cock had more room in my trunks.

"Mercutio," she said, rubbing her hands over her face. "Thou consort'st with Romeo—"

"Consort!" Here was where I kept screwing up. I couldn't remember what came next, something about minstrels and discords, basically a big *no homo, bro.* "Ahh." I let out a growl as I picked up my script and searched for the line. "Fuck."

"You'll get it." She rose out of the water and walked toward me, looking like some fucked-up fantasy version of a forest nymph in her tiny swimsuit. We were in the woods, after all, and as water dripped down all that smooth silky ivory skin, I itched to reach out and touch.

Damn it.

Focus.

I didn't know why I was having this reaction to her. Sure, objectively, Ivy was hot. She had a great body and a killer smile, and I ached to twist that wild hair in a fist and see how hard I could yank. But she was my archnemesis. Carter's girl. Miri's best friend.

My fiancée.

"You think he means fucking?" She wrapped her towel under her arms as she sat next to me. "Consort'st?"

"I think that's implied."

She snorted a laugh and reached for the cigarettes, lighting one and taking a long drag. "Could you imagine? Mercutio and Romeo in a homosexual affair?"

I laughed to hide how close to the truth she'd sniffed. "Romeo's such an emotional twat, it wouldn't have surprised me at all."

She returned the good humor with a small grin before returning her focus to the trees and the rambling water, accented by the cacophony of summer wildlife. "It's beautiful here, isn't it?"

"Yeah." My chest deflated with a forlorn sigh, as if I could will myself to disappear into those woods if I only tried.

"What if we just stayed?" she said. It was low, almost too low for me to hear it. "What if we never went home?"

For one moment, I let myself have the fantasy. Perhaps Miri and Carter could come. We could live together, the four of us, in some cabin where no one would ever take photos of us again. We wouldn't be forced to marry each other, and we could love whomever we wanted every night. Alas, such a thing would never be anything more than a pipe dream.

"They'd track us down." I hated how sad and desperate my voice sounded.

"We could run away." She gave me a shrug, as if the idea was totally feasible.

"Still on your crusade to save us all?" I barked out a laugh, imagining myself going approximately two hours before I broke down and booked us a hotel on one of my family's credit cards. "I'm not built for life on the road."

"I might run away," she said, her hopeless expression nearly cracking my frozen dead heart.

"And leave me to deal with our parents on my own?" I pretended to be outraged at the blind disregard. "Some friend you are."

Her eyes shot to me. "Is that what we are now? Friends?"

"Maybe that's too far," I said, ignoring the lurch in my chest that told me this was a lie. "But we're not really enemies anymore, are we?"

"No, I guess we're not." Her cheeks flushed and that stupid X appeared on her neck, making me desperate to know what she'd been thinking about to put it there. I let it go because at the end of the day, I loved Miri, Ivy loved Carter, and we would never love each other.

"We might have a problem," she said, taking another long drag on the smoke.

"Oh, yeah?"

"I was talking to Kit and Jon a few days ago about our engagement."

I made a sad chuffing noise. *Engagement.* Some fucking marriage we'll have.

"Kit said she would help us find a way out of this, some statute we might have overlooked." Ivy winced and wrapped her arm tighter around her knees. "I'm pretty sure one of the locals overheard the whole story."

A small alarm bell went off in my head, but I didn't know about what. The entire world would find out soon enough. What did it matter if some random stranger overheard a conversation out of context? Still, I asked, "Which local?"

"Her name is Siobhan. She owns the pub in town." Ivy shrugged. "I don't think she knows what she overheard, but I thought I'd tell you in case it comes out somehow."

I sighed and shook my head. "*The Puck's* not over here, X. We're safe for now."

"Yeah, but the paparazzi killed Miri's parents. People are hungry for paydays everywhere."

A question hung between us, one that had gotten louder and more persistent every day we spent with them.

Is it time we tell them?

We should have done it when it happened. Miri and Carter were special to me, to both of us. They deserved the respect of knowing something this life-altering, but the same reasons we didn't say anything a week ago were still there. We had over two weeks left of this intensive, and it was already stressful enough, especially for Miri and Carter, leads of the play, who carried the weight of the performance on their shoulders. This was important. We couldn't afford to fuck it up.

I bit my lip and let the question hang there for now.

In time, I told myself. *We'd tell them when it was right.*

The four of us had lived across the hall from each other for the last three years. We'd spent countless nights hanging out, drinking, and partying until the wee hours of the morning, but we always had our separate space. Miri and I usually went back to her room, and Carter and Ivy to his. A line existed between us as couples, clearly defined, clearly delineated, and even though Miri and I fucked around with other people, there were two who were off-limits.

In four years, we'd never been as close as we were in that Killwater dorm room together. Night after night, Carter and Ivy hung out in her bed across the room from Miri and me. We ran lines until we couldn't read anymore, and then we watched whatever cheesy British comedy we found on TV.

We talked.

We talked in a way we hadn't in years, laughing and teasing. For the moment, I could almost forget that this would all be over soon, that Ivy and I were staring down law school and a future together. A future full of forced smiles and extravagant galas where we'd pretend to be madly in love. None of that mattered in those small moments of joy. I could forget how absolutely fucked my life had become.

But then...things changed.

One morning, I woke up to an empty bed. Miri was in the bathroom, and when I rolled over, I found Ivy's bed empty as well. Carter stood by the closet, his boxers low on his hips with his beautiful muscular body on display. He'd just gotten out of the shower and his hair was in wet spikes on the top of his head.

Good. Fucking. God.

What a sight.

He shook out a T-shirt and turned, locking eyes with me. When he caught me staring, he curled one side of his mouth into a grin, flashing a dimple as his gaze softened. "See something you like, DC?"

His expression had turned hungry, and a depraved part of me responded. I had to physically restrain myself from getting out of bed and yanking him back to it by the waistband of those boxer briefs.

"What if I do, Chicago?" I reached for my cigarettes on the side table, lighting one and sighing in relief as the nicotine buzzed in my veins. "What are you going to do about it?"

He straightened and tilted his chin up at me, looking down from under hooded eyes. When he darted his tongue out over his lips, I zeroed in on the motion. How could a simple pink muscle be so perfect? It shimmered in the morning light, promising temptation and sweet, sinful release.

I inhaled deeper on my cigarette.

"Don't tease me," he said. "Or I'll give you something healthier to suck."

I whipped my focus to him.

What the fuck was this now?

For four years, we'd danced around this line between us. We acted like it hadn't happened, and though we joked with each other in that vaguely fraternal way guys did, we'd never gotten close to that line again. Since landing in Ireland, Carter had not only brought up what happened in London but had also eye fucked me first thing in the morning. Now he was flirting?

"Would you want that?" He raised an eyebrow. "One last time, for old time's sake?"

What the fuck is happening? Am I dreaming?

"C'mon, Lex." He took a step closer to me, moving his hips in a hypnotizing gait that meant he knew what he was packing and exactly what to do with it. "You've always known who I am, and I know who you are."

My eyebrows furrowed.

Why did that sound so familiar? What the—

Before I could think anymore about it, the door opened and Ivy came in, freshly showered and wearing jean shorts with a black tank top. Her long orange hair had been braided down the side, and even though she'd put makeup on, she couldn't hide the bags under her eyes. I knew her well, and she was exhausted.

She threw her dirty clothes by her bag and wrapped her arms around Carter's waist from behind, tucking her head into the space between his shoulder blades. The intimacy in the moment overwhelmed me, and I looked away to give them their privacy.

But I felt it on me—Carter's incinerating stare. I looked back and froze at the heat in his eyes, the possessive way he held Ivy's hands and the cruel twist in his lips mixing with the dominance in his posture. Normally, Carter was all sunshine and rainbows. He could charm the pants off a priest, and everyone who spent any time around him fell in love with him. In the years I'd known him, his light had not dimmed. I'd tried to devour it in the beginning, but he had an infinite supply.

Maybe that was why he'd appealed to me, why I couldn't leave him alone. His light filled my darkness in a way no one else could, not even Miri. But this was new. His stance, the way he held on to her, and the way he glared at me. It all claimed Ivy as his. It sent a message.

Stay the fuck away.

I didn't know how to interpret that. I was relieved when Miri came into the room, bitching about the water pressure.

"I swear, everything about America is better," she said. "Even the smell."

Just like that, whatever was brewing between Carter and me vanished. He smiled and cracked a joke and the day went on as normal.

13

IVY

Carter's hot body pressed against mine from behind, his torso to my back and his hands wrapped around my wrists next to my head. It was so hot in the tiny back-stage closet. We were supposed to be freshly showered and ready to party. We were supposed to be meeting Miri and Lex in the foyer to go to the pub.

Yeah, we had that stupid camping trip with the rest of the theater group early tomorrow morning, but we needed a night to blow off some steam. Carter had other plans. He'd been staring at my ass for hours, so when he'd finally gotten me alone, he shoved me up against the wall and bit my earlobe, making me wilt against him, pliant and ready for anything he wanted.

"You've been teasing me all day," he said. "Wearing your tank top and these fucking cutoffs."

He kneeled behind me, sliding his hands up my thighs to grip the sides of my shorts and ducked his fingers under the waistband of the denim and my underwear. I nearly yelped as he yanked them down to my ankles but not off, keeping my feet tied together. Another shudder went through me at the thought that I'd be at his mercy, completely bound to his whim.

He stood again, his head pressing against the side of mine, and I arched my pelvis into the growing bulge currently at my ass. When he hissed in a breath, I bit back a laugh. I'd never get over how much I loved being with him. He was the only one who unraveled me so completely and who made me feel safe and content and treasured all at the same time.

Who could ever replace him?

Lex.

The thought came to me suddenly, stabbing me in the gut, and I almost recoiled from the weight.

No, I thought. *Not here. Not now. Stay in the present.*

"I live to tease you, Mister Scott." The words tumbled out of my mouth, forced out by a version of me that clung to him like a liferaft.

"Oh, don't I know it." The sound of his metal zipper sliding down filled the small space, and I shivered, knowing what would come next. I wanted it more than anything. It had been a week since we'd been able to have this much alone time, and hell, what an eternity. He poised himself at my entrance and slid home, and I accommodated him, the feeling so familiar and perfect and right.

How many times had he been inside me? How many times had we been this connected? Hundreds. Thousands. Millions, and now, we were down to our last two weeks. It broke my heart.

No.

Determined to forge my own way, I refocused on how good it felt when he gripped my shoulder, how much I ached each time he hit that spot only he could find, and how I spread my knees when he circled around my hip to rub my clit.

"No one else can make you feel like this," he growled. "Only me, right? Only I know how to make Ivy Washington purr."

We'd role-played before. We'd done the possessive, jealous boyfriend thing. But in real life, Carter and I trusted each other. For me, there was no one else, save for one distinctly unavailable princess. Despite this, his rough tone sounded alarms in the back of my mind, his voice ringing too true.

"Say it," he snarled, biting into my shoulder, the back of my neck, and my ears. "Say it."

"Only you," I said. "Only you."

"That's right," he said. "Only you turn me on like this. Make me come undone."

My stomach twisted and my heart sank as I curled my fingers into fists. Then he changed. His arms came around me, holding me close, and his thrusts slowed, the animalistic energy between us dissipating to leave a tender warmth in its wake.

"Remember that," he whispered. "When this is all over. Remember us like this."

"Carter." My voice shook as I struggled to form words.

"Shh," he said. "I'm not done with you yet."

He made me come twice before he did, and at the end, he turned me around so he could stare into my eyes as his release hit. Carter and I had been through everything together. We'd done things that would embarrass me to admit to anyone else, but this was the most connected to him I'd ever felt. This tether between us burned brighter than it ever had, and that made me feel worse.

Very soon, I'd have to sever it, and it would break his heart. I didn't want to do that to him, and I didn't want to do that to myself. With that heavy on my conscience, we righted ourselves and met our friends downstairs.

Irish pubs were different from American pubs. Sure, there were wooden seats around a bar and a few tables at the back with people playing beer pong, but the rest of the space was furnished with couches and recliners, like you'd just walked into someone's home. Which was the whole idea. If a person came to someone's place to drink, they expected to be treated like family. The live music had just started, pipes and fiddles blaring from the stage by the window, and we found spots on two love seats perpendicular to each other in the far corner to enjoy the show.

"There's a beer pong tournament going on tonight," Carter said. "We should sign up."

"Romeo, the Irish drink on an entirely different level," Miri cut in, giving her best mischievous grin. "We'll get our asses handed to us."

"I don't know about that." Carter pursed his lips and gestured to me. "Weeds gets better the more she drinks."

"You two *are* a pretty good team," Miri said.

"What do you say, Weeds?" My boyfriend raised his eyebrows at me, a playfulness in his eyes I hadn't seen all day. "You in?"

"How could I ever refuse you?" I returned his smile with one of my own.

"DC?"

"Sure," Lex said.

Carter bolted up and walked over to the sign-up sheet, looking for spots on the board to put our names. Lex went to get beers while Miri and I clapped along to the music. Around my second drink, she convinced me to dance with her. I didn't know what I was doing, so I kicked my legs and imitated the people around me. When it was my turn to get drinks, I went to the bar and squeezed my way in between the bodies to get the tender's attention.

"Four pints," I said. He nodded and turned to get them.

"I thought that was you," came a voice from my right.

Siobhan.

"Hey," I said. "What are you doing here?"

"I live here," she said. "I own the place. Remember?"

"Oh. Yeah." *Duh.* "How have you been?"

"Fine. You?" She nodded to the dance floor. "I saw you out there. You seem to be in better spirits than the last time we crossed paths."

That reminded me of my conversation with my siblings and the whole engagement thing. "Look, about what you might have overheard—"

"Oh, I didn't hear anything." Siobhan shook her head and shrugged, acting completely nonchalant.

I narrowed my eyes, suspicion warring with the intense urge to believe her. She had an appeal that reeled me in, that made me want to follow her into battle. I had no idea where it was coming from, and a moment passed where I silently debated whether she was telling the truth.

"But let's say I did hear something," Siobhan said. "Why don't you tell your despicable parents to piss off? Move away? Live your own life?"

I cleared my throat and plastered that fake politician smile on my face, the one I'd been trained to fall back on in situations where I felt uncomfortable. "It's not that easy."

She nodded, but the look in her eyes said she didn't buy it.

"I'd ask that you not say anything to anyone, please. I mean, I can't stop you. I don't even know you. But...please."

She held up a hand, perhaps trying to reassure me. "My lips are sealed."

"Thank you." The relief that poured into my lungs made me weightless. The bartender came back with my beers and sat them down in front of me. I reached into my pocket for my money, but Siobhan put her hand on my mine and pushed it away.

"This round's on the house."

"Really?" I asked. "Thank you."

"You guys need it. The shitstorm coming your way?" She blew out a whistle and shook her head, which made me force out this awkward laugh. "I wouldn't want to be in your shoes when your friends find out about your little secret."

"Yes, well—thanks again." This conversation had taken a turn into a topic I didn't want anyone else to overhear, so I gathered the glasses to walk away, but Siobhan stopped me.

"There's a midsummer festival in the woods to celebrate the longest day of the year." Siobhan flashed me a friendly smile, that strange alluring twinkle returning to her soft brown eyes. "We'll have a few bonfires along with some drinking and music. Usually, only the locals are invited, but you and your friends should come. You could use the revelry."

She held up a flyer announcing the celebration, giving me an expectant smile. It was in three days, and by then, we'd be knee deep in final rehearsals. I should have said no. I should have told her our schedules would be too hectic. But *everything* in me wanted to say yes. Bonfires, drinking, dancing. It sounded amazing, and I didn't want to be rude by not accepting.

"Uh, yeah. Sure." I gave her a nod. "We'll swing by."

"Great." She folded the flyer in half and then in half again, tucking it in the back pocket of my jean shorts before giving me a wink. "I'll see you there, Ivy."

"Yeah, see you there." I smiled and headed back to my friends, shoving down the unshakable notion that I might have just agreed to a party with the devil. What *was* it about her that I found so attractive? It wasn't in a sexual way, though she was beautiful. It was more...kismet, like I'd always been meant to find her, and now that I had, I needed to listen to her, to fall in beside her.

Lex, Carter, and Miri were missing from the table, and when I went out back, I found my boyfriend and the princess already engaged in a round of beer pong with their first opponents.

"What the hell?" I gaped, both at the fact that he'd gone on without me and, apparently, they were winning.

"You weren't around," he said, gesturing to Miri as she took a shot and nailed it in the other team's cup. "She was ready to go."

I grimaced, looking at Lex. "Are you saying what I think you're saying?"

"Oh, c'mon, X," Lex flashed me a grin and lit a cigarette. "It's only a few rounds of beer pong. What could go wrong?"

Lex and I were unstoppable. We ran that table, knocking people down left and right. Even Siobhan and her favorite roommate, Donnelly, couldn't beat us. This had the unfortunate side effect of getting me drunker than I wanted.

I was maybe five beers into the night (who was counting?) when the lines between us started to blur. By now, the excitement over team DC had faded. Most of the crowd had relocated back inside the pub, leaving Carter and Miri halfheartedly tossing the ball to try to defeat us.

I hit two more cups, getting another turn.

"Damn," Lex said, tapping his cigarette. "You are on fire."

"The focus of a tiger," I teased, pointing at my eyes with my index and middle finger before pointing back at Carter across the table.

"Hmm." Carter made a noise low and deep in his throat. "You think so?"

"Count on it, Mister Scott."

He raised an eyebrow, his eyes shimmering with that delightful sense of mischief only he could bring to a situation. "Okay." He straightened and turned to Miri. "Juliet, I know a secret."

"Oh, yeah?" Miri said. "What's that?"

"I know how to distract Ivy Washington."

Uh-oh.

My heart raced. I didn't like that glint in his eye or the purse of his lips.

"I know how to get her full, undivided attention."

Oh no.

"*And* I know how to distract Lex at the same time."

Lex's low chuckle echoed next to me, and he took a long inhale on his cigarette, tapping it into the tray on the edge of the beer pong table.

"You have my attention, Romeo," Miri said. "Drive it home."

"If they make another cup, I take off my shirt," he said. "If they make a second one, I take off my pants."

"This is your sad attempt to get naked, Chicago." Lex shook his head and sighed. "You never needed a reason for that."

"If they make a third cup," Carter went on, shifting his eyes from me to Lex in a blatant challenge, "I'll make out with Miri."

My heart kicked in a hot, fiery jolt.

Miri gasped.

Lex snorted. "Is that supposed to make me jealous?"

"Does it?" Carter asked, seeming to purposely provoke Lex.

"I'd be more disappointed to see Miri make out with Ivy," Lex said.

"That can be arranged," Miri chimed in, her tongue curling around her canine tooth like she was remembering our last night at boarding school. I tried not to tremble.

"Down girl," Carter said, and Miri laughed. "You're saying it wouldn't bother you if I grabbed Miri's hair, fisted it between my fingers"—he drew it out, taunting Lex—"dragged her head back, and made her suck on my tongue?"

The visual hit me in the gut, clenching my cunt in a twist of arousal and jealous desire.

I wanted to see it.

No, I didn't.

Yes, I did.

Wait.

He was distracting me. That's all he was trying to do, and it worked.

Focus.

I shot my turn.

Miss.

Plunk.

Carter reached behind his head, his massive bicep flexing as he fisted his T-shirt and ripped it over his head. I may live to be a hundred years old, and the sight of shirtless Carter Scott would still make my knees tremble.

"Would it bother you if I did the same thing to Ivy?" Lex raised an eyebrow, a hint of a challenge in his tone that he normally reserved for me.

What?

Carter laughed. *Fucking laughed.* "You're welcome to try, my friend."

And that? Well, as Carter liked to say, *that* sounded like a challenge. He should have known better. Lex wouldn't back down, and neither would I.

"You think I wouldn't do it?" I put my hands on my hips, heat burning up my neck and into my cheeks at his disbelief. Didn't he know me at all?

"I think you'd rather swim through hot garbage than make out with him." Carter nodded to Lex like he was trash, nothing but scum on his shoes.

How about marry him? The thought pushed into my mind, swirling there for a moment before I shoved it away.

"You'd be surprised," I said.

Carter smiled at what he thought was a bluff. "Put your balls where your mouth is."

I looked at Lex, expecting to see hesitation. Instead, I saw only the thrill of the battle, as amped by Carter as he'd ever been midfight with me. Miri pursed her amused lips and leaned on the table just enough for her summery blouse to hang open and reveal a teasing hint of cleavage.

Memories of the one night between us skated through my mind, and my skin flamed at the echo of her skin pressed against mine. If she was in this, so was I.

"Fine," I said. "If you're sure this is what you want."

"I don't think you have the guts." Carter tilted his head to the side, a proverbial golden retriever bowing down to show it wanted to play.

I wondered why he was egging me on or if there was an ulterior motive, but I didn't focus on it. We were having fun. Just college friends poking at each other at a pub in some random tiny town.

"I accept your terms," Lex said. "You hit another shot, I'll strip. You hit three, I'll make your dreams come true."

The sexual innuendo hung between them like a visible charge, blatant and obvious.

"Don't make promises you can't keep." Carter stared at Lex, and the look Lex gave him in response set something ablaze inside me, like it held more than one meaning between them. Then Carter took his turn.

Plunk.

Plunk.

He got his balls back to try again.

Lex twisted his lips into a wry grin before he removed his shirt, twisting his arms over his head to pull it off. My attention caught on his beautiful tattoos, his entire torso lined with them, as he pushed the button through the hole on his jeans and shoved the denim to a puddle at his feet. I tried not to stare. I tried to ignore the designs snaking up his arms and the trail of hair going down the center of his abdomen, disappearing under his black boxers.

But I was drunk, and the beer goggles were firmly in place. I lusted over his body like I had any right to do so. Especially in front of my boyfriend and his girlfriend.

It was the first time I'd ever looked at him and *wanted.*

Wanted what? I didn't know. All of him, maybe? Just a bite?

When Lex caught me staring, he froze.

Miss.

Miss.

Carter's flying Ping-Pong balls drew my attention back to the game.

"Right." I cleared my throat. "Your turn, Lex."

He sat down his cigarette and picked up the balls, shooting one and then the other across the table.

Plunk.

Plunk.

"That's three," Lex said, calling Carter's bluff. "Pay up."

Carter's eyes lingered on mine for a second, seeming to ask if I was watching, before they shifted to Miri, who grinned up at him like she was seeing the sun for the first time. She licked her lips, and I zeroed in on the motion, remembering how much I'd loved to wrestle her tongue with my own. My pulse pounded as he grabbed the back of her neck and leaned his head down, his lips centimeters from hers.

"Wait," Lex said.

Carter stopped and looked up at him. I half expected Lex to call this whole thing off and to tell him to get away from his girlfriend. I should have known better. Backing down had never been his style.

"Pants off," Lex demanded.

"What?" Carter blinked and glanced to me before back to Lex.

"Two was pants off. Three was making out." Lex inhaled on his cigarette, letting it out in a thick cloud of smoke. "Take off your fucking pants."

I tightened my hands into fists as I waited to see what Carter would do, every part of my body so aware of this pulsing thread between the four of us. Miri's hands went to the waistband of Carter's jeans, and I took a deep breath as she undid them and shoved them to the ground, leaving him standing in his boxers.

Then Carter tilted his head and pressed his mouth to Miri's, tunneling his fingers into her thick dark hair. She grinned against him as his tongue danced between her lips, their bodies pressed against each other, his bare skin against the soft tulle of her shirt.

It was hard to say what I felt in that moment. A white-hot envious rage snaked its way around my heart, that much was certain, but I wasn't sure of who. Of Miri, that she was kissing my boyfriend? Of Carter, that he got to openly kiss Miri? Something I had ached to do for years? A weird sense of longing dripped from my chest into my gut, like I wanted to be in between them, kissing them while they kissed each other.

Miri giggled and dug her fingertips into Carter's sides, tickling him and making him squirm away from her.

"Don't get too familiar, Romeo," she said, giving him a wink before turning to the table. "I'm sixth in line for the throne, after all."

Lex missed his next two shots, so Miri lined herself up, giving me a playful tilt of her lips before sinking both of them.

Plunk.

Plunk.

"That's four." Miri squared her jaw at Lex, raising a perfectly manicured eyebrow. "Pay up."

"We never agreed on what happened at four," Lex said.

"Well," Carter said, his voice dripping with suggestion, "if three is Ivy sucking your tongue, I guess four is you sucking Ivy's."

The energy shifted. What had been flirtatiously sexual only moments ago had now become a power play between Lex and Carter. I opened my mouth to protest, having wanted to shut this down as soon as it started, but the words died on my lips.

"Go on, Weeds," Carter nodded to my partner. "Put your hands in his hair, yank his head back, and make him suck your tongue."

Indecision slithered down my spine, paralyzing me and keeping me rooted with my hands at my sides. If I did this, it would change the dynamic between us, maybe make things even worse than they already were.

But Carter's glare reiterated what he'd said earlier.

I don't think you have the guts.

Oh, yeah?

Eat your heart out, Carter Scott.

I grabbed the back of Lex's head, speared my fingers through his silky dark hair, and crushed my lips to his the same way he'd done to me all those years ago. We could have been those kids again, standing on the coast of the Potomac with the sun setting behind us. I'd meant it to be political. I'd meant it to be cold and impersonal. But the moment our skin touched, I knew the only thing that had ever existed between us was burning and blinding and every connotation of the word *personal.*

His lips were as soft and mesmerizing as I remembered, and when I shoved my tongue in between them, he brushed his against mine in greeting and sucked me deeper into his mouth, delivering on his part of the bet. My blood blistered as the sensation erupted down my body, scalding and invigorating. It raced through my veins, burning me from the inside out, making my knees shake, making me want things that I should never consider.

Warm, callused fingertips slid over my shoulders and across my collarbone, leaving goose pimples on my crackling skin.

Why did it feel so good? Why?

It shouldn't. My cheeks burned, my clothes suffocated me, and the whole world had been lit on fire by this one explosion between us. The palm of his right hand tucked under my jaw and he rubbed his thumb over my pulse...*my X.* Up and down. Up and down. Tracing it. Marking his own X.

I scratched my fingers against his scalp, fisting and yanking him closer, and his mouth worked against mine, just as greedy and primal, seeking the depths of my kiss as fiercely as I sought his. My entire body throbbed, wanting to seek whatever release he could give.

If this was what the rest of my life would be like, what did I have to worry about?

The thought passed through my mind as quickly and as carefree as a Sunday afternoon, but once it was there, it slapped me back to reality.

Oh, God.

Oh. God.

This was Lex. This was my enemy. This was Miri's boyfriend, and my boyfriend was just over there.

Is he still watching? Does he see how much I like it? Does he see how much I want Lex? Do they both see?

I broke away from him, shoving at his shoulders as I wiped my mouth with the back of my hand, gasping for air, desperate for a reality check.

Lex's wide hazel gaze and slack-jawed look meant he'd obviously been just as surprised as I was, and for a moment when our faces were so close no one else could see us, disappointment echoed in his eyes. Like he didn't want to stop. Like he wanted to see what would happen if we let this fire blaze out of control.

I did, too.

Carter's gaze seared my skin, and part of me dreaded what I might find there when I finally peeked. But the other part of me, the competitive part that responded to a challenge, knew Carter had brought this on himself. He hadn't thought I had the guts. He'd goaded me on. I proved him wrong.

I had a moment to revel in my glorious victory before a familiar heavy hand landed on my neck, and Carter's mouth devoured mine. He'd put his clothes back on, but his cock pressed into my hip through his pants. Whatever he'd seen in Lex and me had turned him on, and now he sucked my lips like he was trying to lick Lex off me. I melted into the touch, little tingles of euphoria zinging through my body when I tasted Miri's lip gloss on his mouth. He fisted his hands in my hair, his scent pluming around me, reminding me of how much we loved each other. When he pulled away and smiled, I swayed on my feet, needing my hands on his chest to keep me upright.

Something about the mixture of the four of us, Lex on me, and Miri on Carter, it damn near intoxicated me.

"Let's call a draw, DC," Carter hummed, glancing up to my partner.

They exchanged a look that resembled longing, or perhaps almost yearning, like maybe Lex was seconds away from forcing Carter to suck *his* tongue.

"Fair enough, Chicago." Lex choked on his words, his voice gravelly, his words slurred.

I started to ask what that was about, but Carter grabbed my hand and pulled me back into the pub.

14

IVY

The walk through Killwater Woods back to the dorms vibrated with a magical preternatural effervescence that I'd never experienced before. The nightlife buzzed around us and a dreamy navy blue tinted the sky, painting a romantic backdrop to the way Carter looked at me. We'd both fallen under its spell. Maybe the stories were true and the fairies had enchanted this night for us.

Carter tugged me into the dorm room, his lips consuming mine, greedy and demanding. His hands were everywhere all at once, crushing me to him and like he was desperate to touch parts of me he hadn't felt in years. Even though it had only been a few hours.

We should've talked about what happened or at least pumped the brakes so we could check in with each other and make sure we were both in the same headspace. But I was too lost to the lust and the alcohol, a deadly combination that sucked me into its ravenous black hole.

I pushed him onto my bed and kneeled between his legs, clawing at his jeans, desperate to taste him. He tugged my tank top over my head, exposing my overheated skin to the stuffy, humid night air.

Trying to calm my nerves, I forced my hands to stop shaking as I slid his boxers and jeans off, freeing his cock.

He'd stepped over a line tonight, one I didn't even know existed, and although I enjoyed it, I needed to tease him for it.

"Tonight was a lot," I told him, giving his shaft a long lick, watching as he squirmed and gripped the bedsheets on either side of his thighs. "You shouldn't have provoked me like that."

"You love it when I provoke you," he teased, eyes twinkling in the dim light. "Even more if Lex is involved."

As if they were summoned by some satanic ritual, Lex and Miri burst into the room, the door bouncing off the wall behind it before slamming closed again. They were attached at the mouth, and Miri's legs were wrapped around his waist, her arms around his neck, and her fingers in his hair as he dug his hands into her ass. He maneuvered them over to Miri's bed, and it was only after he dumped her in the center of it that they stopped to notice we were there.

Despite how close the four of us were and how adventurous Carter and I had become, we'd never crossed this boundary. Now, things were so screwed up it was difficult to tell where that line had originally been.

Miri looked at me, bit her bottom lip, and smiled. Lex swept hungry eyes over both of us before going to back to Miri. Unsure, I glanced up Carter's body, my arms on his thighs and his hard, proud cock poised at my mouth.

"Just like old times. Right, Chicago?" Lex said.

I didn't know what that meant, and I didn't care. Carter gave me a nod, and suddenly, my inhibitions disappeared. I sucked Carter into my mouth, fucking him with my face like I could own every inch of him. His hand fisted in my hair, telling me exactly how much he enjoyed it, and tears welled in my eyes as I gagged around him. He liked that the most, liked knowing how much control he had over me in this position. I, likewise, had possession of him, capable of bringing him right to climax, and just when he was about to explode in my throat, I stopped and pulled back.

He groaned, curling into himself and staring down his body with angry, pleading eyes.

"You fucking tease," he snarled.

In the background, Miri moaned and Lex spanked her, the wet sounds of their bodies sliding together punctuated by the bed squeaking. Fuck, that sent a hot lurching jolt right between my thighs, my cunt searching for release, for something to fill me up.

I stood and pushed my jean shorts down to my ankles, crawling into Carter's lap with my knees on either side of his hips. I impaled myself on him and linked my hands behind his neck, slowly working myself against his body.

"Look at them," Carter whispered, grabbing my chin to tilt my face their way. "Look at how beautiful she is. Look at how amazing he is. Look at them together."

I tilted my pelvis against him, his cock hitting that spot inside of me that made both of us hiss in a breath.

"Goddamn it, Weeds," he murmured. "Why won't you stop it? Why can't you stop it?"

I met his eyes again, but before I could question what he meant, he kissed me. Rough and hard and deep, biting my bottom lip and tugging it between his teeth. *Fuck,* I loved that. I pushed him back with my hands on his chest, holding him down and taking what I wanted from him. Working him fast and…Oh…Oh…

Right when I was about to come, I looked across the room and connected with a heady, dangerous, hazel stare.

The soft caress of Lex's lips and the sweep of his thumb across my neck ghosted over my skin, a searing memory that continued to burn. I grabbed the X on my neck, and he widened his eyes.

The connection between us shifted as our souls lined up. I rolled my hips against Carter in time with Lex's thrusts into Miri, like he fucked Carter through me and I fucked Miri through him. Or maybe… maybe we fucked each other.

Jesus Christ.

The filthy nature of everything set me off. I became so aware of everything around me—Carter digging his fingers into my hips, Lex eye-fucking me, the intensity of Miri's moans. My orgasm ripped me under its weight, incinerating me and turning me to ash and dust.

Carter flipped us over so he was on top, and he pounded into me hard and fast, driving himself over that precipice, too. He growled and groaned and murmured, "Yes, fuck yes, yes, yes," into my ear, and when he climaxed, he pulled out to come on my stomach, stroking himself as hot spurts landed across my breasts. I could swear, I felt his ecstasy as if it were my own. He collapsed on top of me, both of us sweaty and panting and exhausted, and somewhere across the room, the sounds from Miri and Lex died down.

Reality caught up to my semi-sober, sex-addled mind.

I'd fucked my boyfriend in the same room where my fiancé fucked his girlfriend, my best friend and former girl-crush.

How terrible is that?

I woke to the sound of Caroline banging on our door.

"You're fifteen minutes late to check in," she said. "Move your asses."

Fuck.

It was only three hours after we'd gotten in last night, and the stench of sex and alcohol still hung in the air, salty-sweet on my tongue.

"Oh my God." I sat up, my head throbbing and my throat burning.

Memories flicked through my mind as I struggled to piece together where I was and what had happened.

Me on my knees in front of Carter, his dick in my mouth.

Miri bent over in front of Lex, his cock buried inside her.

The look Lex gave me right before I came. The way he fucked me with his eyes while I did.

Oh, God.

We'd done something bad, and we had no time to deal with it. Cold, slimy apprehension slicked through me when I met Lex's gaze across the room and quickly looked away. Never in our twenty-two years together had I been afraid to stare him down. Now, this heavy mistake hung between the four of us. I sensed it in my molecules.

Carter sat up behind me. "We had a wild last night, huh?"

Panic seized my chest. These were my closest friends in the world, and if I wasn't supposed to betray two of them by marrying the third, last night would have had an entirely different meaning. But...Lex and I had a secret that was going to crush us. The look we'd shared coupled with the amazing kiss at the pub bordered on a depraved wickedness I didn't want to name.

"I need a shower," I announced, pushing out of bed and grabbing my towel before hauling ass out of the room.

"Weeds, wait." Carter ran after me, catching up to me in the bathroom and slipping inside my stall before I could lock it. We were already late so it would have to be the quickest shower in the world, but I smelled like beer and sex and regret, and I needed to scrub it off my skin as soon as I could.

"C'mon." He rubbed his hands over my upper arms. "Talk to me."

"Last night was—"

"Last night was almost like that time in Atlantic City." He took a step closer, bringing his pelvis in contact with my hips. "Remember that blonde you liked so much?"

My lips pulled into a smile at the memory. She'd been gorgeous and a lot of fun.

"That was different." I turned on the water and stepped into the tiled compartment. "She was a stranger, and we both had masks on. No one knew it was us."

"So what? It's worse because they're our friends?"

I cleared my throat and winced.

No, it's worse because I'm going to marry one of them.

"I love you, Carter." I wrapped my arms around his neck when he stepped in beside me. He put his hands on my waist and pressed his forehead to mine. "I don't want to lose you."

He looked like he was waiting for me to say something else, but when I didn't, he nodded and said, "I know. I don't want to lose you, either."

I fought the tears building in my eyes and cleared my throat, resting my forehead on his sternum, perhaps wishing we never had to get out of that shower again.

By the time we got back to the room, Lex and Miri were already gone, so Carter and I dressed as quickly as we could. I didn't know where my clean pair of jeans was, so I put on the shorts from last night and one of Carter's TWU football T-shirts, relishing in how much his sandalwood scent calmed me.

I was about to leave when I reached into my back pocket for the flyer Siobhan had put there last night. I didn't need that piece of paper poking me in the ass the entire hike, so I went to lay it on the dresser, but as I did, something tiny and green fell out of the folds.

A ring in the shape of ivy vines with little emeralds decorating the leaves. It was beautiful and likely expensive.

Were those real?

I brought it closer for inspection, and a pulse echoed in my blood, like everything in my body recognized this piece of jewelry and urged me to put it on my finger, to wear it as I'd always worn it. I almost moaned at the intensity of the tremble that went down my spine.

Where the hell did this come from?

I figured maybe it was Miri's, so I put it back in my pocket, reminding myself to ask her when we went downstairs.

"You ready?" Carter asked, holding a hand out to me and flipping his hat on with the other.

I took it, nodding and following him out of our room.

ACT III

To say the truth, reason and love keep little company together nowadays.
-Bottom, Act 3, Scene 1

15

LEX

I wished I could say kissing Ivy was only about the game or meeting Carter's challenge because some toxic rule of honor demanded it, but that wouldn't be true. It was just as much about Ivy as it was about her boyfriend.

Watching Carter put his hands on Miri rekindled that same fury inside of me as the first time I saw him touch Ivy—the way he brushed the hair behind her ear and made her smile. I seethed with something sick and desperate.

How dare he touch what was mine?

And how dare Miri touch *him?* Beautiful, shimmering *him,* who I had ached to touch for years. My head was so twisted about it. All of it. I'd gotten tired of holding it in. I saw an opportunity, and I jumped on it.

I had not expected to enjoy myself so much.

Kissing Ivy had been like sticking my tongue on the end of a battery. It shocked me deep down inside. When I rubbed my thumb over that splotchy X and it bloomed to life, I could have bent her over the table and buried myself inside of her.

Some part of me still wanted to.

This was a big fucking problem.

The other issue came the next morning, when we showed up an hour late to meet Stephens. Most of the other hikers had already gone ahead, but because we were so late, two guides had stayed behind to personally escort us.

They were not happy about this arrangement.

"Glad you could join us," Stephens said, superiority and arrogance in his tone. "If you weren't my leads, I'd fire all four of you." He shook his head and ran his hands through his hair. "Carter, Miri, you're with Caroline. Lex, Ivy, you're with me."

"What?" Ivy groaned.

I likewise did not approve. I needed some breathing room from both Carter and Ivy, or I'd do something stupid. It had taken everything in me not to crawl over to them last night, situate myself between Carter's legs, and see if I could make him groan the way he had the first time we met. I wanted to make that mark appear on Ivy's neck using only my tongue and find out how quickly Miri could fall apart while she rode me. My mind was in a depraved place where society's rules didn't matter, and I could get away with fucking three people at once.

What's stopping you? a dark part of my subconscious whispered.

The panicked look on Ivy's face this morning and the way she'd run filled me with hesitation. For Miri and me, last night had been relatively vanilla. But I imagined Ivy, the prude, was freaking the hell out. Carter had been dropping hints all week—first with the talk about London and then that moment when he threatened to give me something healthier to suck.

What had we done?

"Can we switch?" Carter asked. "Can Ivy come with me?"

"Yeah, that would work out better," I agreed, giving our director an enthusiastic nod.

"No," Stephens bellowed, pausing for dramatic flare as he glanced between the four of us, dropping his jaw like he couldn't believe we had the audacity to ask. Then he turned and stalked into the woods.

Ivy kissed Carter goodbye and walked after Stephens. Carter barely looked at me before heading in the opposite direction with Caroline.

"Don't fight with her," Miri said. "She's exhausted. We all are."

"I know," I said, giving her a kiss farewell. "I love you."

"Love you."

I went after my director.

The first twenty minutes passed with Stephens mumbling to himself. "This was supposed to be a relaxing overnight camp before the final push," he said. "We've got less than two weeks to get our shit together. We needed this break, but not as much as you two needed to sleep in, huh?"

I tuned him out and looked over my shoulder at Ivy, who had her gaze set on the ground in front of her, purposely avoiding me. Which was fine because it gave me time to think.

What the hell did we do? What the hell did *Carter* do? What would prompt him to strike up that challenge at the bar? Was it as easy as he got drunk and took it too far? Or was it something else?

As far as I knew, he and Miri were friends. If it were more than that, Miri would have told me. Of course, it was more than that between Carter and me, and I hadn't told her. Still, I knew about her night with Ivy, so she had no reason to hide any desired tryst with Carter. The whole making out with Miri thing couldn't have anything to do with Miri herself. Which meant it had to do with me. Or Ivy. Or me *and* Ivy.

Once the bug had been planted there, I couldn't stop spinning it around in my web, turning it over and examining it from all angles. He knew we hated each other. He knew we could barely stand to be in the same room together. And yet, he'd egged us on, mischief in his eyes, curiosity in his smile, like a cat batting around its prey.

Then he came all over her in front of me.

The words from a few days ago blared to the forefront.

"One last time, for old time's sake. You've always known who I am. And I know who you are."

And the possessive way he'd held on to Ivy when she came into the room.

He knows about the engagement, that dark part of my subconscious whispered. *He knows our secret.*

"Ivy, I need to talk to you," I kicked her shoe to shake her awake.

"Go away, Lex," she murmured, lying on top of her sleeping bag in her tent.

After a grueling two-hour hike into the forest, we reached our campsite. It was still hotter than a lava pit, and by the time we stopped, dehydration had me blinking and shaking my head to see straight. Stephens gave us a few hours to rest before we had to do the stupid team-building shit he had planned. We'd camp here tonight and hike back to join the other group for more rehearsal tomorrow. But right now, I was spiraling, and I needed Ivy's voice of reason.

"It's important." I took a deep breath and shook her again, this time nudging her harder.

"Fuck off."

"It's about our happily never after." I huffed, damn near losing my patience enough to straddle her and slap her cheeks until her eyes opened. "Get up."

She growled and rolled over, glaring at me like that would make me leave, as if I hadn't spent the last twenty-two years perfecting my best eat-shit stare in return. She finally relented and pushed to her feet.

"Fine. Let's go." Her hands clenched into fists, she stalked out of the tent and gestured at me to go first. I led her down the creek, following it until it fell over some rocks and provided the perfect sound barrier. I didn't want anyone else to overhear.

"Carter knows," I said. "About the engagement. He knows."

"What?" She crossed her arms. "What makes you think that?"

"Why was he goading us on last night?" I lit up a cigarette and handed the pack to her so she could light one up for herself. "It's not like him."

"He was drunk. We were all drunk." As if that explained it all.

"He knew what he was doing, Ivy." I was sure of it.

"You're being paranoid." She sighed and rolled her big steel eyes.

Maybe.

"Has he said anything to you?" I asked. "About me? About us?"

"Why would he say anything about you?"

That seemed even more strange. He told me he planned to confess our secret to Ivy, and he hadn't. Maybe he was testing me, seeing how I'd react to knowing he planned to stay with her after he moved to California. No, it made more sense if he knew about the arrangement and that we'd kept it from him. He was screwing with us.

Would he be that conniving?

Ivy didn't know the whole story. She only had half the picture.

"I need to tell you something," I said. "And full disclosure, he said he was going to spill first. I'm only saying it now because we need to figure out our game plan."

I bared my soul to her. I told her everything about Carter and me, the night in London and the years of pining afterward. When I was done, we sat in silence while she processed the last four years under this new lens.

"Shit," she said. "We're officially the most fucked-up group of friends on the planet."

My load lightened at the chance to laugh at her wicked sense of humor.

"I'm serious," she said. "You fucked my boyfriend. I fucked your girlfriend. Now we're getting married. It's a goddamn soap opera."

"Or a Greek tragedy," I said.

That stopped our levity as the consequences of reality sank on our shoulders. Our lovers would hate us after this came out, and what we'd cherished coming here would certainly meet its demise once it did. Like a tragedy, none of us would survive this fairy tale unscathed.

"I don't think Carter knows anything," Ivy said. "He wouldn't be that maniacal. We don't keep anything from each other. If he suspected something, he would say something."

"He's a very good actor." I shook my head and sighed. "You're keeping at least one thing from him, and he kept this from you for four years."

She laughed out a sigh through her nose and shook her head, inhaling deeply on her cigarette before murmuring a quiet, "Why are you the dirty little secret for both of us?"

That made me run hot for reasons I had no desire to examine. "You and I haven't done a great job of being cool about it."

"I know," Ivy said. "Last night was—" She took a deep breath and sighed. "We can't repeat last night."

"We won't."

We locked gazes, and I remembered the way she looked when she came—how her eyes had yearned for me and how much I ached to be closer. To her. To him. Her cheeks flushed and the X bloomed on her neck, and I wondered if she was having the same thoughts, if she yearned to figure out what more that connection between us could mean.

"We should tell them." Ivy looked out to the water and sat with her legs crossed, digging her fingers into the emerald grass. "When we get back."

"What happened to waiting until we get home?"

"It'll be too late." She sighed. "We need to do it now."

I imagined how they would react to the news. Miri would pretend it didn't bother her while slowly rotting away on the inside. We had a good thing, the two of us. We were honest with each other, and we understood what the other needed out of our partnership. It was *above* monogamy. We didn't ask for more than the other could give. Carter, on the other hand, would probably be a jealous, angry mess. He'd want us both and be conflicted about that, as conflicted as I was about him and Miri or him and Ivy. Or, God help me, all three of them.

"What do you think it would be like?" she asked, her voice too soft and broken for my liking. "If we got married?"

I let out a breath and sat next to her. "Exactly the same as it is now."

"You don't think anything would change?" She raised her eyebrows. "We would go on sleeping in separate rooms, sleeping with separate people?"

I barked out a laugh. "I guess that last one's negotiable, huh?"

"You know what I mean." She shoved my shoulder and let out an annoyed scoff.

"Would that bother you?" I asked, curious about her answer. If she had asked me a month ago, it wouldn't have bothered me if she slept around, especially if it was with Carter. Now, it ached like an itch under my skin. Perhaps, after last night, after all of this, some part of me had started to consider her mine.

"If we have children, yes." She stabbed the cigarette out and glanced down at the ground in front of her, considering how this charade would actually play out. "I don't want to be embarrassed the way my mother was."

Understandable. While her father was in office, he'd had an affair with one of his interns. It had taken nearly an act of God to repair the Washington reputation after that. But since she'd mentioned it, I figured we might as well talk about it. "Do you want children?"

Are we talking about this like it's real? What happened to fighting it to the end?

"Sometimes, yes. Sometimes, no." Ivy furrowed her brows together, a soft smile curling on her lips. "It gets in the way of my senatorial plans, you see."

"Ah, yes. The ole kids or career debate." I lay down in the grass, my hangover catching up to me as my head pulsed. I needed to drink more water. "Don't worry about that. We'll have nannies to raise our kids, just like we were raised.

"I don't want to do it that way." She lay down with me, my right arm touching the side of her left, the heat of her body a heady alluring thing, urging me to explore of it. "What about you? Did you and Miri want children?"

"Miri wants a ton of kids," I said. "A whole house full of them. I've never been that serious."

"Our parents will expect at least two."

I turned to face her, hoping she took what I was about to say with the best intentions. "You can have another man's kids, Ivy. I don't care if they're mine."

She looked up to the sky, closing her eyes and taking a deep breath before letting it out in a ragged sigh like she was trying not to cry. "How did our lives get to be so screwed?"

I didn't have a good answer, so I didn't say anything. We stayed like that for much longer than we should have, lying silently together in the violet heather and staring up at the sunny afternoon sky.

I could always sense a storm brewing days before it came. The air had a heaviness to it, weighing down the world with its building intensity. The sky seemed even more radiant, an even brighter blue than before, as if in warning, as if to say it was about to boil over. It was like that with Carter and Miri after the camping trip.

Something happened between Ivy and me on the banks of the creek as we slept off our night of terrible decisions. A simple peace, perhaps. An acceptance of what we needed to face. But something happened with Carter and Miri, too.

When we met with up them the next morning, Carter wrapped his arms around Ivy and pulled her to the side so they could whisper to each other. Miri put on a good show, but I saw the sidelong glance at Carter when he cuddled Ivy close. I saw the small frown on her lips, there for a blink and then gone, a plastic smile in its place.

"Hello, darling." She gave me a kiss. "Did you two play nice?"

"Did you?" I narrowed my eyes and put as much suggestion into that question as I could.

She seemed confused, but her smile never faltered. "What do you mean?"

"What's going on with you and Chicago?"

"Me and Chicago?" She raised an eyebrow and shook her head. An unexpected response. Had I read this wrong? "Darling, the only thing going on with me and Chicago is wondering what the hell is going on with you and X." She jabbed me in the chest with her finger. "And running lines, of course. We're always running lines."

"There's nothing going on with me and X," I lied. "Why would you think that?"

She linked her hands behind my neck and leaned into me, letting out one of those judgmental sighs that said she was playing along for the sake of playing along. She pressed her forehead to mine and whispered, "You're entitled to your secrets, love. Just don't be cruel."

She gave me a sweet kiss, broke away, and called out to Stephens to ask which scene we were starting from.

Just don't be cruel.

Were Ivy and I being cruel by keeping our charade to ourselves? We didn't love each other, not like I loved Miri or she loved Carter. So why did it matter? If nothing *had* to change, then why the smoke and mirrors? Why did I feel this sinking dread when I thought about spilling my guts? Why did I fear what Miri and Carter would do when they learned the truth?

The reason was obvious. Because once we spoke it out loud, everything *would* change. Perhaps it already had. Perhaps it was too late.

We were shit at rehearsal that day, the tension between us clear to anyone watching. After the big fight scene ended with Ivy and me bombing our final lines, Stephens scrubbed his face and let out a groan of frustration.

In the years we'd been performing together, we'd had our disagreements, but we never let it impact us here. This trust and mutual respect had landed us these roles to begin with. Now, everything we did brought us one step closer to an impending explosion. We needed to talk about what happened between us, even if it was to brush it under the rug. Ivy and I needed to tell them about our engagement. We couldn't keep it a secret anymore.

But after we ran through the first three acts again and hiked back to the dorms, we were exhausted and disgusting. Despite the cracks in the foundation of this dilapidated friendship, we showered and slept in the same room that night, decidedly avoiding the enormous suffocating tension between us.

16

IVY

I was barely holding myself together, and the heat had started to make me loopy.

"Come on, Ivy," Stephens groaned, clapping his hands to get my attention. "You're killing me."

"I'm sorry," I said. I couldn't remember my lines. I couldn't think straight. I needed a break. I needed a nap. I needed a week off in the Bahamas.

"Don't apologize," Stephens blared. "Do better. Tybalt is the epitome of nobility, the prince of his house. Surely you can understand what that feels like."

I swallowed down the insult I had brewing for him. I could absolutely understand what that felt like. I could even understand what it felt like to be in Juliet's shoes, forced to marry someone she didn't love, destined to choose between her heart and her family. But Stephens had a reason for his frustration. We were five days away from our first performance, and this was no time to start fucking up.

"Yes," I said.

"Good," Stephens said. "Take it from the top of the scene, please."

"Hey, you okay?" Carter ran a hand down my arm. We were at the part where Tybalt killed Mercutio and Romeo chased him through Verona. It involved fight choreography, making it a million degrees warmer in this stuffy auditorium.

"Yeah," I lied. "It's just hot." I was in a full renaissance costume with a pound of makeup on my face. Basically boiling alive, but that was only half true. I hadn't been telling the whole truth for almost two weeks. I wasn't okay. I would probably never be okay again.

Lex kept staring at me. Not in a creepy way, but the same way he looked at me that night—like he couldn't decide if he wanted to wring my neck or fuck me. Probably both.

"I know." Carter leaned in close, pressing his mouth to my ear. "I was thinking, how about tonight after the midsummer party, you and I sneak off to the creek? I found a secluded spot on my hike this morning. We could cool off and then get *real* warm again. What do you think?" He bit his bottom lip, making me want a piece, and I sighed as my cunt clenched, anticipating this plan.

"That sounds amazing." I could use the alone time with him. Things had been weird since we'd been here. We usually had no boundaries between us, and every day, my secrets erected new ones. Part of it was my fault, but I kept thinking about what Lex told me by the river. Carter still hadn't mentioned London, and if he was keeping that from me, it was entirely possible he was keeping other secrets, too. Did he know about the engagement? And if he did, why go along with pretending he didn't?

I didn't want to believe it, but once Lex put the idea there, I couldn't stop thinking about it. It was in the way Carter looked at me sometimes, possessive and angry, before he locked it down and became the same old lovable guy again.

A night at the creek alone with him? I needed that reconnection, a chance to clear the air.

"Great." He turned to find our friend, Davis, who played Benvolio, and I shook my head against the guilt that snaked through my body.

I'd find a way to fight for him. I had to.

It didn't get dark in Ireland on the summer solstice, not like it did in Virginia. The sun stayed up from four thirty in the morning to ten at night. After it set, the sky turned a radiant blush and violet until midnight, when it finally dipped into "astronomical twilight." That was science-speak for the weird in-between time when the sky wasn't quite the pitch one would expect for the wee hours of night, but not quite sunset either. It reminded me more of the indigo in Carter's eyes.

"Are you sure we're going the right way?" Lex asked for the millionth time.

"No, actually, I'm not." I held the flyer up to him and pointed to a spot on the tiny map in the corner. "But here's what I'm following. Would you care to do better?"

He snatched it out of my hands and looked down at it.

"Now, now," Carter said. "Play nice in the sandbox."

Miri tilted her head back to look at the sky as we walked. "And none of the other students were invited to this?"

"Siobhan gave me a flyer," I explained. "I didn't think about inviting anyone else."

"Wait." Carter paused to grab my shoulder. "Do you hear that?"

Drumming echoed off in the distance to our left.

"We're close," I said.

"C'mon." Carter put his hand in mine and pulled me through the undergrowth toward the music, helping me jump over a mossy log before yanking me up a moderately steep hill. Once we crested the top, he curled his lips into an excited smile, which made me grin to see. Four bonfires burned brightly in the valley below, one at each corner of the clearing. A sea of bodies writhed in the center, drums beating out a rhythm while fiddles and pipes accompanied.

Is that a lyre?

"Holy hell," Lex said.

"This looks amazing." Miri grabbed my hand, intertwining her fingers with mine and yanking me with her into the valley, Carter following on the other side.

There was so much going on that I couldn't rationalize one thing fast enough before my focus landed on something else. A man walked by wearing a kilt, half his face painted like a butterfly. Another person had on booty shorts, glittery flowers etched over their bare chest. A group dressed like elves stood in a circle, their fur clothing held together by leather straps and leaves, twigs accenting choice pieces. Others only had on scraps of fabric, strategically placed to maintain propriety in public.

As beautiful as this place was, the atmosphere itself held a magical quality I struggled to explain. I tasted it on my tongue, salty sin with hints of pure citrusy hedonism. Laughter echoed around me, mixing with moans and squeals of delight. Combined together, I inhaled it like wood smoke and sex and sugar and flowers. It poured down my throat and into my veins.

I was under its spell in seconds.

"Welcome," a beautiful brunette said, shoving a handful of daisies into my hands. She reached into her wicker basket and retrieved a flower crown, placing it on top of my head with a kind smile.

"Thank you." I giggled as she did the same to Miri.

"Here!" Another woman gave me a wooden chalice. I traced over the curling design etched around the cup, ghosting over the text in a language I didn't understand. But it looked like everyone else had them, too, so I nodded and thanked her as well. She tipped a bottle of wine over it, filling it almost to the brim before doing the same thing to Lex and Carter.

Should I have accepted a drink from a stranger? Probably not. That was "being a girl in college" 101. But could I refuse? Also no. *When in Rome, am I right?*

I took a sip of the most exquisite thing I'd ever tasted—ambrosia

—sweeter and more decadent than anything my parents had in their wine cellar. It burst to life in my mouth, overwhelming my senses until there was nothing else in the world, just this party and my friends and this moment. I'd never known what delicious meant before.

We took a few more steps, and someone shoved condoms at me attached to little rectangular packets containing lube and edible oils.

Where the hell are we?

"This is amazing," Carter shouted, stuffing a handful into his pocket. It wasn't until I was doing the same that I realized there weren't any children in attendance. In fact, there weren't any children here at all. All adults. Of course, it was late. Almost ten o'clock. When I took another drink of my wine, I didn't care anymore. It didn't matter. Nothing mattered.

"Come dance with me," Miri said, pulling me into the drum circle as we laughed and swayed to the music. I lost myself in the mob, the pressures of being Ivy Washington melting away with each passing second. Law school? Meh. Carter leaving? Not a problem. Being engaged to the Anti-Christ? Could be worse. Everything felt so right, and so free, and so...perfect.

The social anxiety that normally consumed me by being around crowds of people seemed inconsequential. There were no strangers here. The electricity between us made us one. A girl in a long maxi skirt twirled around me and grabbed at my waist, dragging me with her. I grabbed Miri's hand and off we went. Skipping and prancing and...*oh, holy shit...*

Everyone at the front of the line was jumping over the bonfire. I hadn't had enough wine for that, so I tried to break away, but Miri wouldn't let me.

"Oh no, you don't," she said, digging her fingernails into my hand.

We did it together, screaming the whole time. Flames licked at my cheeks, the heat nipping at my hair and the flowers on my head, but on the other side, I became someone who had jumped through literal fire with the woman of my dreams.

"We did it!" Miri threw her arms around my neck and jumped. "We did it! We jumped the fire." When she pulled away, I held her gaze long enough to see hunger dance behind it.

I want you, too, I almost said.

Then the girl in the maxi skirt came back and said, "You have the prettiest hair. Can I braid it?" Short of any good reason to say no, I grinned and nodded.

After my tresses had been tamed into a long plait decorated with flowers and heather, I ran out of wine, so I told Miri I'd be right back and went to hunt down something to quench my thirst. I weaved through the crowd, looking for the person with the bottle or maybe a bar. Just when I thought I saw a person refilling a chalice a few feet away, I caught a figure watching me in the distance, that same look of indifference on her features.

Siobhan.

Remembering the ring in my back pocket, I took a few steps closer to her and reached inside to pull it out.

"Hey," she said, giving me a wide grin. "You made it."

"Thanks for inviting me." I returned her smile. "We're having a great time."

"You're welcome." She inhaled on her cigarette, letting the smoke out in the other direction. Something about her seemed different, perhaps more entrancing than before. Was it the way she moved? Somehow more graceful and elegant, like she'd had centuries to practice? Or was it her skin that glowed as if lit from within?

Jesus, how much of that wine did I drink?

"I think you dropped this the other night at the pub." I held the ring out in the palm of my hand. "It was folded up in between the pages of the flyer you gave me."

"Oh, yeah." Her features lit up, and she took it in between her fingers. "I was looking for this. But you know what?" She put it back in my palm, its heavy weight now nearly burning. "You keep it."

"What? No." I pushed it back to her. "I couldn't."

"I insist," she said. "In fact, I'm going to take pity on you, Ivy Washington." She paused long enough for me to wonder what she could possibly mean, and then she smiled. "I'm going to give you a gift."

My hackles raised. *A gift? What gift?*

Siobhan leaned in closer, and the light from the fires flickered over her features, making her seem powerful and ethereal. She closed my fingers around the ring and grabbed my hand between hers, one palm on top of mine and one below.

My heart pounded. I'd only met Siobhan a few days ago, and this seemed strange for the less than twenty minutes we'd spent talking to each other. But then again, it felt right. I was drawn to her in the same way I had been the other two times we'd interacted. Nothing about the way she held me in her gaze and rapture was abnormal at all. Her lips touched mine, and she whispered something against them that I couldn't understand, her voice too low to hear. Then she kissed me—softly, gently, platonically, the way one might kiss a sister or a close friend.

She grinned when she pulled away, murmuring in a different language before letting go of my hand. I stumbled back, either unprepared to let go or wanting it so bad that it startled me once I had it. I looked down to catch myself, and when I glanced up again, Siobhan was gone.

"What the—" I scooted away and launched to my feet, blinking against the impossibility of what had happened.

Where'd she go?

"Hey," Lex said, suddenly next to me. "I saw you fall over. You okay?" He shoved his cup in my hand. "Here, drink something."

"Yeah." I took a giant gulp of the delicious wine before handing the chalice back to him. "Did you—did you see the person I was talking to?"

"The brunette with the tattoos?" Lex nodded, bringing the drink to his lips and finishing off the last of it. "Yeah, of course."

"That's the person who knows about us, Lex," I said. "That's Siobhan."

He searched the crowd for her, and when he came up short, he nodded toward the tree line like he needed to talk to me. Grabbing my hand, he led me into the woods for privacy.

17

LEX

I led her out into the woods a few yards away from the party, following the trail that led us down to the creek. The sun was low in the sky, not quite set, but enough to give the world a dreamy peach-colored haze. It had to be close to midnight, but the music echoing through the trees hadn't slowed down since we'd gotten here.

"What did she say to you?" I asked, concerned that this townie wouldn't leave Ivy alone. She kept showing up in the most unexpected places, and if the shit didn't stop, I'd have to intervene on Ivy's behalf.

"When she gave me the flyer to come here, she put this ring in my pocket." Ivy held out the emerald encrusted jewelry in the shape of ivy vines. It was kind of pretty. "When I tried to give it back to her, she told me to keep it. She said she had a gift for me, and she kissed me."

"Well, aren't you building up a little roster while you're in Ireland?" I teased.

Ivy rolled her eyes and shoved my shoulders. "Be serious."

Laughing, I took another drink of the incredible festival wine before asking, "Do you think she's going to say anything?"

Ivy shrugged. "She said she wouldn't, but that doesn't mean she won't."

"We should do it tonight," I said. "Tell them. On our way back from the party."

She took a deep breath, as if steeling herself against the emotions rising in her chest. "And ruin midsummer?"

"It's never going to be the right time." Even though I, too, lamented ruining the highlight of this trip, thus far. But still, the time had come. "Better to rip off the bandage."

"You were right." She crossed her arms over her chest and pulled her bottom lip between her teeth. "Carter knows something's up. He's been acting strange. Something happened on that camping trip. Did Miri say anything to you?"

You're entitled to your secrets, love. Just don't be cruel.

I didn't know what that meant, and I hadn't brought it up. Ivy slumped down on a fallen log and put her head in her hands, her elbows on her knees. I sat beside her and crossed my legs in front of me.

"They suspect," I said, conceding her point. "More reason why it needs to happen soon."

"How?" she said. "How do you drop that into conversation? I love you, Carter, but my shitty parents are forcing me to marry your best friend, my archnemesis, the one person I hate the most in the world."

"Hey," I said, a little offended. We didn't *hate* each other anymore. Strongly dislike was more appropriate.

"I knew it," came a voice from the tree line to my left.

All the blood in my body rushed to my gut when Carter pinned me with an incredulous glare, his arms crossed over his chest. Miri stood next to him, her hands steepled over her mouth while she shifted her wide honey-brown eyes between Ivy and me.

Fuck.

"Marry?" Miri's broken voice nearly made my knees collapse. "You're getting married?"

"It's not like that." Ivy's face flushed and the X on her neck flamed against her skin.

I scrambled for the right thing to say, the right way to bring everyone's emotions back to reality, but nothing came. My heart kicked at the tears spilling down Miri's cheeks and at the utter shock in Carter's eyes.

"Then what's it like, Ivy?" Carter snapped, focusing on his girlfriend, my fiancée.

"Our parents," Ivy tried. "They're making us, but I'm going to fight it. We'll find a way to get out of it."

"Why did you *lie?*" He took a few hesitant steps closer, his eyes burning red with unshed tears.

"I didn't," Ivy started, but her words failed her because anything she could have said after that would also be a lie. We'd been dishonest for almost two weeks now. "I didn't mention it because once I convince my mother to let us out, it won't mat—"

"How long have you known?" I cut in. Ivy's explanation meant nothing. We wouldn't get out of this, no matter what we denied or what excuse we made.

"I saw you two sitting in your Audi after brunch." Carter crossed his arms over his chest, his lips pulled into a thin line. "I was leaving for the gym, and I was going to say hi when Ivy started talking about your sham marriage. *You've always known who I am. I know who you are.*"

My face burned as Carter flung my words at us. That's where I'd heard that before. He'd known the whole time—on the flight over here, at the pub, during the camping trip. He *was* fucking with us.

"Is this who you are, Lex?" Carter said. "The guy who abandons his girlfriend when a better opportunity comes along? The guy who'd marry someone he spent his life ridiculing?"

"Carter—" Ivy put her hands up, trying to calm him down.

"And you—" Carter's voice cracked, simmering with his sadness and fury. "I know we said we wouldn't hold each other back, but goddamn it, Ivy. You're killing me."

Tears streamed down her cheeks, her hands shaking as she tried to wipe them away. "I don't want this. I'm going to stop it from happening. I swear to you, Carter. I will."

"We didn't have a choice." I clenched my hands into fists as the urge to defend her, to defend both of us, took over. "They're going to cut us off. We'd have nothing."

"Oh, cry me a river," Carter said. "Am I supposed to feel sorry for you? My family doesn't have shit, and I'm in the same place as you. Work harder."

"You think this has been easy?" My blood catapulted through my veins, shoving the feral side of me to the surface in preparation for the fight. "This has been a goddamn nightmare."

"Yeah, real hard for you, I bet. Sleeping with a princess. Marrying another one. Blowing your best friend on the side." Carter realized his misstep as soon as he said it. "Shit!" He shoved his hands in his hair, pacing away from us.

"What?" Miri pointed between Carter and Lex. "You two?"

"It was before you," I explained, my heart suddenly weighing a freight ton. "Before us."

"London," Miri said, finally putting the pieces together. She looked at Ivy. "Did you know?"

"Lex told me a few days ago," Ivy said.

Carter looked at me, hurt warring with rage in his eyes. "You told her?"

"Something was going on with you," I said. "You haven't been the best about hiding how pissed you are."

"So you *all* knew about Lex and Carter, and no one told me?" Miri's voice cracked with despair. "You *all* knew Lex and Ivy were getting married, and no one told me?"

Horror replaced the heartbreak on her face. She thought we were making fun of her or we'd purposely excluded her. That, like everyone else in her life, we found her replaceable.

"Fuck *you*." She said it with a broken whimper and stormed away.

"Miri, wait," I called after her.

"If you follow me, Alexei Fairfax," she snarled, "I'll have you murdered. I mean that."

Ivy pushed past me, sneering as she took off after her friend, leaving me alone yet again with Carter Scott.

The woods hummed with the signs of wildlife settling in for what little night they'd get. Insects in the distance, birds chirping overheard, water rushing over the water next to me. It had been a long, hot day, and it was going to be a long, hot night.

My temper matched the scalding temperature, racing through my veins like venom. Four years of holding everything I felt for Carter inside had just reached a tipping point.

"How could you do this to me, DC?" Carter's eyes burned, his indigo irises nearly gone in his fury. "*Me?*"

We were best friends, brothers in arms, roommates. We shared everything, even each other once upon a time. This betrayal had cut him deep, understandably so.

"You know how I feel about her." He choked out his words, his hand gripping at his shirt over his heart. "You know what she means to me."

"What did you expect me to do?" I couldn't believe this. It had happened the day before we came here. I'd barely had any time to react, much less do something about it.

"Say no." Carter said it like it was so easy. "You're an adult. You can do what you want."

A dark, twisted laugh spilled out of my chest as I hung my interlaced fingers on the back of my head. "You obviously haven't been paying attention."

He stared at me, his jaw clenched. "What's that supposed to mean?"

"It means I don't get a choice about *any* of this, Carter." We were dealing with the most powerful people in this bloated nationalistic hellscape of a country. Between Ivy's parents and mine, they had the combined wealth, connections, and privilege of some small countries. "I don't get a choice about Miri or Ivy. I don't get a choice about *you.*"

He winced, and I pretended like it didn't chafe to know I could hurt him, that I had hurt him. I didn't mean to, but the week had taken its toll on me. I was in a horrible mood, sleep deprived and woozy from dehydration, and my tongue was on autopilot. Misery loved company, and I'd become one miserable fuck.

"Why do you care?" I continued, spewing horrible shit just for the sake of being horrible. "You got what you wanted. You got to fuck the rich girl through college and now you don't have to deal with her when you leave to join the millions of other failed wannabes wasting away in LA." I shrugged. "You're welcome."

My insult landed somewhere around his heart, and he hit me. Hard. Right in the cheek.

I deserved it.

I *wanted* it.

Pain skidded down the left side of my body as my brain caught up. For half a heartbeat, I wasn't sure what I'd do. Then, instinct took over and I launched myself at him, shoulder to his gut, taking him to the ground. We were the same height, but he'd buffed up, and he now outweighed me by at least forty pounds of muscle.

Heart pounding in my ears, I scrambled to hold him down, hitting him in the stomach and using my legs to pin his hips in place. A fist to my ribs buckled me to the side, and I groaned, losing enough momentum for him to flip us. He wrapped his fingers around my wrists and pinned them above my head, but I used the weight of my legs to buck him off and rolled so I was on top of him again.

He landed on his back and I reversed our positions, me holding his arms outstretched, my torso on top of his. Our stomachs rose and fell against each other, his thighs on either side of my hips.

He squirmed. I held him tighter. Until...something pulsed between us—an energy, a vibrant, luminous thing that trembled as hard as my hands. It shimmered, there one second and gone the next. But I saw it.

He froze, his wide eyes meeting mine, seeming to ask if I'd seen it, too.

I did.

I became achingly aware of every part of my body touching every part of his. His cock twitched against my lower stomach, mine echoing with a jerk of its own, and I tilted my pelvis so they brushed against each other. He shut his eyes, and I touched my forehead to his, hot breath coasting across my lips as the smell of his sweat and his scent intoxicated me.

Fuck.

I wanted him so much that it hurt. I nearly trembled.

"Maybe it's not about Ivy," I murmured. "Maybe you're pissed you still want me, and no matter what happens, you can't have me."

This time, he laughed, surprising the sick, monstrous part of my heart and poking it awake.

"DC," he said. "I could have you anytime I want."

I rocked my hips against him, pleased when he groaned and laid his head back on the undergrowth. His overheated skin made the humid evening air seem even more suffocating.

"You sound sure," I said.

He kissed me, hard and demanding, and a moan tripped out of my throat before I could stop it. I sagged into him, the feel of his lips radiating over every nerve in my body, and he chuckled again. A sharp sting of embarrassment coated my insides when he broke the kiss with that arrogant smirk on his lips. "Pretty sure."

"You've been holding back all these years." I tilted my weight so I could hold on to his wrists with one hand, spit into the other, and shove it under the waistband of his gym shorts, easily finding his velvet cock. He shook when I stroked him, hitting a spot with my thumb that made him groan. I smiled and sank my teeth into his earlobe. "Why not take what you want?"

"Ivy wouldn't like it." His immediate answer reminded me of where we were and what had just happened between the four of us.

"And now?" I stroked him faster, my grip tighter. He hissed in a breath and rocked his hips against the action, urging me on.

"I don't give a fuck what Ivy wants." His growl turned me on even more, made me fuck him harder. "You get her no matter what. And if I have to share her with you, then she has to share you with me." He moaned out that last part.

It was so deliciously perverted. *I love it.*

I crashed my mouth to his, nibbling and biting, wrestling my tongue in between his lips. Heart racing, I jerked him off, sliding my hand up and down his cock while I watched him grit his teeth and fall apart. I narrowed my gaze in on the perfect O of his mouth and the way his Adam's apple bobbed when he swallowed back his euphoria. Just when he was about to come, I yanked down his shorts and replaced my hand with my mouth, sucking him deep into the back of my throat.

He lurched forward, fisting his hands in my hair the way he did the first time, and he thrashed under me. I held him down with my forearm while his legs shook.

"Jesus Christ, Lex. Fuck...Fuck!" He arched against me, and even in my darkest moments, I'd admit that it made me feel like a goddamn king.

I swallowed every last bit, taking what I'd deprived myself of for so long, and then I crawled up his body, hovering over him and bringing my lips to his ear.

"I'm going to fuck you, Carter," I told him. "If you have any objections, speak now or forever hold your peace."

He met my gaze, but I only saw a flash of anticipation.

He wanted me.

I sat back on my haunches while he flipped over, and I reached into my pocket where I'd stuffed the handful of freebies someone had shoved at me earlier in the night. I ripped open a packet of lube and took a moment to admire the view: Carter Scott, bare-assed and on his elbows for me, beautiful and sinful in his elegance.

Dragging a finger through his cheeks, I dripped lube on his ass and worked it over his hole, dipping one and then two fingers inside him to get ready for just how hard I planned to fuck him. I'd been dreaming about it...obsessing over it...for four years.

Now that he was here, like this, just for little ole me...*Fuck,* my hands trembled and my pulse wouldn't stop pounding. I could barely catch my breath. I rolled a condom over my dick, giving it a few strokes as Carter shook under me, every single muscle tensing with mind-numbing brilliance. He sucked in a breath, and I leaned over him, planting my fist by his ribs so I could press my forehead to the back of his hair, inhaling him deep.

"You have been fucked before, right, Chicago?" I said.

"Yes," he said. "Fuck, yes."

"Good."

That was the only warning I gave him before I pushed the head of my dick inside him. Fuck, he was so warm and tight and perfect. I almost collapsed, and he pushed back on me, urging me farther, deeper.

I inched out and nudged in again. He felt so goddamned good. I pulled back to ease in slower, so much slower than I anticipated.

Pace yourself. If I went too fast, this would be over much sooner than either of us wanted, and I'd be an embarrassed mess.

"Jesus, Lex," he snarled, clearly losing his patience, "just fuck me."

I froze, long enough for the shock of his filthy mouth to hit me square in the cock, and then I shoved myself to the hilt. I could have sworn my heart stopped, my breath died in my chest. I was balls deep inside Carter Scott, and he gasped and arched under me, completely at my disposal. *So good.* I was about to blow my load after only two seconds.

I pretended like my pause had to do with letting him get used to me, but we both knew I was a nervous wreck. I had ached for this, *yearned* for this, and now that I had it, I was ashamed to admit I couldn't fucking stand it.

"Fuck," I said, and it sounded more like a plea.

"C'mon, DC." Carter pushed his body against me, rotating my dick inside him. Holy fuck, that felt amazing. "You've wanted this for four years. Don't disappoint me now."

Goddamn it.

He wanted to be fucked? I'd fucking fuck him.

Grabbing his shoulder with one hand and his hip with the other, I plowed into him with single-minded purpose, chasing my release like nothing else in the world mattered. Carter and I had been made for each other. Him, the ambitious golden child, and me, the famous bad boy, two sides of the same coin, and what a coin it was.

I could spend entire lifetimes fucking Carter Scott. I could wake up every morning just like this.

Pausing to dribble more lube on our connection, I contemplated what I'd have to do to get that. But then I slid inside him again, and my whole damn world skidded to a halt. I fisted my hand in Carter's hair and dug my teeth into the place where his neck met his shoulder, growling like a beast. He tensed and moaned, and fuck, I was coming. It hit me behind the eyes, and I saw stars. I froze inside of him as it seized my muscles, my chest drenched with sweat, and my lips salty with his.

Good. God.

I couldn't catch my breath. My blood sang for this man.

"You should have done that years ago," Carter said, panting down his own climax.

"Fucking hell." I rolled off him, lying on my back so I could dig through my pockets to find my cigarettes and lighter. I put two between my lips, lit them, and handed one to Carter, grateful when the nicotine buzz soothed my shaking nerves. "Does this mean you forgive me?"

"No." Carter took a long drag and let it out on a puff. "Do you forgive me?"

"No. I think I'm in love with you. As fucked-up as that sounds."

He sighed. "Trust me, my feelings about you are just as fucked-up."

"Are you still pissed?"

He looked at me. "Are you still going to marry her?"

"Probably." I didn't see how I had another choice.

"Then I'm still pissed." He took a deep breath of his cigarette and blew it out in a desperate exhale.

"What would you do if I didn't?" I asked. "Would you face down her mother and ask her for her permission? Stand up in front of all the world and proclaim yourself her Prince Charming?"

"No. I'm not worthy of her," Carter said. "But neither are you."

I sighed but had no response because he was right. Neither one of us was worthy of Miri nor Ivy.

18

IVY

"Miri," I shouted, trying to catch up to her. The sky had turned a shade of rosy pink, casting the forest and everything in it with an enchanting glow. The crickets chirped and the frogs sang, the nocturnal beings of Killwater Woods waking despite the fact it would never get truly dark.

My heart pounded, and I cursed all those cigarettes I had smoked since arriving. Miri could book it when she wanted to, and I was in terrible shape.

"Wait," I said.

"What?" She whirled on me, her teeth bared and tears streaming down her cheeks. In all our years of friendship, I could count on one hand the number of times I'd seen her cry, and this might have been the most heartbreaking because I'd done it. "What could you possibly have to say to me?"

"I'm sorry," I said.

"I don't care." She tried to leave again.

"Wait." Panic tightened my chest that she might disappear into the woods, never to be seen again, just like all those old stories we'd been warned about.

"Why didn't you tell me?" Her voice cracked as she wiped under her burning brown eyes. "Why didn't you say anything?"

"I'm planning to fight it," I confessed, "when I get back to the States." I rubbed my hands over my face, hoping I would scrub myself awake and realize this was a horrible, terrible dream. "There hasn't been any time to deal with it. We only just found out the day before we came here."

A tense moment of silence passed between us, all the things we'd swept under the rug in four years weighing a thousand tons.

"I'm going with Carter to Los Angeles," she said.

My heart dropped into my gut, my knees shaking as they threatened to give out. "What?"

"At the end of the trip, we're going out there together." Miri crossed her arms over her stomach, looking surprisingly small and delicate despite how angry she was with me.

I blinked back my confusion, struggling to catch up. It didn't make any sense. She and Carter were never together. They'd never had what I had with either of them. "Why?"

"I know some people who can help him," she said. "An agent or two. Right now, he's just Ivy Washington's *maybe* boyfriend. He's going to need to shed that image if he wants to be taken seriously."

My chest tightened into a fist and my stomach churned, agony in my veins and tears burning my eyes. Miri and Carter, together, in California. And me and Lex in DC, an entire country away.

"Which means a clean break," Miri continued, pouring salt in my proverbial wounds. "You understand what I'm saying? Especially now that...Well..." She swallowed and held her head higher, staring me down. "Especially now."

I understood what she was saying, and it sliced me open, pulling my insides out. My muscles tensed, and I fisted my hands at my sides.

"For four years, I've acted like it doesn't hurt to see him pine over you, over both of you." She took a step closer to me. "He loves me, but he'll never love me like he loves you."

I furrowed my brows, unsure of what she meant. "Carter?"

"No, dummy," she said. "Lex."

"He doesn't love me—"

"And the worst part"—she continued, stalking closer—"is that I get it. I know why he loves you. I know why they both love you." She was inches away now, her breath hitting my lips and the heat from her forehead radiating against mine. "Because I'm in love with you, too."

I had ached to hear those words for ages, and not in the friendly way she said them when we were in public. I wanted them the way she meant them now. They shot through me like adrenaline-laced desire, and I pounced, crushing my mouth to hers. I cupped her jaw and tangled my fingers in her soft hair, inhaling every last bit of her that she'd let me have, and she melted against me, tugging me closer, crushing our torsos against each other. When I pushed my tongue into her mouth, she sighed and brushed hers against mine, sending a surge down my body to my clit, pulsing in time with my heart.

Yes. Finally, I get to have her.

This wasn't like last time, when I'd been all virginal innocence and blushing naivety. I now had four years of taking what I wanted from life, and now I wanted everything *from her*. I pushed her up against a tree and forced my leg between hers, where she ground down on it, rubbing her pussy against my thigh while I licked my way down her throat. She dug her hands under my shirt and under my bra, rubbing my nipples. I sucked in a breath at the contact, a jolt of electricity surging, sparking to life between my own thighs. I tugged at the fabric of her skirt, inching it up until I grazed her bare skin. Her muscles trembled, and I ventured farther north, finding her panties soaked.

"If you don't want this," I told her, "tell me to stop."

There was hardly a moment's hesitation before she said, "I want this."

It came out on a breathy sigh, and I crushed my lips to hers again. I took my time exploring, rubbing, and teasing her, shoving her thong to the side so I could spear through her silky wet skin. She was already so aroused, and it pained me to know she'd wanted this as long as I had. Wasn't that a damn shame? All this wasted time.

I captured her moans on my tongue and rubbed her the way I remembered, the way I knew she liked, inching closer to her entrance, working her clit with the heel of my palm.

"Yes," she moaned, twisting her fingers into my shirt. Pain mixed with euphoria when she sank her teeth into my bottom lip, and I chuckled into her mouth, slipping a finger inside of her. Fuck, we were desperate for each other, and she was so warm and slick, her muscles tightening when I worked my middle digit in with my index. When she fell apart, I memorized the way the pink glow from the sky made her seem otherworldly—like an angel, like she'd fallen from the heavens to drag me down with her.

I pulled her to the ground, and she rolled us so she was on top, but I wasn't done with her yet, so I twisted, rolling back over her and making her squirm under me. She dug her fingers into my sides, tickling me, making me collapse and give her leeway to switch positions. When she was in between my legs, she put her hands on either side of my head and leaned over me with that post-orgasm glow on her face.

"I've missed you," she said. "I've missed this." I darted my gaze between her eyes, looking for any shred of insincerity. When I found only earnest adoration, I fell just a little more in love with her. "I don't think I can pretend any longer, darling."

"Are you sure you want me?" I rubbed the back of my fingers down the side of her face, memorizing her satin skin, the most delicate thing in the world.

She leaned in to kiss me before muttering a quiet, "I'll always want you."

Miri disappeared down my body, dragging my shorts and underwear with her, and I yelped when she bit the inside of my thigh. She licked with her fiery tongue over my clit and sucked at me, sending sparks of euphoria up my spine and down my legs. She slid her fingers inside me while she licked and lapped, and every molecule in me shook with fulfilled anticipation, the delight that was this moment with her.

"I remember this." She kissed the side of my knee and looked up at me. "I remember how much you wanted me. How hard you came that first night. Do you remember, darling?"

She was so gorgeous, and I had wanted her so much. I still did. I feared I always would. She nibbled at the sensitive parts of me, being rougher than I was with her because she knew I liked it. The quick little slice of pain set me off. I came with my hands fisted in her hair, her fingers deep inside of me, and her teeth in my skin.

When my hormones leveled and I panted down my euphoria, I rolled us so I could explore her with my mouth, kissing and flicking and licking that pulsing flesh. I loved the way she curled around me when she came. I loved the way she cried my name. I realized, with heartbreaking certainty, that I would miss her when this was all over. More than I'd ever missed her before.

Because I was also certain I loved her as fiercely as she loved me.

The world hummed around us. The earth vibrated, echoing through me. Like some kind of link tied me to the very soul of the planet. Magic pulsed in the air, tasting like the sweetest honey in the world, or maybe that spiced wine from the party. It yanked me under its rapture.

When I looked up Miri's body, her glazed-over eyes told me she'd been taken in by the same force.

A high.

A drug.

Overwhelming.

Potent.

Omnipotent.

I sensed them the way most people knew which direction the sun was shining. Heat radiated in the pull between us, tugging Miri and me closer to the water—almost as if it were a tangible thing, almost as if I could reach out and touch the tether to them.

I broke the tree line and found them bathing in the creek, their foreheads pressed together and their arms over each other's shoulders, Lex's tattooed skin a stark contrast to Carter's blank canvas.

I didn't know what happened between them, but I could guess. The same thing that had happened between Miri and me. Now that Pandora's box had been opened, why would we deny ourselves a dance with the demons inside? All except hope because there was no more hope for us. There never was.

I stripped my T-shirt and bra over my head and pushed my shorts down to the ground, grabbing Miri's fingertips after she took off her dress. We walked hand in hand into the water like the fight between us had happened ten years ago instead of an hour.

We said nothing.

Nothing needed to be said.

When Carter looked up, I knew all I needed to know. Instinctively. We'd done this a million times before. We'd been doing this since the dawn of time. The drums from the party echoed in the distance, the music a soft accompaniment to the leisurely way we explored each other's mouths. He put his hands on my waist and pulled me closer so I could wrap my legs around his hips.

In one fluid motion, Carter slid inside me like he'd been waiting for me, like his whole life had been bringing him to this moment, and he had only one purpose, to connect us. Now that he had, he gasped and clung to me, his nails digging into the skin on my hips. I ran my fingers over a bite mark on his shoulder, understanding on some level that it must have been left there by Lex, but I didn't care. I didn't care about anything.

I felt free—truly and unequivocally free.

He rocked into me like we had all the time in the world. Slowly.

Gently. Not so much to fuck as to have as much of our skin connected as possible, because we might never get to touch each other like this again.

Hands crept up my spine, Miri's perhaps, and lips trailed across my shoulder. Another set of hands roamed across Carter's chest, and he let his head fall back against Lex's shoulder. Lex bit Carter's ear, trailing his mouth down the side of his neck. The sight made my cunt pulse, and Carter let out a pleased laugh, pulling me tighter against him. He felt it, and he liked it.

Miri found my mouth, and in a dizzying frenzy, she pushed her tongue between my lips, licking at my teeth and asking for entry inside. I felt her anticipation like it was my own.

The energy of this time and place molded to my molecules, grafting itself to my DNA, like the woods were inside of me. The night sounded louder, the music more intense, the coral-colored sky more vibrant, Miri's taste and scent more enticing than ever before.

My thoughts barreled through my mind, chaotic, incoherent, speeding like a rocket.

Touch. Lick. Take. Kiss. Hands. Skin.

Take. Take. Take.

Miri teased my nipples, and Carter slid his hand up the center of my body, interlacing his fingers with hers somewhere around my sternum. Lex's hand disappeared below the water, and I soon felt a thumb brush up against my clit, sending a shock up my body that had me gasping into Miri's mouth.

Carter surged deeper inside of me, Lex rubbed me harder, and Miri explored every inch of my skin with her hands, her lips like velvet on my neck and mouth. It could have been a minute or it could have been an eternity, but my climax hit me like a sledgehammer and broke me into a thousand jagged pieces.

I moaned and cried out and tensed as a powerful wave crashed into my spirit. I let it take me. Carter's cock twitched inside me and he groaned, holding me tighter, like my ecstasy had become *his* ecstasy and I could feel the weight of our union tying us together forever.

Lex gave Carter one last kiss and circled around his body, a rush of heat going through me when he pressed a tender peck to my lips before setting his attention on Miri.

Yes. Beautiful, lovely Miri.

He wrapped her legs around his waist and leaned his forehead against hers, sliding into her as easily as Carter had slid into me. Carter went behind Lex, and I positioned myself next to Miri, granting myself the privilege of her silky skin, soft breasts, and pebbled nipples. I sucked them into my mouth, licking and biting my way up her chest to her neck and taking the opportunity to mark her the way Lex had marked Carter. She hissed, but held my head closer like she wanted more.

I gave it to her. I gave her everything she wanted, and when she hit the peak of her own orgasm, it rang through me, too. Her emotions were my emotions. Her joy, my joy. As I held her and kissed her, my attention drifted to whatever Carter was doing behind Lex.

My enemy's head lay back against Carter's chest, his hand on Lex's forehead and a look of pure rapture on Lex's face as Carter did something between them under the water with his other hand. When Lex came, groaning and curling into Miri, something shifted between us. I felt it instantly. It zapped through my stomach, down the back of my legs, and up over my scalp. A knowing. A feeling.

Almost as if I could see it, burning and blinding, a permanent aura around us, cocooning us in this safe idyllic heaven for eternity.

Years might have passed while we touched each other in the water. Decades or millennia, I didn't know.

It felt like a dream, like I'd wake up any second alone in my bed. Maybe I'd gotten too intoxicated and the world refused to right itself —not as we dressed and sought a drier place to spend the night, not as we followed the mossy emerald trail farther into the woods, not when we discovered a stone ruin covered in clover and ivy.

Perhaps it had once been a small castle or a military outpost, ornate and opulent, and while the walls were intact, most of it had long since been reclaimed by nature. I'd hiked all over these woods in the ten days we'd been here, especially this close to the creek. I didn't remember seeing this, but now my heart swelled at having found it.

"It's fantastic, isn't it?" Miri grinned at us, running a finger down a wooden window frame as she walked closer. "Maybe we could live here forever."

I wrapped my arms around her waist from behind and put my head on her shoulder. "Who says we can't?" Pure ecstasy rattled through me. Her happiness. Mine. They were so interconnected, I couldn't tell where one ended and the other began.

"C'mon." Lex grabbed my hand and I grabbed Miri's. He led us through a door and into a large rectangular space with the remains of a hearth at the far end. Vines stretched the length of the walls, and the floors were compacted dirt, as if they'd never been finished. It reminded me of a witch's cottage from one of those fairy tales I used to read to my siblings when I was younger, and truthfully, I wasn't entirely sure that it could be anything else.

"We might as well stay here tonight," Carter said, hands on his hips as he assessed the small space. "No sense in getting lost in the woods trying to find our way back in the dark."

"No complaints from me." Miri spun around with her arms out to her side, seemingly lost to the romance of it all. I still felt high. My head swam and my heart raced. I might never come back down again, and that was sooooo okay with me.

Carter and Lex built a fire so we'd have more than the glow from the sky to see. None of us had any idea if it was safe to burn wood in the ancient space, but who the fuck cared? When it appeared like the smoke billowed out of the top, we stopped worrying about it.

Peace fell between us, the first peace I'd had in years. I didn't hate Lex. I wasn't angry at Miri or Carter. I wasn't angry with myself. I lay in the dirt with my head in Miri's lap, her fingers running through my hair in a sensual rhythm that set calmness in my soul. Carter's head lay on my chest, his ear over my heart, and Lex sat parallel to me with Carter's legs sprawled across his thighs. We'd been teasing each other for hours, laughing and giggling about the things we'd done. The things we wanted to do.

"I can't believe you're going to marry him," Miri whispered. Lex and Carter talked among themselves, not paying us girls any attention.

"Shh." I put my fingers over her mouth to silence her. "Don't ruin it."

She kissed my knuckles and leaned down to do the same to my forehead, making me feel cherished and adored.

"What if..." she said. "What if you married me instead?"

"I would marry you in a heartbeat."

"Would you marry me tonight?" Her eyes lit up, glittering with mischief in the firelight.

"Of course." I'd like to say I felt completely in control of my actions, that there was a part of me that still had agency and would be able to remember everything that came after. In that moment, the words spilled out of my mouth before I could consciously stop them, like whatever coursed through my veins made the decision for me and I was only a puppet on a stage.

"Carter is ordained," Lex cut in. "He married two of his friends from home. Isn't that right?"

"That's true." Carter nodded. "But I won't wed you to Miri. The only person you get to marry is me."

"Wait." Lex grinned and tilted his head to the side. "What if I wanted to marry you, Chicago?"

"Why can't we all marry each other?" Miri giggled like she'd meant it as a joke, but in the transcendent glow of everything about that night, it made an incredible amount of sense.

What if we all married each other? What if we made vows between the four of us to love, honor, and protect each other until we died? So it didn't matter if I had to be with Lex in DC? So it didn't matter if Miri went with Carter to California?

In our hearts, we would be together. Forever.

Some part of me knew it sounded ludicrous. I should've listened to that little voice and thought this through, but I was caught up in the fervor of the night. The taste of sex hung in the air, the drums echoed in the distance, and the sounds of every other animal in the immediate vicinity erupted with exactly what we were doing, loving and living and copulating.

"I would marry all of you." Carter spoke low and sultry, using the tone as when he whispered dirty things to me.

"I would, too," Lex said.

"Really, Lucifer?" I rolled my head so I could meet his gaze. He looked as buzzed out as I felt, his eyes shimmery with a pleased smile on his lips. "Even me?"

"Especially you, X." He pulled his grin wider, staring up at me like a villain in a fairy tale. A rush of fire exploded in my chest at the ravenous lust in that expression, the same one he'd given when I came, like it was only a matter of time before he got his hands around my neck again.

"Then it's settled," Carter cut in, bringing me back to this transcendental reality. "We marry each other and be done with it."

"I can think of a couple of governments that would have a problem with that." Lex huffed out a laugh and leaned his head back to stare at the beautiful sky.

"Who says we have to tell them?" Carter said.

"We'll know," Miri added. "And that's all that matters."

"You're okay with this?" I looked at Miri, furrowing my eyebrows. "I thought you never wanted to get married. I thought you never wanted to settle down."

"Well, it's hardly settling down if I have three spouses, is it?" She tucked a piece of hair behind my hair and kissed the tip of my nose.

My heart beat harder.

"And I've never felt about anyone the way I do about you three," she added. "I don't think I ever will again."

"That's the truth," Carter agreed.

Lex pushed to his feet, determination furrowed between his brows as he patted down his jeans. "We don't have rings."

"That's okay." Miri stood. "We'll do it the old-fashioned way."

I didn't know what she meant by that until she ripped a piece of fabric from the bottom of her dress, a long strip of pastel lavender.

Hand fasting.

Literally tying the knot.

I did the same to my shirt, white cotton that bore the TWU logo across the chest. Lex tore off a piece of his black V-neck and Carter added a length of Bears navy. Miri tied the ends together into one ribbon about three feet long.

"Okay, hold out your right hand," she said. I put mine in Carter's, and Miri put Lex's over ours and placed hers under the group. My stomach churned with giddy excitement while she wrapped the fabric around our joined palms, over and over. Lex and I helped her tie the two ends into a bow on top.

"Uh—okay. Vows," Carter said. "I'm going to wing this. I've never married four people at one time before."

"I vow to love you," I cut in as inspiration hit me in the vocal chords. "All of you. I will honor and cherish you and treat you with respect." I didn't know where this was all coming from, only that it poured out of me like it had been there for ages, waiting to spill over. "I will never betray you." I met Carter's indigo stare, saying this part especially for him. "I will never hold you back from your dreams." My heart gave a little girlish skip when he flashed those dimples at me. "Or each other," I said to Miri. And finally to Lex, "I promise honesty. From today. Until the end." I cleared my throat, emotion starting to overwhelm me and tears prickling at the corners of my eyes.

"Yes," Carter said. "I make the same vow." He repeated it back, putting his own spin on a few words. Lex and Miri said the same.

And once our promises hung between us, a violent sting hit me in the center of my palm. Like an insect bite. Or a hot poker.

I winced and tugged against Carter's hand, trying to let go and get out of the knot. Compared to the otherwise dreamy world around us, this was agony.

"Fuck," Carter said. "What is that?"

"Ahh." Miri scrambled and clawed at the fabric to get free. "I don't know."

It burned, and when I finally got my hand out, I opened my fingers to find scratches in the center of my palm, like someone had taken a branding iron to my skin along the lifeline. Tiny letters.

Until the end.

"Until the end?" I said, wincing against the ache. I looked over at Miri's hand, and she had the same marks in the same spot. "Where did that come from?"

"How the fuck—" Lex started.

"Whoa." Carter buckled at the knees, his hand going to Lex's shoulder to keep himself upright.

The world started to go wonky. A warmth spread from my palm up into my heart and down my spine, coating the length of my legs and toes. It radiated up my neck and over every piece of hair.

I'd never know pain again. I'd never know loss or death.

My world was perfect. And I was perfect. And so were *my husbands*. And so was *my wife*.

We weren't the first to stand in this spot and say these words. We wouldn't be the last. In that moment, we were so connected to all that had come before us and all that would come after us that we were *infinite*.

Time blurred by so fast, I could barely comprehend it.

Hands.

Hands everywhere.

Lips and tongues and mouths.

Skin.

Fiery, hot skin.

And ecstasy.

I drowned in my pleasure. I let the lust wrap itself around me and crush me in its shiny, sparkling grasp. We were a mass of electric life, pulsing and vibrating with the need to consume everything about each other.

We didn't fight it, we couldn't any longer.

We didn't even come up for air.

19

LEX

I would have sworn we were drugged.

But any drugs I'd ever consumed had never come close to the rush of feel-good chemicals coursing through my body that night. I didn't know where they came from. I didn't know what caused the marks on our hands. I didn't stop to think about it.

I dined on that forbidden fruit like Persephone sucking down pomegranate seeds, only vaguely aware that whatever I'd done might never be *undone.* But fuck it, right? It tasted so good sliding down the back of my throat.

And I wanted more.

Carter lay with his arm draped over Miri's waist, her body tucked against his chest and the sounds of their heavy breathing confirming how lost to dreamland they were.

Ivy was on her side, facing me and with her back to Carter. I had my arm tucked under my head and her right hand was in mine, our marks achy and scratching against each other.

Until the end.

A testament of our vow, right there for all to see. Forever.

The high had started to wear off, the rush of endorphins

returning to pre-vow levels. Now, I was restless and too big for my skin. I needed *something*. If I were still popping pills, I might have reached for a downer to help me sleep.

But I didn't have anything naughty with me, and part of me sensed Ivy remained just as itchy. So we kept each other awake.

"You feel it, too, right?" she said. "Tell me you feel it, too."

"Feel what?" I kissed the knuckles of her fingers, our hands clutched together in between our faces.

"This rush, this energy, this…" She sighed. "Pulse."

"I feel it," I said. "I don't know what it is, but I feel it."

"How did those words get on our hands, Lex?"

"I don't know," I said, leaning a little closer to her. "I don't care."

"Me neither."

The entire night, she'd held no more or less fascination for me as the other two. I found her just as appealing as Carter or Miri, an essential part of our square, as important as its other members. Now, in the fading afterglow of whatever magic had possessed us, I found Ivy to be the most singularly perfect thing in the world—her glassy gray eyes that begged for adoration, her strawberry-tangerine hair that felt like satin between my fingers, her soft, delicate skin, just asking to be marked.

I traced the curve over her shoulder with my finger, pleased when she trembled, and I let myself wander down her upper arm and over her forearm to her hand, bringing it to my mouth. Sucking on her index finger, I swirled it with my tongue, my cock kicking to life when she sighed and pushed it in deeper. I tasted us on her. Miri and Carter and *Ivy*.

In the chaos, it had been difficult to tell whose hands belonged to whom, which mouth was which. I was certain I already fucked Ivy. I was certain she'd already fucked me. But this was a different kind of intimacy. I had never given myself permission to touch her alone. I had never thought she'd willingly spread her legs for me and let me spear through her skin with wanton possession. I never thought she'd be this close.

Perhaps our life together would not be as terrible as I feared.

I rolled us so she was on her back and my hips were slotted between her thighs.

My sore dick, abused but delighted to be involved again, jolted to life at the connection to her hot, puffy pussy. Balancing my weight on my elbows by her head, I caged her in and brought my forehead to hers, our bodies connected all the way down our torsos.

I trembled, and I didn't know if it was because I was nervous to be doing this with Ivy or if it was because I'd come so many times that night that my balls were literally spitting air.

I slid inside her. I didn't ask, and she didn't protest. It was more of a compulsion than anything else. She winced and arched her back, clearly just as tender as I was, but still wet and tight and inviting.

"Fuck." She felt so good. Too good.

I rocked against her, taking my time to draw the pleasure out and unwilling to admit this was at its end. Slow. Leisurely. Private. Just between us. She flushed, sighed, and tilted her head to the side, displaying that rosy-pink X.

I couldn't resist. I dragged my tongue across it. Once. Twice. It burned, tasting like sweat and skin and making me so greedy for her. I licked it again, and Ivy moaned. That sound...*Fuck,* that intoxicating sound. I would spend hours chasing that noise, that purr of pleasure, knowing I could draw it out of her.

I was close.

So was she.

I sank my teeth into her neck, right over that X. Not enough to break the skin, just enough to leave a mark, and she clenched around me, moaning again. I slammed my hips into her, seeking that spot that made her wild. She sank her nails into my back, scoring a path along my ribs. My vision swam as I exploded deep inside of her with whatever I still had left to spill, milking the last little bit of this madness out of me. It drained away completely, leaving me an exhausted, shaking mess.

I collapsed, landing on my back at her side, gasping for air.

After a few moments, I padded around for my cigarettes, but Ivy found them first, lighting one for each of us before handing mine over.

We smoked in silence, not needing to say anything. Our bodies had said it all. And once we were done, we stabbed out the butts, and I tucked her in close, my arm around her waist, her back to my chest, and my lips on the small of her neck.

And we fell fast asleep.

What the fuck?

That's the first thing I thought when I woke up.

What the actual fuck?

The sun hit me square in the eyes, and a blinding, splitting headache shot straight through to the other side. I winced, squinting as Ivy's ginger hair came into focus. My arm was draped over her waist and my fingers intertwined with a heavy palm that felt like Carter's on the other side, their foreheads touching. Miri had an arm over Carter's ribs and her hand was latched on to Ivy's.

Fucking hell.

Everything hurt. People say they feel like they got hit by a train the morning after doing hard drugs, but I really did. Every nerve ending I had screamed when I moved. I disentangled my hand from Carter's and sat up, running my palms over my face to try to figure out where I was or what we'd taken.

Ecstasy, maybe? A shit ton of cocaine? My head pounded like the comedown from a serotonin overdose. I'd probably feel like hell for another twelve hours.

Wait...

No.

We hadn't taken anything. I didn't bring anything with me from the States.

Agony blazed up my arm from my right hand.

Until the end.

Jesus Christ.

We branded ourselves?

I ran my fingers over the marks, maybe about a half inch by two inches total, right in the center of my palm, on the edge of the mound by my thumb. They were little, but real, and they stung.

I had no idea how they'd gotten there. I looked around the space, my gaze landing on the length of fabric a few yards away. We had to have taken something. There's no way I would have agreed to this unless I was on some serious shit. But I couldn't remember. Not all of it, anyway.

I'd always considered myself a rational person. I didn't believe in God or fate. I definitely didn't believe in fairies or any of that supernatural bullshit. Any bumps in the night were usually explainable, but even I had to admit, this seemed surreal.

I lit a cigarette, my mind grappling for any memories it could conjure. The orgy in the creek. The walk to the ruin.

The wedding.

Then after that, a fat load of nothing...until I held Ivy down with my teeth and fucked her while she clawed at my ribs. I ghosted my fingers over the angry red marks.

Fuck.

We were so fucked.

The problems that had been there yesterday were still here in the bright light of today. One doped-up orgy in the woods would not fix the two weeks Ivy and I had spent lying to Carter and Miri. Nor would it fix four years of keeping my relationship with Carter a secret from both of them. This would only make things worse.

How far away those problems seemed. I could barely remember our argument.

"Shit," Ivy groaned, rubbing at her eyes and blinking awake. "What time is it?"

Carter stretched, kissed Ivy on the mouth and ran his hands over Miri's arm, rolling so he could look at her and give her a peck on her nose. I found my phone, miraculously still in my pants but unfortunately dead. The same fate had met both Ivy's and Miri's, and Carter hadn't brought his.

"Maybe nine, maybe ten?" Carter said. "Judging by the sun."

Ivy let out this sad laugh. "We're so screwed. Stephens is going to fire us."

"No, he's not." Carter pushed himself into a sitting position. "We'll tell him we got lost. It'll be okay as long as we figure out our shit on stage."

"Bloody hell." Miri examined the bite marks on her inner thighs, violet and pink against her skin. "I can't tell whose are whose." My gaze landed on the matching ones on Carter's shoulder and Ivy's neck.

I'd marked them.

Mine, a depraved part of my subconscious shouted. *All of them, mine.*

My teeth marks.

My vows in their skin.

Mine.

A burning possession rolled around in my chest, curling my hands into fists as I thought about any of them with anyone else. I chided myself for being such a greedy, perverted fuck.

"Christ," Ivy said, finally taking notice of the wounds on her palm. "What did we do?"

"I can't remember." I shook my head and pinched the bridge of my nose. "I'm still pretty fucked-up."

"Wait," Miri cut in. "Did we take something?"

"I don't remember taking anything." Carter pursed his lips. "I'm pretty straight-edge these days."

"It feels like we did." Ivy winced and rubbed at her temples. "It was that wine. From the party."

Miri stood and walked over to the tied-up strips we'd torn from our clothing, barely a ball of fabric now. She picked it up with one finger like it was radioactive. "I think we tied the knot last night."

"What happened after that?" Ivy rubbed one of her marks with a grimace.

No one said anything.

"We had to have been drugged," I said. "That's the only explanation."

"Who is going to drug four college students at a theater retreat in the middle of Nowhere, Ireland?" Ivy smirked and rolled her eyes, clearly set on giving me a migraine before I'd even found my pants.

"I don't know, Ivy," I said, returning her petulance. "Maybe someone at the orgy you took us to last night."

"It wasn't an orgy." She sneered and shook her head.

"They were literally passing out condoms and lube. I'm not judging, I'm just saying—" I cleared my throat and shrugged. "It was definitely an orgy."

"Well, I can see the honeymoon's over." Carter pushed to his feet, grabbing his boxers and gym shorts to slip them over his legs.

"Or things are back to normal," Miri added.

In my heart, I knew that wasn't true. Things would never be normal again. I had changed. I could feel it in my skin, my blood, my bones. Whatever happened to us last night would stay with us long after we went home. Maybe for the rest of our lives. We had made a vow of forever.

Until the end.

Ivy groaned and rubbed her hands through her hair. "What if someone messed with us while we were asleep?" She gasped. "What if somebody *saw* us?"

"Who?" Carter wrapped an arm over her shoulders and tucked her in close to his body. "Like you said, we're four theater kids out in the middle of nowhere."

"That doesn't mean there's not someone out here looking to make money," she said.

"Ivy's got a point," Miri said. "We have to be careful about how this appears. We can't be all 'mushy gushy here's my boyfriend and my girlfriend and their boyfriend' in public."

"Aw," Carter teased, wrapping his arms around her waist from behind and pulling her into him so he could rest his head on her shoulder. "After our wedding, I'm your husband, too, Juliet. Does that make me seventh in line for the throne?"

She poked his ribs and smiled. "Don't push it."

"I can't go back to hiding how I feel about you," Ivy said. "I won't do it."

Miri's cheeks turned a brilliant shade of rose, and she linked her fingers with Ivy's, leaning in to give her a sweet kiss. I liked the sight of it too much, the way Miri's mouth curved into a joyful grin and the way Ivy looked at her like the girl hung the moon.

I didn't want this to end.

I didn't want to lose this the minute we stepped out of the woods.

Panic gripped me at the idea that it could happen, that Ivy would slip back into her former self, the one where she hated me and wouldn't let me touch her. I couldn't be that guy again. I wouldn't. But Ivy was scared of change. She wouldn't roll over and accept that this had happened, that we had something between us, whatever it was. I felt it last night. I knew she did, too.

"There's a difference between hiding from each other and hiding from everyone else," I said. "We promised honesty last night, or at least, I think we did. We made a lot of promises. It's all a mess, but what if—what if we kept them? What if everyone gets what they want?"

"You're talking about a poly relationship with your best friend and your archnemesis," Carter said. "Just so everyone's clear on that."

"So?" I said. "I have to marry Ivy. I don't have a choice in that. Neither does she." Carter winced. Maybe I was being a little brutal. "But *we* have a choice about how we react to it." Once I said it, an enormous weight lifted off my shoulders.

"Meaning?" Carter said.

"Miri is right," I said. "Why can't we all have each other? What's so wrong about that?"

"Aside from the media scrutiny and the guaranteed disapproval from our parents?" Ivy said. "Possible disinheritance and the complete and utter breakdown of every ten-year plan I've ever created."

"You can still have law school," I continued, ignoring her pessimism. "You can still have the Senate and the presidency and whatever else your entitled ass wants. I think not holding anyone back from their dreams was also part of our vows, no?"

"And what do you want, Lex?" Ivy said.

"I want to fuck Carter whenever I want," I said. "I want to fuck Miri whenever I want. I want you to not be a pain in the ass about every goddamn thing."

"Well, two out of three ain't bad, right?" Carter said.

"Fuck you both." Ivy raised her eyebrows and put her hands on her hips, part offended, part amused.

"Sure, why not?" I teased. "You can have that, too, if you want."

"I'm in," Carter said. "If I go to LA knowing I've got the three of you in my corner no matter what, I'll sleep a lot easier at night."

"What if you meet someone new?" Ivy cleared her throat and shifted on her feet, a blush creeping up her neck and into her cheeks. "What happens when you want to marry someone else? We were going to break up, Carter. Before all this."

"We'll deal with that if it comes to it, Weeds," he said, taking a step toward her so he could wrap her in his arms and tuck her under his chin. "Together."

"I'll keep him in line, darling." Miri gave them both a wink.

"*You* will be the worst influence of them all," Ivy said with a deep sigh and a laugh.

"There are a million things that could go wrong." Carter kissed her temple and hugged her tighter. "But imagine if it went right?"

As soon as he said the words, I saw it. Our life together—the four of us at Miri's cottage in Scotland, streaks of gray in Carter's hair and wrinkles at the corners of his eyes, Miri's timeless smile and her unyielding loyalty, Ivy's piercing stare, not a day less intimidating for all the years it had spent incinerating people where they stood. I imagined the days spent chasing after our children and the nights drawling slowly by as we sipped from this forbidden chalice and made love under the Milky Way, pretending the rest of the world didn't exist.

I'd never wanted anything more in my life.

Shame and guilt stabbed my heart because I knew every move I made from that moment on, every decision, every conscious *choice*, would be to bring me closer to that one pure vision.

"I'm in," Miri said.

"Me, too," I instantly agreed.

"Weeds?" Carter said.

Tears brimmed at the corners of Ivy's eyes, but she pushed them back down and cleared her throat.

"God help me," she said. "Yes. I'm in."

20

IVY

Why did I ever agree to such a stupid, silly thing? We already had matching words carved into our hands. What else could they want from me?

Everything, it turned out, my whole future, theirs, and I would have given it to them if it belonged to me. Which it decidedly did not, and the closer we got to reality, the more that sank in. Carter and Lex talked about rules and not fucking around with people outside of our square.

"We're more like two triangles," I argued. "Seeing as you and I don't like each other."

"That's not what you were saying last night." Lex winked and lit a cigarette.

"I was *high* last night." I seethed with his accusation, the memory of his teeth on my neck and the way that made me come so hard that I'd almost passed out ghosting to the forefront of my memory. I'd also been mostly sober. I remembered it, but I wasn't about to share that with the rest of the class.

"No way. You two?" Carter whistled. "Hell, and I thought *I* made some bad decisions."

I resisted the urge to scowl at him.

"Look, I think it's easier if we play it by ear," Miri said. "*We* are each other's home, and we'll always know that, but life does happen."

"Miri's right," Carter said. "And if things change or we start to feel different, we'll tell each other. We'll talk about it."

My mind was a million miles away. They were so concerned with figuring out the dynamics of a relationship that had barely left its infancy, but I couldn't stop thinking about how deep we were in the forest. We'd been walking on the trail for almost an hour, and we hadn't even passed the spot where we'd gotten into an argument and swam in the creek. *Fucked* in the creek, I corrected myself. I couldn't remember if it was a long hike to the ruins last night, and my brain hurt anytime I tried.

Everything hurt. My head. My hands. My poor pussy, which ached every time I took a step. We'd torn each other apart, and I didn't regret it, but I was certainly paying for it.

And the mark on my palm?

Had I put it there?

I vaguely recalled scrambling to get my hand out of that knot because it burned.

No, I thought. I had to have imagined that. We had to have done it to ourselves. I must have agreed to let someone cut my skin. But who? No one remembered doing it, and no one had anything small enough to form words. That was problem number one.

Problem number two was whatever caused us all to feel so drugged up that we'd promptly fucked each other and passed out on the dirt floor of a ruined castle. To be sure, I would have had to be sky-freaking-high to let Lex bite my neck. Even more so to enjoy it.

Which I didn't. I definitely *did not* enjoy it.

My hand went to the spot where his teeth had left a bruise; I could feel it there today, sore and tender.

Some sick part of me hoped it never healed.

Stop it.

I refocused on the larger issue. Like why weren't they more worried about the acid trip we all went on together?

"You okay?" Carter put an arm over my shoulders while we walked, pulling me into his warm, safe embrace.

"How can you be so cool about this?" I said. "I don't like feeling like I don't have control of myself."

"You know my mom's into all that new agey stuff, right?" he said. "She says that sometimes people can get into these deep, meditative trances and sort of project their consciousness out of their bodies. Like go on spirit walks together."

"Tell me, what about our argument in the woods pre-orgy put you in a deep, meditative trance?"

He rubbed the back of his head and sighed. "Fair point."

"Maybe it was the fairies," Miri teased. "Ashley warned us not to piss them off."

"Yeah, and we didn't," Lex said. "Why would they fuck with us? We've been pleasant houseguests."

He and Miri kept talking, but her suggestion slid into the crevices of my brain like a splinter.

No.

Fairies?

It was laughable.

Is it?

I believed in God, didn't I? Why would fairies be any different? I couldn't see or touch God to feel their presence in my everyday life. But could I, reasonable, rational Ivy Washington, really convince myself the mind-blowing euphoria I experienced and the random wounds on my hands were the work of small woodland humanoids?

Even if I could suspend disbelief enough to consider it, why would fairies waste their time with us? Why wouldn't they just go on living their fairy lives and leave us to self-destruct?

Siobhan.

Her name echoed out of the depths of my memory like a siren.

"I'm going to take pity on you, Ivy Washington. I'm going to give you a gift."

She'd kissed me. I patted my jeans, finding them empty.

The ring.

It was gone. I'd shown it to Lex before Carter and Miri found us... and now?

Fuck.

It was too late to go looking for it; I didn't even know where we were. Siobhan had fucked with me, and I didn't even have proof. She'd kissed me and then she'd disappeared. Was she even real at all? No, Lex definitely said he saw her. Was she responsible for doing this?

When we finally reached the campus, we emerged from the tree line holding each other's hands. Mine in Carter's and Miri's and Lex on the other side of her. It looked exactly the same as it had yesterday. The same tall stone buildings, the same gray facade, the same trees in the same spots with the same sidewalks connecting them.

It was all so normal...*so perverse.*

A part of me screamed to turn around and run back into the woods, to find the ruins and fix it up and live there for the rest of our lives.

Why had we come back? They wouldn't understand anything, not us, not me. My entire world had shifted. Everything about my life had changed. And for all these people? More of the same.

Students milled about, carrying books, talking to each other, and dressed in everyday, ordinary clothes. A group of women walked by, collectively giving us a once-over and a sneer as they passed.

I could only imagine how we looked.

Dirt caked every inch of exposed skin, my hair was in a matted plait down the side of my body, exposing the bite mark on the side of my neck. Out of the four of us, I might say I was the most presentable.

I dropped my hands to my sides as my heart sank. We'd been kidding ourselves for thinking we could have each other.

Look at these people.

Look at this world.

I would never fit in again. I couldn't. None of us could.

ACT IV

My lord, I shall reply amazedly,
Half sleep, half waking. But as yet, I swear,
I cannot truly say how I came here.
-Lysander, Act IV, Scene 1

21

IVY

Everything seemed fine as we stumbled through the dorm halls to our room. Sure, people gave us sideways glances, but we were covered in mud and caked with sex, so I understood. We did the walk of shame up to the showers. After we washed away the grime and made ourselves presentable, we headed to the auditorium, ready to face the music. We were a few hours late, but nothing we couldn't explain or make up.

"Well, look what the cat dragged in," Davis shouted.

Someone else laughed. "Oh, you four are in deep shit."

"Yeah, what the hell?" Piper said. "You can't disappear for a whole day and show up like nothing's wrong."

"Stephens is pissed." Davis sang that last word.

"What the fuck do you mean?" Lex asked, his eyebrows furrowing.

A whole day?

I grabbed for my phone, and sure enough, it was June 23. We had spent the entirety of June 22 in the woods, in those ruins. It didn't feel like a day. It didn't feel like more than a few hours. My heart beat so hard that I expected it to leap out of my body and flop around on the ground like a fish.

"How is that possible?" I whispered to Carter as we walked in between the curtains to the stage.

"It's not," Carter said.

"Fuck, we're so screwed," Miri said.

As soon as we stood center stage, Stephens froze and stared at us. Anger poured off him like a sickness, and he held his arms out to the side, shaking his head.

"You're fired," he said. "All of you. Pack your shit. I'm hiring a cab to take you to the airport tomorrow."

"Stephens," Caroline said, holding up her hands to try to calm him down.

"No, I'm done. I'm done with all of them. I give them the lead and they squander it."

"Wait," I cut in. "Wait, Stephens. Please. Can I talk to you in private?"

"Weeds, what're you doing?" Carter murmured.

I had an idea. I hated to use this card, but I didn't see any other way out of this, and we didn't deserve what happened to us. We didn't ask for it. We were still struggling to figure it out ourselves.

"We were lost in the woods for twenty-four hours," I told him once we were a few rows away from everyone else. I crossed my arms and stared him in the eye, determined to make him understand. "You're upset, I get it, but imagine how we feel? We didn't show up for breakfast, and we didn't show up for rehearsal or for dinner. No one here batted an eye, much less looked for us."

Stephens straightened, his hands on his hips and his shoulders flexing as he considered it from this new perspective.

"You showed up late to the camping trip," he said. "You've been so miserable you can't remember your lines. Tell me why I should give you another chance."

I was exhausted. The heat and this thing with Lex and the orgy and being drugged had stressed me out, and I'd had enough.

"What do you suppose my mother would do if she knew you lost her eldest daughter somewhere in Ireland? That no one even looked for her? Or *Alexei Fairfax*? I mean, c'mon, Stephens."

Low blow.

We hadn't told anyone where we were going, and I hated using the *Mommy-get-out-of-jail free* card. But Stephens needed us. He knew he did. I watched him come to this realization himself.

"Fine," he said, "but you'll make up your time. Every morning. Until showtime."

I'd like to thank the Academy…

"Fine," I said, walking away even more certain that law school was a bright beacon in my future. My mother would have been proud, disappointed in my behavior, absolutely, but I worked Stephens like goddamned putty, and even she'd admit he folded like a cheap suit.

After rehearsal, we ate dinner with the rest of the group and told stories about wandering around the woods, trying to find the creek so we could follow it back. Some of them probably believed it, but we knew what really happened. To us, we'd been out in those woods overnight, maybe twelve hours max. Not twenty-nine. Not enough to lose an entire day. But it wasn't until we got back to our dorm room that night that we could talk about it freely.

"Okay, what the fuck is going on?" I asked, doing my best to keep my voice down.

Carter shook his head and grabbed our double bed, scooting it along the floor so it was in the center of the room. Then he helped Lex do the same to theirs.

"We had to have been drugged," Miri said. "That's the only thing I can think of."

"You think it was the townies?" I said. "The locals at the bonfire?"

"Maybe," Lex said. "Or maybe just some bad actors. Who knows?"

"Who knows?" I balked at him. "You're not concerned about this?"

"We're fine," Lex said, gesturing around to us, his hazel eyes exhausted and shimmering with apathy. "It's out of our system by now, so even if we went to the doctor and they ran tests, they wouldn't find anything."

"Lex is right," Miri said. "We were irresponsible, but there's not much we can do two days later."

I met Carter's gaze across the room, his soulful eyes indicating he felt the same way. Whatever happened was more than being roofied at some festival in the woods. It felt bigger than that, like I needed an exorcism or...a blood transfusion. I wasn't the same person anymore.

Molecularly.

After Lex and Carter pushed the two beds next to each other, Miri and I climbed in and the boys bookended us. My worry over the fact that something terrible had happened sat in my stomach like stale coffee, but my exhaustion won out and sleep took me quickly.

In my dreams, I ran through the forest barefoot on the balls of my feet, tree branches hitting me in the face as the wind whipped through my hair. I was running from something.

No.

I was running *to* something, the pull to it growing heavier and more tangible with each pulsing step.

The ruins.

I was close, so close.

"Ivy," someone said. "Wake up. You're having a nightmare."

I opened my eyes with a dying sob in my throat, my hands clamped around Miri's and her brown eyes inches from mine. It took me a moment to remember where I was—in my dorm with my friends. My *spouses.*

Miri leaned in and kissed my cheek.

"You're okay." She yanked me closer and wrapped an arm around my shoulders, holding me as tears spilled over my cheeks. "You're here with us. It wasn't real."

It wasn't real.

Jesus, it felt like I'd never get out of that forest again, like I had to reach the ruins or something evil was going to devour me. Kill me. Take my soul and never give it back.

A flash brightened the room, a loud boom following it and making me jump.

A thunderstorm.

The unusual summer humidity had finally given way to rain, and the room already seemed less stifling than it had the entire time we were here.

I listened to her breathe and the sounds of our husbands' deep sleep echoed from either side of us, creating a hypnotizing rhythm that lulled me back to a hesitant peace.

"Do you regret what we did?" she whispered. "The four of us? Together?"

"No," I said. Despite the blank spots in my memory, the tension between us had eased considerably. Like it was always supposed to be this way, and we'd been fighting it for too long. Like Lex and I had always been waiting for Carter and Miri to even us out and give us that rubber buffer around our live-wire relationship. "I just wish I remembered how it happened."

"Me too," she said. "This is our last week together. I don't want to spend it fretting over something I can't change."

I understood, even as the reality of it hit me like a battering ram straight through the heart. *This was it—the last days we would ever be like this.*

That pit in my stomach lurched when I remembered everything that had been on our plate before we went into the woods, everything we'd have to deal with again once the intensive was over. Carter and Miri would go to California. Lex and I would stay in DC. The charade would begin, and my parents would be watching; the whole world would be watching. I'd fight to find a way out of this engagement, even if it took everything I had left. This wouldn't be the last time I spent with them, it couldn't. I'd rather die first.

"Miri, what if someone was there last night? What if someone *did* drug us and record the whole thing?" Terror shot through my chest, slicing me in two, making my muscles tremble. "What if our orgy makes front page news?"

It was silent for a minute, and then she giggled to herself, soft and low. "I hope it does. I suppose then we'll know what happened."

I balked at the horror, the sheer chaos, that would cause. My mother might never speak to me again, and the public would decry our debauchery. If I thought I they were bad before, I could only imagine the lengths the paparazzi would go to in order to get the exclusive scoop on that headline.

"What?" Miri said at my expression. "It's not like anyone would *believe* it was us."

"People have believed a lot worse," I said.

"Let them think what they want," Miri murmured, shaking her head. "I'm not ashamed of loving you. Any of you."

"It sounds so easy when you say it like that." In reality, a public relationship like the one we'd formed in those woods would destroy everything we'd ever taken for granted about our lives.

"Love *is* easy, darling," she said. "It's them who make it difficult."

It reminded me of boarding school, when she'd told me sex didn't have to be a big deal and that the public made it more than it ought to be. I'd gone out and hooked up with random strangers as a result, but I'd found that none of those emotionless encounters did anything for me.

She's wrong.

A love like ours would never be easy. It would break my heart to let Carter go, to send Miri with him, to live with Lex and know we both pined for two people neither of us could have. I didn't want to think about it. We still had a week, a whole week, left together. I vowed to make the best of it, so I tucked myself tighter against her chest and fell asleep cuddled in her safe embrace.

That draw to the ruins stuck with me. Even if I didn't dream about it again that night or the night after, the stinking, blinding fear of it pulsed in the back of my mind every time I looked down at those words on my hand. It raged inside of me anytime I caught a glimpse of the forest beyond the campus. It burned in my blood on a constant unending simmer, refusing to let me forget what we'd done.

I knew, even then, the forest wasn't through with us.

Maybe it never would be.

22

IVY

The rain continued well into the next day, a torrential downpour that kept us inside. At least the heat had broken, and everyone's mood lifted by being able to breathe in the auditorium.

Stephens damn near died on the spot when we got to the fight scene between Romeo, Mercutio, and Tybalt, and the awkwardness that had been there three days ago was now nonexistent.

"I don't know what it is between you and Lex," Stephens told me afterward, "but you two showed me something tonight I want you to lean into. How different would this scene be if Tybalt and Mercutio were secretly in love?"

I snorted a laugh and buried my face in my hands.

Jesus Christ.

"Secretly in love, huh?" Lex said, twisting his lips into that smug, arrogant grin that I *hated*. "Well, I don't know if Ivy and I can pull that off, but we'll try."

"Play around with it tonight," Stephens said before turning his attention to Carter and Miri.

"I have about a thousand things I'm thinking of playing around with tonight," Lex purred next to my ear. The heat from his breath coasted down the front of my shirt, and he lifted a finger, delicately dancing it over his bite mark on my neck.

The entire left side of my body broke out into goose pimples, and I shivered.

"Well, that's too bad." I took a step away from him. "I was going to do some research, so I guess you'll have to play with your girlfriend instead."

"Maybe I'd rather play with your boyfriend."

"I'm sure he'd be happy to oblige." It should have made me jealous, and perhaps a small jolt of fire surged through my blood before I quickly smothered it down. The thought of Lex and Carter fooling around turned me on, and that confused me. Shouldn't I find it audacious? Shouldn't I be upset that they had something I didn't? The whole poly thing was still new, and until I figured out what happened to us in those woods, I didn't have time to focus on it.

"What are you researching?" He raised his eyebrows, looking genuinely interested.

My various subjects flitted through my mind—the town, fairies, ruins, ancient rings, disappearing women, fairy gifts, the words on our hands, this indescribable urge to disappear deep inside of the woods and never come out again. Ya' know, the usual things a twenty-two-year-old prelaw student wants to know about. No big deal. Still, I didn't want Lex to find out. He'd wanted us to drop it, but I couldn't tame my curiosity.

"None of your business," I said in that same tone I'd always used with him, the one that told him to screw off. But this time, it held less bite.

I headed to the library. Ashley had said there was an entire section devoted to the local legends, and I planned to stay here until I read them all or until the library closed. The rain pelted against the windows while I flipped through the pages of a dusty old tome I'd pulled out of a shelf that clearly no one had touched in ages.

Killwater Woods: History and Grounds by J. M. McMurphy

I'd been here for two hours and so far all I'd learned was the college had been founded in 1645. Prior to that, the land was completely undeveloped. The college had kept the surrounding forest in trust since then, allowing no one to build on it since at least the 1680s, which meant the ruins we found were older than the college.

No way that could be true. It looked old, but not five hundred years old. Maybe two or three hundred tops? Of course, what the hell did I know about ancient Irish ruins? I'd been a poli-sci major. I closed the book and put it back, trailing my fingers down the shelf as I read each title, hoping one would jump out at me.

Legends of the Killwater Area. I grabbed that one and balanced it on my hip.

The Curse: Plague in Sixteenth Century Northern Ireland. That one sounded fun, so I grabbed it as well before returning to my stack at the table.

My research led me down the windy rabbit hole of disappearances in Killwater, at least forty in the last hundred years, which hadn't been enough to raise alarm at face value. The police chalked them up to drunk college students never finding their way out again, but combined with the local legends about fairy curses, it gave the woods a sinister vibe.

There were as many legends about fairies as there were books in the entire library—maybe the world. Some of them weaved a frightening tale of child abduction, of human infants replaced with fairy changelings. They mentioned light and dark fairies that used to live in Ireland before men destroyed their realm and speculated that there might still be fairies living in the woods today. But I didn't put much stock into these tales. They were, after all, stories.

Explain Siobhan's kiss. Explain disappearing for twenty-four hours when it felt like twelve. Explain the vow on your hand.

Until the end.

Our vows carved into the same spot on each of our palms, curving along the lifeline on our mound of Venus. There was no way any of us could have held a knife steady enough to cut something this small.

And what was up with that ring? Did it mean something? Was it important?

A throat cleared from the spot in front of me, and I looked up, my eyebrows furrowing when I met Lex's incredulous gaze.

"You've been down here all night," he said.

"And?"

"I told you, I had plans for us." He stuck his hands in his trouser pockets, his button-down shirt rolled up to the elbows. His dark hair fell in his face, unkempt from how much he'd evidently run his hands through it, and his pouty lips pursed even more as he waited for my response. Lex had always been so undeniably attractive, and after what we'd done together only a few nights ago, I should have gone running right back into his bed. But no...my feelings for him couldn't have changed that quickly, so I needed to keep researching, keep figuring out what made us react this way.

I snorted a laugh and went back to my reading. "I didn't think you were serious."

"Why wouldn't I be?"

"Because we don't like each other, Lucifer." I flipped another page in my book. "We never have."

"We married each other."

I rolled my eyes and turned another page. "That was pretend."

"Was it?"

He grabbed my hand and flipped it over, revealing those stupid scratches, and I tried to act like the pulse of excitement at his touch had more to do with how warm his palms were compared to mine. I whipped away from him, brushing my thumb over the vows like maybe I could rub them away if I tried hard enough.

"What were these *plans*?" I said.

His lips lifted into a slow, devious smile. I got his meaning loud and clear.

"We're not high anymore." I sighed, pretending like his heavily implied innuendo didn't annoy me...didn't make me run hot for reasons I'd rather not investigate. "There's no reason for us to pretend like that was anything else."

He hummed a noise and tilted his head, his eyes wandering over me as I resisted the urge to squirm. I hated when he looked at me like this, like he was peeling my layers away and baring my soul, whether I wanted him to or not. Yet, hate and love were so close to the same thing, weren't they? I clenched my hand into a fist to keep from dragging him across the table so I could see if his lips tasted the same way sober as they did when I was drunk.

Needing to put space between his mouth and this clawing, aching desperation in my soul, I stood and pretended like there was another book I wanted to find. Lex stalked behind me as I meandered down an aisle, looking over the spines for something to grab.

"You can't ignore me forever," he said.

I sighed and ran my eyes down the books on my right. "That sounds like a challenge."

"Whatever this thing is between us, it's only going—"

"There is no thing between us," I cut him off with a curt look over my shoulder.

"Oh, sure there is." He took another step closer, his hands in his pockets. "Everyone sees it now. Even Stephens."

"That had nothing to do with any *thing* between us. That had to do with a drunk night in the woods."

He ran a finger over wisps of my hair, brushing a piece back from my face, and the soft caress of his fingertips sent a flush of wanton heat down my neck. Flames spread up my cheeks and into my chest, my palm instinctively going to cover the X on my throat. He smacked my hand away, widening his eyes as he gripped my windpipe and traced his thumb over it the way he had the night at the pub.

His touch on me made me shake, as if I had a direct line from that spot on my neck down to my clit. I shivered with need for him, so agonizingly aware of it that I clenched my jaw to keep from reacting.

No.

This was Lex, and he was off-limits, always off-limits. I didn't like him. He didn't like me. We'd already defined our roles together. There was no reason to change them. Even if we were going to be married.

I took a step away.

"I know your secret, Ivy Washington," he whispered, narrowing his hazel eyes, that dark hair falling on his forehead.

"I don't have any more secrets, Alexei Fairfax," I said, gulping against my suddenly dry throat.

"Yes, you do." He leaned in closer, the heat of his body radiating into my skin, making me sweaty and flustered. "The last time, the time just between us, I know it was you."

I swallowed, avoiding his gaze and everything about him. The way I wanted him shouldn't be real. It *wasn't* real.

"*You* you, not *high* you." He pressed his mouth against the curve of my ear. "You liked it."

I trembled, squeezing my thighs together to curb the pulse between them. I had liked it. I liked it so, *so* much. But I couldn't tell him that.

I moved away, but he shot his hand out and wrapped it around my wrist to tug me back. I collided with his chest, the smell of deodorant and cigarettes and *Lex* hitting me in the face, making me want to bury my nose in his neck to breathe him in until I suffocated.

"Let go of me." I struggled against him.

"You and me? It's fucked-up, X," he growled. "But you like that, too."

"I *hate* you," I snarled, baring my teeth.

"Yeah?" He brought his face closer. "That's the thing I like the most."

"You're a sick fuck."

"So are you," he hissed. "Aren't we a pair?"

I could have killed him. I could have dug my fingers into his eyes and smacked at his head like I used to do when we were kids. Now that I raged with all the scalding, furious passions of a woman, I wanted to hold him down by the neck and fuck him until I couldn't think.

He must have read that in my gaze because he shook his head and laughed out a dark, demented noise that made him seem villainous, like a creature out of a horror movie.

"I bet if I shoved my hand in your pants right now"—he ghosted the tip of his teeth over my earlobe—"I'd find out just how much you love hating me."

"Hmm." I narrowed my eyes at him and backed up, my entire body flush against the racks, his thigh between my legs, his heart pounding in rapid time with mine. "I bet you're so thickheaded that you actually think this hate-to-lust thing is working on me."

"Is it?" He grinned, brushing his lips over mine in an electric sizzle that amplified the untenable connection between us.

I scoffed. "You should be so lucky."

"Oh, X. Luck has nothing to do with it." Lex chuckled and leaned back a millimeter, just enough to meet my gaze. Then his attention darted to my mouth and back again. "You look like you want me to kiss you. Do you want me to kiss you?"

Yes.

"No." The word came out on a squeak.

"You're such a liar." His mouth descended on mine, mesmerizing and commanding, and I tunneled my hands through the hair on the back of his head, my nails against his scalp. He growled and bit at my bottom lip while our tongues wrestled for dominance, and I moaned when his cock twitched against my pelvis, revealing that he was as into this as I was. Our dance had been going on for far too long.

He teased at the button of my jeans, plucking them open with a simple flick. Then he shoved his hand down the front and cupped me, his middle finger playing over my clit and going right for my entrance, already slick and ready for him. Shame rolled through me at how much I wanted it. That chuckle echoed low in his chest, urging me on, making me desperate and needy in ways that I shouldn't be...not from him. But oh...it was like my desire for Lex had been dormant in my soul for eons, and now that it had gotten loose, I struggled to contain it again.

"I knew it," he murmured, breaking the kiss and resting his forehead against mine. "You want me so bad that you can't stand it."

Glaring up at him, I yanked at the leather of his belt, the metal jingling as I snapped open the button on his pants. Just when I was about to shove my hand down the front, a throat cleared behind him, and we both jumped. Lex ripped his fingers out of me and I rushed to grab my jeans, holding the seam together as I glanced at our intruder.

"Excuse me, Ivy," the librarian said. "We need to close up. Should I hold your books for you?"

"Uh—yes. Please." My voice cracked, and I cleared my throat to try to hide it. "Thank you."

"No problem." A heartbeat of silence. "Hey, maybe you two could...I don't know...Go find a room. The whole library can hear you. Good acoustics, you know."

Lex let out a deep belly laugh while mortification rolled through me, and I stalked away, buttoning up my jeans before running my panicky fingers through my hair to make myself presentable.

I did not want Alexei Fairfax. Not one bit.

As long as I kept telling myself that, it would be true.

It's called manifestation.

I flung my messenger bag over my shoulder and grabbed the book about plague, hoping the disgusting topic would cool my sexy time jets. I pretended I didn't like the way Lex smiled at me as he casually followed me back to the dorms, like how a lion might leisurely trail after a baby gazelle, if only to give it a false sense of security before tearing it to pieces.

Except I *wasn't* a baby gazelle. If Lex was a lion, I was a lion. And I would sink my claws into his pretty face as soon as I could.

We walked down a dimly lit corridor. It was late, almost ten thirty, so the overhead florescent lights had long since been replaced by the navel orange of the low-wattage bulbs over the doors. No one was around, just the two of us and our footsteps on the hardwood.

A few feet from the main corridor, a flutter kicked in my lower gut, sort of how it felt right at the start of sex, right when a cock slid inside me, a poke right up against my G-spot. I paused, furrowing my brows as I decided it must be residual effects from my encounter with Lex in the library...not that I'd liked any of it. Not at all. He'd all but attacked me. So I ignored it to put my head down and keep walking.

The flutter kicked harder this time, and I dug in my heels as my eyes clenched shut, a moan barreling out of my throat. Tingles of pleasure shot through my body, and need vibrated through me, my body suddenly so aroused, so desperate to be filled, I thought I might combust.

"Fuuucck," Lex said in a starved tone, his body next to me. I fisted my hands in his shirt as another wave of lust rocked through me, this one more intense, arching my back and frying my nerve endings.

I couldn't stop myself. I pushed up on my toes and devoured Lex's mouth as he tugged me over to the shadow cover of an alcove between two doors, pressing me up against the cool brick wall. The sharp contrast to his overheated body added to my shivering muscles, and I parted my legs on instinct to make room for him, my knee going to his hip so he could get that rock-solid cock right up against my clit.

How I moaned when they finally connected. How I loved it. How I had *craved* it.

For, undoubtedly, he had been correct.

I wanted him so badly I could barely stand it.

I wanted his tongue in my mouth and his hands on my neck, his thumb pressed right up against that X he was obsessed with. He rutted against me like the world might end, like we were figuring out how our bodies smashed together for the first time. The friction of the denim and my panties and his dick against my aching clit added to the growing sense of urgency building inside of me, seemingly coming from nowhere and everywhere all at once.

Like I could feel every person in the world who was doing exactly what we were doing, who was reveling in their own debauchery.

"Don't stop," I whispered. "Please don't stop—"

A crescendo hit, and I tightened my hands around the fabric of his shirt, my nails digging into the chest underneath, every molecule pulsed with the weight of my orgasm pulling me under its grip.

I couldn't resist it. I gave into the rush of euphoria racing through my veins, squealing and laughing while it had its way with me.

Lex thrust against me two more times before his cock gave a jerk, and he froze, groaning in my ear, sinking his teeth into my earlobe, clinging to me like he might fall over if he let go.

Once those feel-good hormones died down, he leaned back and looked at me, his mouth agape and eyes wide, shock and horror mixing in that hazel stare, mirroring my own.

My body raged like it did out in the woods, like I was high on life and the world would never end. Except this time, I hadn't had any wine. I hadn't kissed a stranger who offered me a gift I promptly lost. This had come out of nowhere.

When we got back to the dorm, we discovered it had hit Carter and Miri even harder.

I opened the door to a hushed, "Shit" and "Is it them?"

Miri sat on top of Carter, her legs on either side of his thighs, her skirts plumed around them. Her hands were on his knees, and his fingers gripped her ass, but his jeans appeared to still be on. They hadn't gone much further than Lex and I had in the hallway. I didn't remember much from that night in the woods, but this couldn't have been the first time they'd been so close. I'd slept with both Miri and Lex, so who was I to judge? Yet the two of them here by themselves hit me in the chest with a fiery righteous stab that I had no right to feel, tingling all the way down to my fingers, which had intertwined with Lex's.

I wanted to sob. I wanted to join them. I wanted...I didn't know...I just *wanted.*

"It's okay, X," Lex whispered, leaning into me. He moved the hair over my shoulder and brushed his fingers against the side of my neck. "Look at how beautiful they are together."

They were. The strength in Carter's chest matched the elegance and softness in Miri, and together, they were the most elegantly made people I'd ever seen. I loved both of them so incredibly, so completely, that watching them together turned me on. It shouldn't, but it did.

"We're married," Lex whispered. "Remember? We made vows."

I turned to face him, his mouth so close to mine, so frustratingly close. It hit me again. This overwhelming power, this urge to consume everyone in this room.

I had to have him. I just...*I had to.*

Lex kissed me and tore at my shirt, yanking it over my head. I scrambled for the button on my jeans and shoved them down to my ankles, stepping out of them. He had that look in his hazel gaze again, the one he'd given me in the library, like he couldn't wait to devour me. His hair fell over this face and I raked my fingers through it, brushing it out of his eyes. My bra went next, and Carter whispered something to Miri that made her chuckle, and the sound of their combined joy radiated through my soul.

I fell back on the bed right next to Carter, holding myself up on my elbows as I spread my legs for my nemesis. My fiancé. My *husband.* The heat radiated from Carter's body, from his shoulder down to his legs, and when Lex stripped right in front of us, Carter and I made similar groans of excitement. He wasn't as muscular as Carter, but that did not make the long lines of his body any less desirable. His tattoos contrasted his skin, swirling and sparkling in the dim light, making him out to be the villain he always claimed he was.

"See something you like, Chicago?" Lex drawled, making Carter laugh and throw back his head, sighing and groaning and gripping Miri's hips harder while she worked to free his cock from his pants. Lex paused to wrap an arm around Miri's neck and pull her lips to his.

"Hello, darling," she whispered with a big grin.

"Hello, Princess," Lex said, and then he crawled over me, bringing his mouth to mine again and spearing his cock deep inside of me in one quick movement. I arched into the mind-numbing sensation, gripping Miri's calf and sinking my teeth into Carter's shoulder at my side.

I should fight it, I told myself. *I should push this away—this high, this unknown craze that had abducted us and taken our sensibilities. It's not real. None of this is real.*

It seemed so much easier to simply sink into its abyss, to let Lex bite my neck and hold me down and take me while our husband fucked our wife in the bed next to us.

In an upside-down version of what had happened the other night, Lex grabbed my chin to force my gaze back to his, holding me with his stare while I met his thrusts blow for blow. That tension sparked to life again, that familiar pull to Lex Fairfax that had started the night his brother died. Perhaps no matter what we'd done, no matter what happened, we would have always ended up right here.

Carter grunted and Miri moaned, clearly as caught up in the pheromones as Lex and me, and their pleasure echoed inside of me as if it were my own. Because they were. We were one. We had promised each other unconditional eternity and then we'd consummated it for an entire day. There was no going back now. We were truly connected on every molecular and meta-physical level, and this was the proof.

I grabbed Lex's satiny hair and arched into his assault, and when Miri came, it exploded inside me, shoving me into my own orgasm.

Nothing in the world was more exquisite than the heaven we'd found inside this room.

"Fuck." Lex groaned, kissing me as he climaxed, his cock jerking, his muscles tensing. What a magnificent sight. "Fucking hell, X."

Carter's orgasm erupted next, a warm fiery thing, and then it was over. Whatever had hit us, whatever caused the madness, it dissipated as quickly as it had come on.

Lex rolled off me and Miri fell to the other side of Carter, her legs spread out over him, and her feet resting on my stomach. For the moment, we basked in the moonlight creeping in from the slits in the window.

My body ached. My mouth felt dry. I tasted like old books and Lex and sweat, and we all smelled like sex. But none of that mattered, because it could mean only one thing. Whatever happened to us out in those woods had followed us back to reality.

"This is bad," I finally said.

No one disagreed.

23

LEX

"**S**omething is seriously wrong with us," Ivy said the next morning from her spot across from me at the table. We were in the dining hall, surrounded by dozens of curious eyes and ears, hardly the right place for this conversation. Carter looked up from his oatmeal and raised an eyebrow. Miri picked at her fruit salad. I drank coffee, hoping it would nurse away the headache brewing between my eyes.

"We all felt it." She raised her eyebrows and looked between us.

"Understatement," Carter winced and rubbed at his eyes, like they burned as much as mine did.

We'd spent a large portion of the night rehashing everything we'd already talked about. No one knew anything more than what we'd already said. No one remembered anything differently. But whatever had gotten us so messed-up in those woods was still in our system. The lust, the overwhelming need to consume and devour my three spouses, that feeling of being unable to stop...I'd never experienced anything like it before, so its sudden reemergence, after all this time, terrified the shit out of me.

Ivy cleared her throat and glanced at the table between us.

Despite it all, the thought of Carter and Miri together on their own kind of ticked me off, but I didn't know if that was because I wanted a piece of Carter or Miri. Or because I'd been left out of it to begin with.

And Ivy? Sweet hell.

What happened was only a problem because of the urge, the high, the dreamy whacked-out state that had overtaken us until we were together. Dubious-consent didn't even begin to describe the levels to which we'd taken bad kink etiquette and made it worse. But even a depraved fuck-up like me could admit, being with the three of them seemed...*right*.

In any case, we had to figure this shit out because we only had a few days left until we went back to reality. Performance week was here. We were in the final push. None of us had the time for this bullshit.

"We should go to a doctor," Ivy said. "Run some tests. See what we were dosed with."

Under any other circumstance, I might have agreed with her. But I had a secret, one I'd planned to share with Ivy last night before this happened, one I now considered keeping to myself. I should have left well enough alone. I should have convinced myself we'd been drugged and we'd done some depraved shit while we were high and moved on with my life. Except—I'd done everything under the goddamn sun, and nothing had ever affected me like this. Nothing had ever made me feel so out of control, and now that it had, I couldn't get it out of my head.

What was it?

I didn't know, so yesterday, while Ivy was in the library, I'd gone in search of the ruins. Stephens had forbid us from going back into the woods and it was raining its nuts off, but I lied about where I was headed and went anyway. There was a good possibility I'd get lost and never find my way out again, but fuck it, because I had to know. I had to stand in the spot where it happened and force myself to remember.

I followed the path until I reached the beach where Carter and I had fought and made up...*many times.* Smiling to myself at the haughty memory of holding him down and finally taking what I wanted, I continued on to where we'd met with the girls and bathed. Which meant the ruins had to be close.

For hours, I had trudged that trail up and back, my shoes soaked through and my shirt and pants heavy with water. Nothing. No crumbling, moss-covered stones. No opulent decaying staircase. No hearth containing the remains of a fire Carter and I built. Which had sent me straight to the library looking for records of *anything* being out that far.

Anything.

A mill. A stable. A whorehouse for woodland creatures. *Something.* There never had been. It had been preserved land since the college bought it. That meant that not only had we gotten so high we'd fucked and branded each other, but we'd also hallucinated an entire building that had never existed. All of us. Hallucinating *the same* building.

I had no other explanation. I didn't know what to think. One thing became clear almost immediately. No one could ever know about this. Our parents would slam a psychiatric hold on us so fast, we'd get whiplash from how quick we'd end up in a padded cell.

I needed Ivy to keep her mouth shut. No doctor could fix the can of *oh shit* we'd opened. No high-quality therapist could repair what had already been damaged. The best thing we could do would be to forget this ever happened and hope for the best.

"And what exactly are you planning to tell them?" I cut in. "That we had an orgy in the woods which none of us remember?" She glared at me, preparing for a retort I could already see building on her lips. "That we get random intense urges to fuck each other?" I lit a cigarette, raising an incredulous brow at her as I bit out a harsh laugh. "Jesus, Ivy, it sounds delusional. *We* sound delusional."

"Well, I can't shove my head in the sand, Lex," she snapped.

"What do you suppose your mother will do when she hears?" I

tapped ash out in the crystal bowl between us, refusing to back down now. "Or my father? Do you think they'll approve of us running around telling a bunch of doctors and psychiatrists we randomly disassociate and screw around with our exes?"

"Lex," Carter cut in, grabbing onto my shoulder. He gave me a look that said, *knock it off*. But I had never backed down from Ivy, nor did she want me to.

"And Miri's gran? You think she'll ship her off to America again like it's no big deal? What if *The Puck* gets a hold of it?" I blew out a breath, pretending to be dramatic. "You think my reputation's fucked right now?"

"You've made your point," Carter said.

"Of course you would feel that way," Ivy hissed, ignoring Carter's attempt at peacekeeping. "As long as you get what you want, right? What happens when we get back to the States, and you're stuck with only me? You sure you want to be the only one in the house the next time something like that hits?"

"Stop it," Miri cut in. "Arguing like this solves nothing."

No one said anything for a moment, too humbled by Miri's rightful chiding.

"Does anyone have any other ideas?" I tapped ash out and looked between my spouses.

"Ivy, you said you found some books in the library, right?" Miri pursed her lips and furrowed her eyebrows, seeming to work through something in her mind.

"I don't know." Ivy sighed and shrugged, returning to poke at her cereal. "There's no *orgy-with-your-best-friends* section." She filled us in on her research—the disappearances, the fairy lore, the history of the woods and the castle. "Maybe I'll go down a more psychological route," she said. "I've heard of intense empathetic responses, like being so close to someone that you can feel when they're in pain. Maybe it's something like that."

"Yeah, but isn't that usually with twins?" I asked.

"Sometimes with mother and child," she said. "I don't know. I'm heading back to the library after rehearsal tonight."

"We have eight shows over the next five days," Carter cut in. "When are you planning to do this research?"

She took a deep breath and softened her features. "In the evenings, I guess."

"Weeds, this is our last few days together." He said it so low that I was sure he only meant for her to hear it. But once he did, her features softened and she hung her head between her shoulders.

A heavy weight settled in my gut when I came to the same realization. Miri and I hadn't talked about what would happen when we got back to the States, and now that she planned to go to California with Carter, I didn't know if the conversation was worth it. For four years, she'd been that rock I broke myself against—the steady, calming force in the avalanche of my life. I struggled to think what it might be like without her. Not to mention, whatever had been rekindled between Carter and I would only have this time to burn bright before we'd have to smother it out again. It would be difficult to say goodbye to both of them.

"I know," Ivy said, resigned.

"Table it until we get home," I said. She snapped her gaze up to me. "When we do, I promise I'll help you figure it out. I'll help you fight our parents. I'll help you do it all."

"You hate me," she balked, scrunching her adorable features together. "I hate you. Why would you help me?"

"We'll be stuck together," I said. "I won't have a choice."

Carter and Miri shifted the conversation to how tough they thought the two-a-day shows would be, but Ivy crossed her arms and narrowed her eyes like she could read every guilty thing on my conscience. Like she was rifling through my memories until she figured out what it was I was keeping to myself.

"What?" I said.

She shrugged and shook her head.

"Nothing, I guess," she said, returning her attention to our friends.

When Ivy and I leaned in to the relationship between Mercutio and Tybalt, Stephens lost his mind with excitement. It was the last dress rehearsal before the matinee tomorrow. We'd do two shows a day for the next three days, and then two final evening shows before we headed home. He seemed pleased that we figured it out, even if it was on the last day possible.

But that night, as I showered and thought about the plethora of ways my life was completely fucked, the sinking weight in my chest grew heavier. I didn't want to face Ivy's relentless pursuit of the truth or Carter's and Miri's inevitable departures or what it meant that the ruins didn't exist.

Shove it down, I told myself. It helped no one to spiral so close to the end.

I wrapped a towel around my waist and walked back to my room, thinking maybe I'd spend tonight here to get some space, but as soon as I walked through the door, I froze.

Carter sat on his bed in his boxers, his long legs stretched out in front of him, his weight balanced on his hands behind his back, displaying all that skin just for me. The fading remains of my bite mark glowed on his shoulder, sending a strange sense of pride and longing through my chest. I wanted to sink my teeth into the rest of him.

I closed the door and took a few steps closer.

"We need to talk," Carter said.

"Oh?" I tossed my toiletries bag over by the closet and raised my eyebrow, curious about where this was headed. Talking wasn't even in the top five things I wanted to do with my mouth after finding him practically naked and alone in my room, and as I stalked closer, I licked my lips with the thought of which one I'd get to do first.

"About Ivy," he added.

"Oh," I said again, this time disappointed. I went to stand between his knees and looked down my body at him, memorizing the curve of his pouty mouth and the shape of his cheekbones. *What a beautiful boy.* I ran the back of my fingers down the side of his face, relishing in his stubble and the way his jaw became his thick strong neck. "What about her?"

"About how you talk to her," Carter said. "About how you'll talk to her after I leave."

"Are you defending her honor?" The thought almost amused me.

"No, I'm making sure you two don't kill each other."

I narrowed my eyes and assessed him. Despite how good of a liar Carter could be, I'd always been able to read between his lines. He loved Ivy. I didn't see that changing any time soon. He wanted to make sure I was prepared to treat her right, that I wouldn't go too far and hurt her, and honestly, his apprehension might have been warranted.

He saw Ivy as something he had to protect.

I saw Ivy as fully capable of protecting herself, even against me.

I made a noise that sounded like a growl and a hum, leaning down so I could hover centimeters from his lips, the heat from his broad chest reinvigorating my chilled skin, still wet from the shower.

"Why would we kill each other?" I tucked my nose against his throat, inhaling him deeply, reveling in the summer and soap and sweat, and I ghosted my lips across his shoulder, just barely touching him in a decadent test. It took everything in me to keep from licking him, and when he trembled, I smiled, pleased I still unnerved him.

"You need to go easier on her." Carter put a hand on my chest, trying to shove me away. "She acts tough, but she's fragile."

Ivy? Fragile?

"Don't be ridiculous." I grabbed his hand and brought it to my mouth, my gaze catching his as I took his index finger between my lips. "She likes when I'm mean to her."

"Sometimes." He gulped, watching as I sucked his digit into my mouth and licked like I ached to do to other parts of his amazing body. Then he closed his eyes and gulped before continuing. "But after you're mean, you have to kiss it better. Or it festers."

I let the first finger go so I could move on to its longer, thicker neighbor. "Are you telling me to play nice with my favorite enemy?"

"No, Lex," Carter said, tensing his shoulders to try to hide a tremble. "I'm telling you you're going to have to put her back together after you two are done tearing each other apart. I won't be around to do it."

"Ivy's fine." I balked, only half paying attention to him so I could kiss the remaining fingers on his hand before dropping to my knees, nibbling down his chest to his stomach. "She'll be fine."

My cock throbbing, I grabbed at the waistband of his boxers, frantic to get my mouth around him. He grabbed my wrists. Hard. Hard enough to make me wince and send a pulse straight to my balls.

"Stop it, Lex," he said. "Look at me."

I glanced up, damn near blinded by the intensity in his expression.

"You have to take care of her, do you understand? If I find out you hurt her, if I find out you neglected her, I don't care what pact we made in the woods—"

"Threats, Chicago?" I didn't know whether to be pissed or turned on...and in a fucked-up way, I realized I was both. "And here I thought we were friends."

"Lord knows I could never threaten you," Carter said. "But if you break her heart, this ends. You get me?"

Yeah. Got it. Loud and clear. In the war between me and Ivy, no one would ever come before his Weeds. The thought shouldn't have squeezed my heart as much as it did. Hadn't I laid claim to him first? Hadn't he been my secret love affair in London? Didn't Carter belong to me before anyone else?

They all did, my dark possessive monster thought. *Ivy and Carter and Miri. They're mine. They belong to me.*

"All right," I said, shoving that voice aside to accept my defeat. "What do you want me to do?"

One side of his mouth pulled into a grin, and my gut churned because I knew that look. It meant he had an evil mastermind plan that would probably make me want to shoot myself in the face, but I'd go along with it because I doubted there was anything in this world that I wouldn't do for him. He stood, bringing me with him, and switched us so I was the one with the back of my legs against his bed before he dug his warm fingers into my lower stomach to tug the towel away. My cock sprang against his and I buckled at the hips, letting out a small groan before I could stop it.

Fuck.

"Be gentle," he said, one hand on my shoulder, bringing me back to our conversation. *Be gentle? With Ivy?* That was something she and I would never be capable of. Then he lowered himself between my legs, pushing me back with his big palm on my chest, urging me to submit to him. I thought about fighting it, some toxic idea of me wanting him to force it out of me, but I ultimately relented because who the fuck wouldn't want their cock in Carter Scott's mouth? My spine hit the mattress and his scent plumed around me, reeling me in and making me dizzy.

"Dealing with Ivy is a lot like dealing with you." He dug his teeth into my inner thigh and coasted his other hand up my leg to my hip and over my stomach, soothing and steady, like how one might calm a skittish horse. "Like trying to disarm a bomb."

I huffed out a laugh and dug my palms into my eyes. "I don't know whether to be proud or offended."

"Try being silent." The hand on my chest slid up my neck and clamped over my mouth.

My heart pulsed at his dominance, sending a jolt straight down to my cock. He'd play this part with Ivy, but never with me, and fuck, it thrilled me.

"You can't go in guns blazing," he said, flicking his tongue over the tip of my shaft. I moaned, excitement mixing with whatever this thing was in my chest that kicked at the sight of him like this. "You have to take your time. You have to be patient."

He ran the length of me, kissing and sucking at the place where my dick met my balls. I shook like a virgin, so amped up and shamefully desperate for him that by the time he took me in his mouth, I hissed and squirmed against his hold like I might explode.

"If you set off the bomb…" Carter said, releasing me with a pop that sent sparks through my bloodstream. I took a deep breath in through my nose, the crook of his palm pressed against my upper lip. The rough scabs of our vows scraped against my mouth, making this experience even more demented than it already was. "You have to clean up the mess."

He worked me harder, sucking and handling me like he'd been doing it for years, and my whole body lit on fire, like I'd been frozen in ice since the last time he'd touched me. I trailed my fingers through his hair, but he smacked them away, clearly wanting to maintain control. Which was fine by me.

"Don't make me hold you down," he growled, glancing up with those shimmering indigo eyes, curling his lips into a grin. "Unless that's what you want? You want me to hold you down while I take what I want from you?"

"Fuck," I mumbled against his hand.

A sharp sting zapped up my right side as Carter bit my thigh harder—marking me.

"I said be silent," he murmured. "You make another sound, and I'll edge you all night."

Promise?

"Believe me, I get it. You like to rile her up." He lazily stroked me, teasing and toying with me, like we had all the time in the world. "She's cute when she's pink and fiery."

Cute wasn't the word I'd use. More like annoying. Or mesmerizing.

"But you play too rough, and if you don't take care of her when she breaks, you don't deserve to break her." Another long lick had me moaning and arching forward, desperate for more, despairing for him. "Do you understand?"

He looked up at me, his eyebrow raised and his fist closed over the tip of my dick, expecting a response. I was in the most vulnerable position a man could find himself. A pulsing, aching erection in someone else's grip and a willing mouth inches away, but unable to move or speak.

I nodded.

"Good." He slowly sucked me, warmth and adoration spreading through my torso at the sight of his lips around my dick. I took a deep breath, trying to slow the pounding behind my ribs, but I couldn't help bucking against him, urging him to go faster and take me deeper. He held my hips down with his forearm and drew it out, making me sweat with the need to come. And finally, *finally,* he let me put my hands in his hair and fuck his face the way I wanted. I took him, my balls throbbing as my orgasm claimed me hard behind the eyes.

Good. Fucking. God.

He let me do it, swallowing me down like a good little husband, and when I was a panting, shaking mess, he stood and shoved his boxers down to his ankles. He didn't let me breathe. He didn't let me pull myself together. He clawed at my hair and tugged my face to his hips, shoving his dick past my teeth.

Which I gladly obliged. I took him the way I knew he liked, hard and fast and deep, like I couldn't get enough of him. I couldn't. I would stay here all night if it meant I wouldn't have to go another four years of wanting him.

He moaned and thrust hard into my throat, making me gag. My eyes watered. But I let him do what he wanted. He ran this scene, and I'd given my control over to him with very little fight. He fisted his on the top of my scalp and yanked me off him.

"Lie back," he said, leaning down to kiss me. "I'm going to fuck you now, Lex, so that you'll remember." He cupped my face, pressing his forehead to mine to give me a sweet peck on the lips. "You'll remember your promise to me." He tasted like both of us, which made me want him more. "To protect her. To keep her safe. To put her back together again."

He climbed up my body as I lay back, his torso hard and hot against mine. He tucked an arm under one leg, hooking my knee in his elbow. I reached into the nightstand next to the bed, retrieving the lube and tossing it down to him.

It occurred to me as he dripped the cool liquid down his fingers and over my ass that I'd be losing him in a few days. I never got to fully have him. Just like last time, I'd get a taste, barely a sampling, before he slipped through my grasp.

He pressed a digit inside of me, balancing his weight on his other hand by my ribs while my legs spread for him. My cock pulsed back to life, squeezed between me and Carter's big body, but fuck, even that ramped up my excitement. Carter controlled my body, my pleasure, and I never wanted it to stop.

"Do you like that, DC?" He tucked his nose under my chin, tilting my face up to his, forcing me to look him in the eyes. "Do you want me?"

"Jesus Christ, Chicago," I teased. "Fuck me already."

He made an adorable chuckling noise and nipped at my jaw.

"You're impatient and spoiled and uncontrollable." He pressed another finger inside of me, all the way in, and I gasped at the pleasure and pain of it, a half-hearted jerk hitting me in the balls. "She's going to eat you alive."

"Why are you being such a prick to me?" I bucked my hips against him, urging him on. "Go lecture her."

He smiled and shook his head, positioning his cock at my entrance before he slowly, so slowly, pushed inside of me—just the head at first, letting me adjust—and then all the way in. I felt so full and so achingly aware of every agonizing inch of him. It hurt, and it sent ecstasy sending through my body. I loved it. I'd been dying for him to fuck me since I met him...since the beginning of time.

"I want you to remember that you love her," he murmured,

pressing his lips to the corner of my mouth, tenderly caressing my skin with his mouth.

I started to argue, but he bit my bottom lip to shut me up, and the contrast of his gentleness to his roughness made me melt further into the mattress.

"You love her," he continued, "and you love me, and you love Miri. What we have is special." He rocked against me, inside me, sweetly taking over my senses until all I knew was him. "Even when you want to destroy it. Especially when you want to destroy it. I'm asking you not to."

I realized what was happening as it was too late to stop it. Carter held me down, kissing and caressing me...*making love* to me. My chest tightened as panic uncoiled in my stomach. I didn't know why it scared me, but it did. I loved him, and perhaps I never wanted to lose him.

"Hey." Carter froze against me, perhaps sensing the shift in my mood. "Tell me what you're thinking."

I opened my mouth to say something horrible, to tell him something terrible to get him off me, to stop being so tender. But when I did speak, it wasn't what I expected.

"I never get to have you, do I?" I said. "Every time I get close, you disappear."

Carter flashed that boy-next-door grin and hung his head, touching it against mine again. "You get to have me for the rest of your life, Lex." He thrust again. "Just call, and I'll come running."

He held me down by the chest with one hand and stroked my cock with the other, fucking me, reaching places inside me that radiated with complementing sensations. I scratched and bit at him to egg him on, but he refused to give in. He wrestled that feral part of me into submission and kept me there, panting and moaning and begging for release. My toes curled when he slipped his hand over my tip, gripping me just right and when I finally came in hot shooting spurts up his stomach, the weight of world lifted off my chest for one brilliant moment.

After he found his release deep inside of me, we clung to each other, breathing each other's exhales like they were all we'd ever need again.

I found his lips, and he smiled into our kiss.

"Now you promise me something," I murmured.

"Anything."

"You go and be a big movie star and I'll take care of her. But when you're done, you come home to me. You understand? You come home to me, and you come home to Ivy and Miri. In the end, it's us."

His eyes darted between mine for a moment before he grabbed my right hand and flipped it over, revealing the matching words on both of our hands. "Until the end."

"Until the end."

It hit home three days before we left. Miri and I lay on a blanket in the gardens behind the college, staring up at the cloudy, overcast sky. We only had an hour break before we had to get back to the auditorium, but at least it wasn't raining anymore.

"Are you upset with me?" She furrowed her brow and pulled her bottom lip between her teeth. "That I'm going to California with Carter?"

I sighed, ignoring that ache in the center of my chest.

"No, Princess." I gave her hand a squeeze and leaned in to kiss her. "Are you upset that I'm staying behind with Ivy?"

"I was at first," she said. "I thought it would work out differently. Though I suppose that was ridiculous now in hindsight. You and I would never have made it."

"Why is that?" I recalled that vision of us, the one I'd had in the woods. She'd been a big part of that, we all had. There was no us without Miri.

"Because I won't have a choice either," she murmured, her beautiful eyes dropping to look at the ground between us. "When the time comes. Our lives are not our own."

Maybe not right now, but we were young. We still had a lot of our lives ahead of us, and despite what our families might want, I wouldn't let either of them go that easily.

"You promised us until the end, Miri." I shook my head, steeling my jaw when I ran my fingers down the side of her face, forcing her to meet my gaze. "And we promised you. Go to California. Take care of our boy."

Miri smiled and blinked back tears, visibly swallowing before clearing her throat and muttering a quiet, "You too. With Ivy."

I lit a cigarette and blew out the smoke. Miri rolled over on her side to face me, stealing it from me.

"Ivy can take care of herself," I said.

"Oh, I know," Miri giggled and wiped at her cheeks before inhaling on the cigarette. "I meant you, darling." She poked me in the ribs and handed the smoke back to me. "I know how you are when I'm not around. You're positively obsessed with me, and my absence makes you cranky." I rolled my eyes, trying to hide my amusement when she threw herself across my ribs and stared up at me with that dreamy grin. "My prince of darkness. You'll be okay, right?"

"Yes, Your Highness." I tapped her nose and chided her with a tsk of my teeth. "I walked and talked and fed myself before you came along."

She laughed but seemed unconvinced, leaning down to give me a kiss. "Good."

I put on a good show, but the thought of my life without her made my chest ache. At least I'd have Ivy. At least we'd have each other.

24

IVY

The final days of the intensive passed much like the years before it. Two shows a day were exhausting, and by the time the sixth performance was over, I looked forward to performing only once in the evening. Of course, with each passing show, we came one step closer to reality and I got one step further away from answers. I spent as much time as I could in the library, but nothing I found was anything more than myths and legends. What happened to us was real.

Very real.

Once it happened again, I could no longer ignore it. My dreams about the ruins wouldn't go away. I needed to find something I'd lost while I was out there, probably that ring Siobhan had given me, but now I had questions. She'd been the one who invited me to the festival in the first place. If anyone could give me answers, I had to start with her.

On our second to last day at Killwater, I told everyone I needed some privacy to figure out what to do about my upcoming nuptials, but instead, I slipped into town. I hadn't told Carter or Miri about Siobhan and the ring. The only one who knew was Lex, and he'd said he saw me talking to her, which meant I wasn't completely out of the realm here, right? Siobhan must have been a real person.

I fought with myself the entire walk, debating if I should outright accuse her of drugging us or admit I'd lost the ring, despite knowing it was likely priceless. And what the fuck was up with that kiss?

"I'm going to give you a gift."

What gift? A night I didn't remember? Drunken orgies with friends I'd known for years? Why were we still experiencing the high days later?

I'd always considered myself logical, rational, perhaps a little over imaginative and anxious, but otherwise, of sound mind, especially in a crisis. So did I really think everything that happened to us was the result of some ring a woman had given me at a bonfire? No. Did I think there was something in the wine everyone was passing around? Plausible.

Doesn't explain the marks in your hand. Doesn't explain the time lapse.

I couldn't trust my own reality anymore, and if I couldn't do that, then what the hell *could* I believe? *Who* could I believe?

When I got to the pub, it was packed with locals. Music blared from the same corner, pipes and guitar hollering a rhythm that reminded me of when the four of us had come here last week. I searched the crowd for her, and when I didn't find her, I went to the bar.

"Hey, is Siobhan here?" I asked the bartender.

The stranger shrugged. "Haven't seen her. Ashley's around."

"Her sister?"

He nodded and pointed to a booth in the back, where the woman who'd spoken to our group sat with her laptop in front of her. Stephens had introduced her as a folklorist, someone who studied the myths and traditions of the area.

Bingo.

"Hi there," I said, brushing hair behind my ears as I approached.

Ashley blinked up at me, flashing a genuine smile. "Hello."

"I'm Ivy," I said. "From the theater group up at Killwater. You might not remember me."

"Of course I do. Sit." She gestured me to the spot opposite her, where I scooted into the spot and tried to remain casual. "What can I do for you?"

"I was wondering if I could talk to Siobhan. She said something that's stuck with me and I wanted to ask her about it."

"Oh?" Ashley raised her eyebrows, balancing her head under her chin. "What did she say?"

Like her sister, she had a way of pulling me in and making me want to tell her everything even when I knew I shouldn't. Being in her presence was oddly soothing, like a warm blanket in a blizzard. Her big brown eyes implored me to keep her gaze, and her genuine smile encouraged me to talk, like I'd known her for eons, like I could trust that she'd keep my secrets safe. It was oddly entrancing, and I had to shake my head to break its spell.

"Something about giving me a gift," I explained. "She whispered in Gaelic."

"Where was this?"

"At the festival."

"Ah." Ashley gave me a nod. "Did you have fun? I saw you and your friends dancing."

"Uh—sure." Until I didn't. Until things went so wrong so fast. "Look, I really need to speak with her. I think—" I scratched at the back of my head. "I think something happened."

"Like what?" Ashley seemed perplexed, curious—all too eager for me to divulge everything. I paused and looked for signs that my paranoia might be valid. She seemed a little...off—her face too perfect, her smile too friendly. Her reluctance to say where Siobhan raised alarm bells, and I hesitated. What was I going to tell her? That I'd had an orgy in the woods with my friends? That we'd gotten so intoxicated, we lost a day somehow? That we kept experiencing aftereffects of whatever we'd been given?

Lex was right. I sounded outrageous, and I didn't want anyone running to *The Puck*. I shouldn't have come.

"Actually—" I sighed. "This was stupid. I better go."

"Siobhan went on a trip," Ashley explained. "She won't be back for a while. Not until your class has gone home, I'm afraid."

Of course. Just my luck. Defeated, I huffed out a sigh and went to stand, but Ashley spoke again, stopping me.

"But if you show me the gift," she said, "I can look at it. See if I recognize it."

"I don't have it with me." I narrowed my eyes at her outstretched hand, pulling mine a little closer to my chest.

"Shame." Ashley shrugged, seemingly nonchalant. "Well, Siobhan's not here."

"Right." I stood to leave. "Thanks."

"You know..." Ashley snapped out to grab my wrist, stopping me from rising, and leaned in close, focusing her entrancing eyes on me. "Outsiders generally aren't welcome at the midsummer festival. That's why I didn't mention anything about it to your class. We'd appreciate it if you and your friends didn't talk about what you saw there."

The way she looked at me when she said it sent a cold shiver down my back. She didn't make her threat lightly, and the set in her jaw meant she'd come for me if I didn't obey. I didn't know how she'd know, but her wide eyes suggested that she had her ways of finding out.

"Code of guest right and all," she continued, softening. "It's sacred. You understand."

For one frightening second, everyone in the bar stopped to look at me, their eyes menacing and narrowed and a scowl on their lips. My heart pounded, and I thought they were about to attack me like some kind of zombie movie. Then, in the next blink, they were back to normal, carrying on conversations with the people next to them.

I jumped out of my seat, whipping my hand away from her.

"What the fuck?"

"Anyway," Ashley said, once again bright and bubbly, like that horror show hadn't just happened. "Hope you have a great performance. I got tickets for tomorrow night. Can't wait!"

I looked around. Everything seemed so normal. The patrons were eating and drinking, carrying on as if I wasn't there. I'd imagined that whole thing.

Welp, I've had just about enough of this, so...

I made my way through the crowd and out into the summer afternoon.

I probably should have hightailed it back to the college, but my curiosity plagued me. Maybe if I went and found the ruins again, the dreams would stop coming. Maybe if I just found the damn ring, this would all be over. I could research it or use it to contact Siobhan.

I found the trail that led down to the creek, and despite it being a muddy mess, the undergrowth was surprisingly clear. The rain had stopped yesterday, but everything was still wet, so I stayed close to the trees until I got to the shoreline. The water had swelled from all the rain, so if I had lost it somewhere between the ruins and the college, it was long since gone to the tide.

From there, I turned and walked as far as I could remember. I'd lost the flyer to the party, and there weren't any mile markers on the path, so I wasn't exactly sure where I was going, only that instinct pulled me in this direction. I had an hour or two to get back to Killwater before roll call, and if I stayed out too long, Carter would come looking for me.

It had to be around here somewhere—the remnants of the festival and the enormously large bonfires.

I walked along that path until I had to turn around or I'd risk being late, but I never found the ruins.

What does it mean?

Did we hallucinate? If we did, how was that possible?

Get a grip, Ivy, I scolded myself. Was it enough for me to say I'd been irresponsible at a party and gotten so high I'd blacked out, and that was the end of it? Was it enough to say we'd managed to brand ourselves in a different language none of us knew? Could I believe that whatever we'd taken had stayed in our system for three days and we'd all had a reoccurrence of it at the exact same time?

Pissed and confused, I turned around a tree to pick up the trail again and ran smack into a hard, broad chest.

"What the fuck are you doing out here?" Hazel eyes met mine, Lex's lips pursed around a cigarette.

"Are you stalking me?" I asked.

"Stalking you?" Lex scowled. "You're stalking me!"

"No way," I said. "I was out here looking for—" I stopped myself, caught in my lie. I'd told him I was working on a plan for us to be free, not wandering aimlessly around in the same woods we'd gotten lost in a few days ago.

"They're not out here," he said, stuffing his hands in his trouser pockets.

I paused, neither confirming nor denying what I was looking for.

"The ruins," he said. "They're not out here."

I swallowed and sighed, hoping he was wrong. I had to find them, I had to know what happened to us. "How do you know?"

"I've been looking for them for days."

"Days?" My fury rose, and I shoved at his shoulders. "You told me not to worry about it, that we should move on with our lives."

"Yeah, because I didn't want you blabbing to some shrink about how we're all having an extended acid trip together." He turned around and headed on the trail back to the college. I matched his pace, seething with annoyance. We promised each other honesty. We promised each other freedom. Of course...I was keeping a secret from them, too.

"Lex, something really messed-up is happening."

"Yeah, no shit." He forged ahead, throwing the words over his shoulder.

"No, listen." I grabbed his arm and stopped him, turning him to face me. "I told you about Siobhan and the ring, right?"

"You mean the townie that invited us to an orgy?"

"She kissed me," I said. "She gave me a ring and I lost it."

"What do you mean, you lost it?"

"I don't know. I had it in my back pocket and then on the way home from the ruins, I didn't have it anymore."

He shrugged and turned to keep walking. "Well, that's a bummer. It was pretty."

"You don't think—" I ran my hands through my hair and shook my head, hating that I was even saying it. But I had to get it out there. I had to tell someone. "You don't think losing the ring had anything to do with this, right?"

Lex raised an eyebrow. "Are you asking me if I think drunk-kissing an Irish pub-owner and losing a piece of jewelry led to us having two nights of raging, drugged-up sex?" He snorted out a laugh. "No, X. I don't."

"Do you think the ring is cursed?" I bit my bottom lip and a stab hit me in the gut. What if he didn't believe me? Lex and I had always had a rocky relationship, but he'd never lie to me. If he thought I was having a psychotic break, he'd be the first one to say something in his cruel, horribly accurate way.

He stopped and put his hands on his hips, turning to face me with his features scrunched in consideration. Finally, he shook his head and muttered, "I don't believe in curses or fairies or God. We make our own fate."

Well, that settled that, huh? I scrubbed my palms over my face as I realized my link to sanity had been slipping. It was this horrible place, like it was stuck in time or something. I needed to get back to reality.

Lex's features softened, and in a rare act of solidarity, he wrapped his arms around my neck and pulled me into a hug. I circled my arms around his waist and relaxed into him, peace spreading through me at his familiar scent and constant presence. All alone out in these woods, I had almost convinced myself I was going mad and couldn't rely on my own mind. Being here with him reminded me that there were three other people who had experienced the same thing. Lex and I had been together since we were born, and as much as I hated it, I trusted him.

"We'll be okay, X," he said.

I nodded against him, hoping he was right. "We leave the day after tomorrow. Are you ready for this?"

He sighed, knowing as I did what that meant. When we got home, things were business as usual. Lex and I had to put on the great show. We had to face the big boss at the end of our story. We had to unpress pause, and perhaps that didn't terrify me as much as it once had, not if I had Lex there to fight it with me.

25

IVY

"Hey loser," Kit said over FaceTime. "You look like hell."

It was the morning of our last performance, and I'd broken away from the group to give my sister a call. She had already arrived home for the summer and spent a good deal of time texting invites for the movie nights she wanted to have once I got settled in to my new place.

"Thanks. You look like you're adopted," I said, though really she'd always been the spitting image of our mother's great-aunt Edna. She'd piled all her dark hair on top of her head and sat in her room at Mount Vernon still wearing the same tank top and boy shorts that she'd likely worn to bed last night.

She stuck her tongue out at me. "How's the luck o' the Irish treating you?"

Not good. Not good at all. If anything, I was pretty sure I'd been cursed.

"That great, huh?" She raised an eyebrow and scooped cereal into her mouth.

"What is it, like noon over there?" I said. "Are you eating cereal for lunch?"

"Don't judge me," she said. "Why do you look like you haven't slept in ten years? Mother's going to shit a brick if you show up at the press conference like that."

"She can go to hell," I murmured under my breath.

"Look," Kit said with a sigh and raised her eyebrows, clearly preparing to drop an epic truth bomb. "I love you. But things are getting shifty around here. I think they're planning to announce it as soon as you land."

"I'm sure they are." I sighed, rubbing at the space between my forehead.

"I've got nothing for you as far as intel, but I'm going to keep digging." She shook her head. "Our family has been in political marriages for centuries, Ivy. Unless you up and run away, this is going to be tough to fight."

I had considered that option, and to be fair, it wasn't completely off my list of things to do. "Thanks, Kit. Can you do me one last favor?"

"Sure."

"You're good at like...tracking people or whatever, right?" Computers were a second language for Kit. She'd placed first at every hacking competition she'd ever been in, much to our mother's chagrin. Evelyn would rather she be another political animal like me, but my sister preferred to walk on the nerdy wild side of life.

"You mean skip tracing?" Kit cleared her throat and looked around her to make sure she was alone. "Yeah, I've heard some things."

"Do you think you could try to find someone for me?" I'd started planning this when I found out that Siobhan had disappeared, but I wasn't sure I had to pull this trigger until Lex told me the ruins weren't real. I had other priorities, but I couldn't let this go. I needed to know what happened to me...to us.

"All right," she said in her skeptical tone. "Promise me you're okay. I'm getting a weird vibe."

"I'm fine, Kit," I reassured her, trying to put on my fake smile, the one I showed to the world. But Kit had known me her whole life, she probably could see through it. I pushed past the awkward silence. "I'll email you everything I know."

She talked about undergrad and this new guy she was sleeping with, and at the end of the call, she made me promise her again I was okay.

"I know Carter's leaving soon," she said. "And so is Miri."

I forced a smile and blinked back tears.

Shove it down, I told myself. *Don't let it show.*

"I'm okay," I said. "Lex and I are kind of getting along now."

Kit snorted a laugh. "Yeah? And hell froze over when?"

"Har har," I said.

"Call me when you land. Hate you."

"Hate you more."

I took a few minutes to type out an email to her, giving her Ashley's and Siobhan's names, and any other names I could remember before heading back inside to find my spouses.

The rest of the day passed quicker than any of the other days before it. The four of us spent it together, wandering the forest to look for ruins that didn't exist and packing our things to return home. My memories were no clearer for having had a week to dwell on them, and now, the whole thing seemed so far away that I could barely remember what Siobhan looked like. After that wave hit us in the dorm rooms, we hadn't had another spell. It had been five days now, and we hoped it was over for good.

When I told Carter and Miri about Siobhan and the ring, they agreed with Lex.

"Fairies aren't real, darling," Miri said, intertwining her fingers in mine. "I don't know how we got the marks on our hands. Maybe someone is fucking with us. But I think we took something we shouldn't have, and that's the end of it."

We were lying in bed after the last show, having spent the majority of the evening tangled in a sweaty, confusing ball under these sheets. Now we soaked in oxytocin and dread. Things would change tomorrow, and I'd been doing my best not to think about it.

My gaze landed on Carter.

"Is that what you think, too?" I asked him. "That this happened because we took something at the party?"

Carter lay on his side, his head balanced on his hand and his elbow propped up on the pillow.

"I don't know." His mouth fell open, and he shook his head. "Something unbelievable happened, that's true. Ashley tried to convince us fairies were real, but then she turned out to be weird, too. Maybe it's more likely they were both fucking with us. Siobhan and Ashley."

"Why?" It didn't make any sense. Why single us out? Was it just for a laugh at the expense of some rich American snobs?

"I don't know." Carter sighed and ran his hands back through his hair.

I agreed to let it go. I didn't have any other explanation, and we'd run out of time. Even though it chafed, I would have to concede that something strange occurred, and I might never know the whole story.

I woke up the next morning wrapped in my lover's arms. Carter's warm body pressed up behind me, Miri's hands were in mine, and Lex's fingers brushed against my stomach as he breathed. I paused and let myself have this rare moment of purity. I let myself drift in the exquisite wonder of the four of us, *all of us,* together.

In six hours, we had to be on a plane to DC. This was over now.

"Hey," Carter whispered, tugging me tighter against him. "Get dressed. Let's go for a walk."

I narrowed my eyes and looked over my shoulder.

"Okay." I climbed out of bed and went to the bathroom, brushing my teeth and making myself presentable. By the time I got back, he was dressed, so I changed into jeans and sneakers before following him downstairs.

"Where are we going?" I asked with a laugh.

"Somewhere we can be alone."

I trailed after him, a somber shiver going through me when he brought me back down to the creek and pulled me into his arms. I wrapped my hands around his waist, and he kissed me on the nose.

"I'm going to miss you most of all, you know," he said.

I blinked back tears and tried to ignore that slice of agony in my chest. "It's not forever, Carter. I swear. I'll find a way out of this. I will."

"I know you will." He nodded and kissed me again. "You're still my favorite girl."

I buried my head in his shirt and let the tears come, hating how much I loved him and how much I didn't want this to end.

"I didn't know if I'd get a chance to be alone with you again, not after we get home. So I wanted to give you this." He held out a little square box.

"What is this, Carter?" I narrowed my eyes at the black velvet.

"Representation." He opened it, revealing a silver ring with a moonstone in the middle. My birthstone. "He gets to keep you, but I had you first." He took it out of the box and put it on the ring finger of my right hand.

"Carter, you sap." I pushed up on my toes so I could kiss him as deeply as I wanted. "I'll always be yours."

"I know, Weeds," he said. "Don't ever forget it."

I thought maybe if I kept that ring on my finger and his voice in the back of my head, I might actually convince myself it would be possible. But reality always had a way of cold-cocking me square in the face, especially when I didn't see it coming.

At the airport in Dublin, Carter and Miri went ahead to a restaurant to have a few drinks before we boarded the plane to leave. Lex and I stopped by a coffee shop to buy water and chips for the flight. He put his hand on the back of my neck, brushing his thumb over the skin next to my shoulder. He leaned in next to my ear to whisper, "You should get the Chex Mix so we can split it."

There was nothing sexual about it, and in the end, I bought the salty snack precisely so we could share it on the flight home. He liked the pretzels, and I liked the Chex. But in the time it took for us to get from Dublin to Washington, DC, a picture of Lex Fairfax with his hand on the back of Ivy Washington's neck blasted across the internet. My family's branding manager, the one assigned to market this charade, used the opportunity to officially announce our relationship.

Since the four of us had been gone from the public eye for three weeks, people had forgotten Carter and I were rumored to be an item. Or that the Princess Miriam had quite a similar situationship with Alexei Fairfax. Now, the hunger for more pictures of us had taken the world by storm.

We were trending on social media. We had our own hashtag, *#Fairington,* and more than two hundred people had DMed me asking for a comment. We got off the plane and four bodyguards the size of tanks greeted us at the gate.

"Ms. Washington, Mr. Fairfax, this way please," the largest one said, gesturing us to the left and away from Carter and Miri.

"Wait," I said. "We're supposed to go—"

"I have strict instructions from your mother," he said. "You need to come with us. Both of you."

I pressed my thumb into the scabs on my palm, a quick reminder of where I'd been living for the last few weeks. I noticed Miri also had her own guard, probably hired by her grandparents, and poor Carter had to go with the rest of the class.

Everyone in the airport turned to look at us and to see what the fuss was about.

What were they looking at? Couldn't they see I was human? Just like them?

My heart pounded in my head and tension tightened in my chest.

"There are photographers waiting outside for you," the bodyguard said, but it sounded like he was hundreds of yards away. Couldn't he see all the onlookers? He was causing a bigger scene just by being here. "Hundreds of them. We need to get you back to your apartment safely."

Lex wrapped his hand around my palm, intertwining his fingers with mine, and suddenly, I'd become that kid again, starting fights with my counterpart to keep from going on stage and being seen. The one that dug my nails into his hand because his brother had died and my heart was broken. We had called a truce so we could hold each other through that loss together.

Lex's touch grounded me and reminded me of who I was. It always had. Standing there in the airport, I realized it always would.

I took a deep breath.

We'll be okay, X.

His voice rang loud and clear, almost like I could hear it, almost like he'd spoken the words without his mouth moving. *Weird.* With my chin up and shoulders back, I went with them. They escorted us out a side exit and down to the tarmac, where a black Escalade waited. Lex and I climbed in the back seat, a sinking terrible weight settling in my gut as the door closed behind us.

I knew then before I even looked at him.

Whatever we found in Ireland had been left on that plane. Whatever fight we paused when we were arguing in the Audi, we now had to put on our gloves and square up. Just because our parents had announced it to the public didn't mean we were out of options. I'd been so focused on what happened to us in Ireland, I hadn't thought about a strategy to dissolve our inevitable matrimony.

As soon as the Escalade rounded the airport and pulled on to the main straightaway, press surrounded the windows. Cameras flashed. People shouted questions.

Ivy, Lex, how long has this been going on? Have you two been on a lovers' getaway? What about the Princess Miriam?

The questions went on and on. I sank lower in my seat and put my hands over my face, but the cushion shifted next to me and Lex's scent plumed in my nose.

"We're in this together," he said, bringing my knuckles to his mouth for a sweet kiss. "I've got your back."

26

LEX

"Jesus, it's a nightmare," Ivy said, scrolling through her social media feeds. We sat on the floor of her empty one-bedroom, smoking cigarettes, while the media went overboard with conspiracy theories. Her king-size mattress was still made up on its box spring, but that was only because we planned to spend one more night here before our spouses left tomorrow.

The movers had come this morning to pack my things and take them to our new apartment closer to law school—some pretentious two-bedroom loft on the penthouse floor of a swanky complex in Crystal City. Our mothers had arranged the whole thing while we were in Ireland. We didn't even get to decide that.

Carter had already boxed his shit up before we left. Miri would keep her stuff in storage through the summer and have it shipped over to the UK once Carter was settled in LA.

This would have happened anyway. This had always been the plan. But the timing couldn't have been more sensationally perfect.

The Puck reported: *Ivy and Lex take their relationship on the road. Princess Miriam heads back to UK in disgrace.* With a picture of the moving vans out in front of our complex and candid shots of the four of us going in and out.

SophieLennon98 posted: *Lex and Ivy are so cute together. Carter who?*

Imogen83 reposted with: *Miri deserves better than this. Where is she? #TeamPrincess*

It didn't bother me. I genuinely didn't give a shit what they thought, but it irritated Ivy and *that* aggravated me.

"You should stay off the socials for a while," I told her, ashing my cigarette in the tray between us. "Let it die down."

"Why did they do this to us, Lex?" She tilted her head back against the drywall and took a puff of her smoke.

I'd been talking about *The Puck* and the internet, but that's not who she meant.

"Because it was done to them." Why would they think any differently about doing the same to us? *Because Mother promised. Because I made a deal, and she went back on it.*

My phone buzzed again, and I ignored the thousandth call from her.

Speak of the devil.

I could only put her off for so long, but today wasn't the day. I couldn't handle her on top of saying goodbye to the loves of my life. I was already depressed enough.

Miri came into the room and frowned. Her swollen, puffy eyes said she'd been crying instead of helping the movers pack, and I opened my arms to her. She came willingly, folding into my lap the way she'd done for years, her legs on either side of my hips. I wrapped my arms around her, a widening chasm in my heart stealing my breath.

I tried to clamp it down. I tried to tell myself we still had twelve hours.

Twelve more hours.

Then she'd leave in the morning and take Carter with her.

Ireland felt so far away, ages and ages ago instead of a few days.

If our parents had their way, this would be the last time we were like this, the four of us—happy and married and in love.

"I don't want it to end," she whispered, giving me a soft, wet kiss. Then she leaned over to Ivy, who rested her head on my shoulder. They kissed just as sweetly, and tears spilled over Miri's cheeks again.

"We need to promise each other that it's not the end," Ivy said. "We need to promise we won't drift away, that the vows we made are forever. Lex and I will get out of this, I swear we will. I just need a little time."

"Until the end," Miri said.

"Until the end," Ivy agreed.

But I knew how these things worked. Proximity was the key to any relationship, especially with someone who craved wanderlust as much as Miri did. We agreed it didn't have to stay between the four of us, but this weird peace I had with Ivy would likely not continue after Carter and Miri were no longer here to temper our rage. We were fooling ourselves if we thought we'd be able to keep this going for any significant period of time with all of us on opposite ends of the world.

Part of me wanted to hope we could. Instead of ruining the moment, I let them have it. I let them have this sweet, unbelievable fantasy.

Carter joined us and closed the door behind him. He had on a pair of light blue jeans and a white V-neck, a little dirty from having been moving shit around all day. He turned his Bears football cap so the brim sat backward, and he collapsed at Ivy's feet, crawling into her lap with his head on her thighs and his arms wrapped around her knees.

"Today sucked," he said.

"Tomorrow's going to be worse," Ivy said.

"Let's just...Let's just pretend we're back in those woods," Carter said. "Like no one else exists except for us."

"Is that what you want, Chicago?" I said. "To go back to the woods?"

He shrugged. "It's peaceful when it's just us."

"It feels right, doesn't it?" Miri said. "It's always sort of felt right."

"I was thinking." I ran my hands through my hair, pushing it back from my face. "Since it's our last night here, we might as well make the best of it."

"And what did you have in mind?" Carter asked.

"Well," I said. "There's something I've been meaning to ask you."

"Yeah?" Carter said.

"Yeah." I dropped my tone to one I usually used with Miri. The one that flirted and teased and demanded obedience. "That night. At the pub. When you made that challenge. Were you hoping to make out with Miri? Or did you just want to see me make out with Ivy?"

"Does it have to be one or the other?" Carter flashed a playful grin, and I shook my head at his deviousness.

Miri leaned back and looked down at me, narrowing her eyes. Did she recognize the game? Was she interested in playing?

"And when you kissed Miri?" I asked, guiding her off my lap so I could push to my knees and move toward Carter, feeling a bit like an interrogator aiming to crack a suspect wide open. "Did you think she'd let you bend her over the table and fuck her in front of me?"

"No, but a guy can hope, right?"

I almost laughed at his brute honesty. What was the point in lying anymore? We knew the truth about each other now. Miri scooted next to Ivy, their shoulders touching and her dark brown hair a stark contrast to Ivy's ginger blond.

"You knew about Ivy and me, and you urged us on anyway," I said.

"I wanted to see if my suspicions were correct," Carter said.

"What suspicions?"

Carter raised an eyebrow and tilted his head, shifting his shoulders in an obvious attempt to keep himself from trembling under my scrutiny. "That you wanted Ivy as much as I wanted Miri."

The minute it was out there, the energy in the room shifted. It had been playful at first, all of them going along with my line of questioning because it was jovial and took our minds off the impending reality of tomorrow. But now we'd wandered into personal territory.

Had it been that obvious?

In hindsight, I suppose I hadn't been great about hiding my reaction to either of them. Of course, Ivy wanted me, too. I hadn't forgotten how she moaned when I slid into her in the woods, or how desperately she clung to me in that alcove. But that Carter had wanted Miri? That Carter knew I had wanted Ivy? This prick would be an Academy Award winner in no time. He'd been playing us for weeks. I knew it. Now we needed to square up for that.

I looked at Miri next to Ivy and asked, "Were you in on it?"

Miri wrapped her tongue around her canine and shrugged. "No, but I'd never turn down a chance to kiss a beautiful man."

I made a noise low in my chest and swung a leg over Carter's waist, straddling his hips and holding him down by the torso. He widened his eyes and gave me that lopsided smile I loved, his dimples making that famous appearance. The position made his cock poke my ass, and I liked that, too.

"We've been hoodwinked, X," I said. "By our closest friends."

"To be fair, darling," Miri said. "You lied to us. Kept secrets from us. You were cruel."

"You deserve worse," Carter added, glaring up at me.

"Do we?" I acted surprised, glancing at Ivy for a reaction. "Do you think we deserve worse, X?"

"I think Chicago needs to be punished for manipulating us like that," she said.

The moment she said punished, Carter let out a noise that was part sigh, part growl. He tried to hide another shiver in his shoulders, but I felt it, and then Ivy, ever the mastermind, wrapped an arm around Miri's shoulders and pulled her closer.

"But so do you," she said, continuing to stare at me.

Well, I wasn't expecting that. I licked my lips, sitting back on my haunches while I regarded my wives and their new debauchery.

"You two hooked up in London?" Ivy said. "And neither of you said anything?"

"How salacious," Miri tsked her teeth and shook her head. "Quite the secret to keep."

"Yes, yes," I said. "We're all fucked-up little monsters. Get back to the part where you think Chicago needs to be punished."

"No," Ivy said, a mischievous gleam in her eye. "The Princess and I deserve retribution. You both knew about our dalliance years ago."

"What did you have in mind?" Carter said, the acceptance in his tone making my heart race. He had an idea about where this might be going, and he planned to participate.

"I think," Ivy pushed to her feet, "we need to see what happened that night in London." She dragged Miri up with her, and both of them moved to the bed. Ivy sat, pulling Miri down in her lap and wrapping her arms around her from behind.

"To get the full experience," Miri said.

I looked at Carter, a silent question in my eyes, and he shrugged with one shoulder as if to say, *Why the fuck not?*

"That will require audience participation," I said.

"We both had dates that night," Carter explained.

"Let's skip to the part where you two hooked up." Ivy pointed between us and bit her bottom lip, clearly focused on getting to the goods.

Were we doing this?

Carter rubbed his hands over his face and sighed, licking his lips before smiling up at me and flashing those dimples.

Yeah, we were doing this.

Carter's hands went to his jeans, and I fisted the back of my shirt to pull it over my head, explaining how the night started and how we'd both been at the pub because of our dates with other people.

I pushed my pants and boxers down to my ankles, and then both of us stood naked in front of our wives. Carter's cock stood straight out in front of him, glistening with precum on the tip, and the sight sent something hot and wicked through my body, made even more depraved by the way Miri and Ivy looked at us. Like we could move the heavens.

I ran my hands through my hair, letting myself relish Ivy and Miri as they watched us. Ivy traced her fingers up the inside of Miri's thighs, parting them to reveal her lace panties to Carter and me. The sight of it made my cock twitch. They were beautiful on their own, but together? The love between them made me love them both even more.

Carter's cock twitched and he wrapped his hand around it, tugging at the tip. I pushed him back into the only other furniture in the room, a chair across from the mattress, and sank to my knees in front of him. Carter dropped his focus to me, tucking his bottom lip under his teeth, and I gripped his cock, giving the tip a gentle kiss that made his mouth fall open.

I sucked him the way I'd been sucking cock for years. He let out a groan as his head fell back. Miri moaned from across the room, and all of it made me so hot and so hard. My heart raced, banging away against my ribs. I'd never been so turned on, so desperate for release, or so anxious to see what would happen next.

"Look at them, Carter," I said, jerking him and giving his balls a squeeze. "Watch Ivy get Miri off. Watch me touch you. Do you like this? Having my hands on you like this?"

"Jesus, DC," Carter said, fisting his hands in my hair. Something about it set him off. Whether it was my words or what Ivy was doing to Miri across the room, but his thrusts turned angry. I elbowed him in the stomach to hold him still, his grip on my hair so tight that it stung in the best way possible.

He let out a growl, and I memorized the sound.

Hell, I would miss this man so much.

He was close, so close. I knew it. I could feel it. I let him go with a pop and sat back on my haunches, making Carter groan and buck against me, trying to find that delicious friction again, but I pushed him back down.

"Not yet," I said. "When you come, it'll be with my dick in your ass."

Which made Carter give me a pleased, goofy grin. My heart melted again. I loved everyone in this room, and I never wanted anything to change.

27

IVY

It should have pained me to see my arch nemesis on his knees for his best friend, my boyfriend, but the love they clearly had for each other emanated out of every shared glance, every touch. I couldn't fault Lex for falling in love with Carter, and I'd stopped wondering why anyone felt the same about Lex in return. The truth was that the four of us needed each other. We were always meant to be this way, and I never understood that more than I did while facing down the end of such a tremendous thing.

Carter yanked Lex to his feet, but I continued my ministrations on Miri, and when Lex saw us, splayed out and rubbing against each other, he paused to gaze, twisting his lips into a smile that made me ashamed of how much I liked it.

"I thought Carter would be ashamed," Lex said, plopping down in the chair Carter had just vacated. Carter sank to his knees at Lex's feet, and Lex looked down at him, running the back of his knuckles along the side of his cheek. It struck me how tenderly he touched him, even after the aggressive way they'd taken each other in the woods.

"But I only wanted to know what it felt like to break you apart."

Carter licked Lex's cock from base to tip and sucked it deep in his mouth, making Lex groan and melt into his seat. Miri writhed against me, bucking into my hand, her pussy so wet. I would miss Miri, too—my first love, my first crush. Our hearts were so inexplicably linked that losing her severed a vital part of my soul. I loved her as much as I loved Carter.

"Remember our first time," she murmured, running the back of her knuckles down the side of my face. Perhaps she sensed my desperation, perhaps she wanted to keep me in the present. "Remember how hard you shook."

"I couldn't believe someone like you wanted someone like me." I laughed out a sad noise and kissed her to remind myself that she was real, that she was still with me, after all this time and all we'd done.

"Darling," she murmured, tears brimming the corners of her eyes, "I'll want you until I die."

Miri turned and dropped in front of me, pushing my dress up and snuggling her body in between my legs. She dragged my panties down my legs and off my feet, and then that soft, delicate mouth fluttered against my vulva, kissing and nuzzling and licking at the most sensitive parts of my body.

She was so beautiful, and I loved every inch of her. She circled my clit with her lips and curled her fingers inside me, sending jolts of pure pleasure down my legs and up my spine. Somewhere in the distance, Carter sucked Lex off, or perhaps they had moved on by now. Either way, the thought of the four of us together like this overtook my senses, and my climax hit me hard. Unexpectedly. Miri fucked her fingers inside me harder, making it more euphoric and sending chills and tingles to every inch of my skin. It made me weak, and I fell back on the bed where Miri let me ride it out, and after I was a panting mess, she crawled up my body to claim my mouth in a searing kiss.

How I loved her. How it hurt that she'd be leaving. How I hated that it had to happen.

"You're so beautiful when you come," she murmured, just low enough for me to hear.

I rolled us so I was on top of her, my hips in between her thighs, and I kissed my way down her body, pushing her dress up and tugging her panties down to her ankles as I went.

"Mmm, so are you," I said, digging my teeth into the side of her thigh. She still had bruises here from the night in the woods, faded to a dull yellowish purple. I kissed them, relishing in the way her thighs trembled under my touch. She moaned when I brushed my tongue against her clit, and her fingers found my hair when I licked her completely.

"Oh, look, Mr. Fairfax," Carter said. "I believe we're being treated to a retelling of what happened that fated night at Mount Oberon."

"It's a reimagining," Miri whimpered, and a giggle burst out of me, blowing hot breath against her skin, which made her gasp and shiver.

Carter moved in behind me, his angry cock cradled at the juncture of my thighs, and dug his fingers to my hips to hold me in place. His chest radiated heat against my back as he leaned over me, kissing Miri's knees and thighs and the back of my shoulders. Worshipping both of us. Revering our love with his own.

"There is one part we left out," Lex said, and I perked up to look at him, resting my head on one of Miri's legs.

"Oh, yeah?" I said.

"Yeah," Lex sat on the bed next to Miri, shifting her weight so she sat in his lap, her legs on either side of his with Carter and me in between them. He positioned himself at her opening and slid home, her hands going to his legs to support herself. She peered down at me from her perch on top of Lex, truly embodying the princess and her prince. Her pretty pussy was spread open right in front of us, glistening and swollen from abuse, but truly inviting as Lex slowly pumped in and out. "Carter, if you'll do the honors."

My husband leaned forward, his body so heavy on top of mine, and he dragged his tongue from Lex's root over their connection to

Miri's clit, sucking and nursing until Miri moaned and fell back against Lex.

"Fuck," Lex said, his legs shaking. "I'll never get over how good you feel."

"Bleeding hell," Miri said. "That made my toes curl."

"Do it again." Lex pushed inside Miri harder, right in front of my face, and I knew I should have felt ashamed of how much I loved it. Instead, I raged with lust. I wanted to lick her next. I wanted to watch them both fall apart in my mouth.

Carter reached between us and rearranged his cock so he could slide inside of me in one quick thrust, filling me to the brim, sending sparks of energy through my molecules. I moaned and almost collapsed onto the ground. He was so hard and watching Lex fuck Miri was so arousing, I couldn't help myself. I dragged the flat of my tongue over Lex and up to Miri's sensitive skin, relishing the taste of both of them, tangy and sweet and *mine*. Both of them...so incredibly mine.

Carter groaned and dug his nails into my waist deeper, his nails biting into my skin in a deliciously violent assault—hard and rough and dirty. I played with Lex and licked Miri, and in the heat of the moment, I let myself be overcome with this powerful connection between us.

Like we had in those woods, the boundaries between us disappeared. Carter's pleasure became mine, and Lex's surged through me at the moment he came, gripping at Miri while he rutted into her. That set off Miri's orgasm and she rode me through it, her fingers gripping my scalp while she pointed me where she wanted me, her moans a chorus to my own euphoria. When they were spent, Carter pulled me upright, holding me close with a hand around my neck and his teeth on my earlobe.

But Lex wasn't done with us yet. He grabbed his cock, quickly hardening again, and climbed off the bed.

Oh, no.

"I made you a promise, Chicago," he said, bending over for his pants, where he pulled a small bottle of lube and a condom out of his back pocket. Carter chuckled and lowered down my body so his mouth could lap at my overheated flesh. I hissed in a breath, my pussy too tender for his warm tongue, but he held me still, that look in his eyes warning me not to move. If Lex was going to fuck him, he wanted his face in my cunt.

"I've got an idea," Miri said, sinking off the bed as well. She kneeled down in front of where Carter leaned over the bed, lining up her face with his cock. From this vantage point, I couldn't see what she was doing, but when Carter moaned into my pussy, I figured she'd slotted him into her throat.

Lex walked up behind him and opened the bottle of lube with a quiet *snick*. He squirted some down Carter's ass, eyeing me over our husband's body while he lined himself up. He pushed into Carter. Slow. So slow.

Carter moaned and sucked at me, gripping me harder to hold himself steady.

Lex's thrusts got faster. Stronger. The sick, twisted nature of watching my fiancé fuck my boyfriend while my best friend blew him rocked through me like a sledgehammer. I met Lex's eyes and when he gave me that wicked little grin, I fell apart again.

I'll spare the goodbyes. They were hard enough as it was.

I tried not to cry in front of them. I wanted to be strong. I wanted them to know it was okay to go and that I loved them no matter what, so I held it all inside. Carter and Miri left together, tears in their eyes, kisses on their lips, and promises to call on the wind.

Then Lex and I shared a quiet ride across town to the apartment our parents had rented for us in Crystal City. Movers were unpacking our things by the time we walked in the front door, but something felt different already. Incomplete. Our square broken.

It reminded me of stretching a rubber band so far it almost

snapped—that jittery sensation in my stomach, the pounding in my heart, the clenching in my jaw, the anticipation of *any second now, any second now, any second now.* With each mile Carter and Miri put between us, I sensed the breaking point encroaching and wondered when it would recoil to sting my exposed heart.

On that first night in the new place, as I lay alone in my bed in the dark, listening to Lex move around the apartment outside my door, I finally let my heart crack.

I cried. A lot.

I hated that I had to go through the pain and shame of losing my spouses in front of the world, in front of the one person I *sort-of-kind-of* hated and loved most. A sob barreled out of my chest, and I slammed a pillow over my face, hoping I could stifle it.

I froze when my door creaked open. "Leave me alone, Lex."

He didn't say anything, but the bed shifted as he crawled in next to me and lifted me by the arms. He tugged me closer, resting my head on his chest, and running his fingers through my hair to brush it away from my face.

"Your incessant blubbering is giving me a headache," he said. "If you won't shut up, I might as well stay here until you do."

I wanted to claw his eyes out, but I tucked my head under his chin and held tighter to him, letting the sound of his cold, dead heart lull me to sleep.

ACT V

And as imagination bodies forth
The forms of things unknown, the poet's pen
Turns them to shapes and gives to airy nothing
A local habitation and a name.
-Theseus, Act V, Scene 1

28

LEX

SIX MONTHS LATER

After Miri and Carter left, things just carried on.

Ivy and I started law school. She buried herself in books and legislation and trying to find a way to fight back against our parents. I buried myself in weed, booze, and tattoos. A forest on my lower back in the free space between my ribs and my hip. A square with an X in the middle of my forearm. A symbol that only we would understand.

I tried with Ivy for a while. I tried to cuddle her when she needed it, attempted to pick up the pieces and put her back together like I promised Carter I would. But I would never be Carter. And she would never be Miri. We both were dreadfully aware of that resounding devastating fact.

As much as we tried to be civil, our heartache simmered below our skin. Looking at her reminded me of *them*. As I'm sure looking at me reminded her of the same. It drew me to her and broke me apart me at the same time.

Were it not for this splinter in my heart and the scabs on my hands, I could have easily moved on with my life. Cut the cord with them as I'd done with every other lover I'd ever had. Except...they weren't any other lovers. I'd married them. *They* married *me*.

They were mine.

Mine.

And we should have been together.

Until the end.

Ivy tried to text them, but her messages went undelivered. I tried the same, only to learn our numbers had been blocked on their phones, which didn't make any damn sense at all.

"Have you heard from them?" Ivy asked a few days after they'd left.

"No." I ran a hand through my hair. "It's driving me batshit."

I wrote again, pleading with them to call me, to talk to me, to either of us. I sent direct messages on their socials, creating new accounts to try to reach out that way, but nothing either of us did made them react. It was almost like they'd gone out there and forgotten we existed altogether.

It stank of political puppeteering, and just when I was about to go to my father and accuse him of fucking with my life again, Carter sent a group text.

"Weeds, DC...listen. We've given it a lot of thought. Stop reaching out. This hurts too much. I love you both, but we knew this would only last so long. Please don't contact us again. This is the end."

Miri added, *"This is the end."*

It shattered what little hope Ivy had left. I'd never seen her broken like that before. She never gave up fighting and she never backed down. She was as stubborn as a fly at a cookout. But believing Carter didn't want her anymore?

Well, if my heart wasn't just as broken, I would have flown to that Malibu dream house myself to strangle him in his sleep.

Take care of her, he'd said. *Put her back together,* he'd made me swear. And then he pulled this shit? *Over text message?*

The next time I saw him and my princess, I was going to take it out on their asses.

Part of me didn't want to believe it was them, that my father had something to do with it. But...*Weeds...DC...Until the end?* How could anyone else know about that shit? That was insider info only. Maybe it was easier to quit them cold turkey. Maybe that would end up killing us all in the end like a more grotesque version of the DTs.

Life went on.

We put on the good show like the political monsters we were, but six months after we'd returned from Ireland, things got fucked-up...a lot more fucked-up.

We were two weeks out from finals, and I had to get an A in my litigation class in order to beat Ivy for best GPA. (I said our *affection* for each other had dissipated, not our competitiveness.) I studied all day and any free time I had was devoted to busting my ass at my internship or helping Ivy take down our parents' political aspirations.

Stressed didn't begin to describe my agitation when my father invited me to family dinner. But fuck it, at least I got a free meal while he berated me and my mother acted like the secret to life was at the bottom of a wine bottle.

"I've confirmed the wedding will occur right after you graduate from law school. Three years lines up nicely with my re-election." He chewed his steak, the jowls on his chubby chin rattling with the movement. I refocused on my mother, who pursed her lips and pushed food around on her plate.

"Whatever makes you look good," I said on a sigh, clawing at my cigarette box. My appetite had been soiled by the invitation to this shit show, and all this talk of marrying Ivy made my stomach even tighter. We'd been scheming all these weeks and had nothing to show for our efforts. Short of jumping on a plane to California, adopting new identities, and going into drowning debt for facial reconstruction surgery, our options were pretty limited. "My opinions obviously don't matter."

"I'm happy you've left that English whore alone," he murmured, cutting into another slice of meat. "What a hilarious charade that was."

I snapped my gaze to him, and the nights spent holding Ivy while she cried went through my mind—the depression we'd both sunk into, the yank on my heart at having been split in half by Carter and Miri's rejection, how terrible it felt to see them on social media looking so damn happy.

Why would he bring her up now?

I narrowed my eyes, and suspicion clawed its way to the forefront of my consciousness again.

"Was it you?" My voice came out low, like a growl.

He stopped and looked up at me, his eyes perplexed. "What?"

"Did you send that text to us?"

"What text?" He bit another piece of steak. "Alexei, what are you talking about?"

"The text from Carter. The one that ended things."

"Things?" My father seemed genuinely confused, but he *was* a politician after all. One of the best. "What are you talking about?"

It had been a long day in a long month in an even longer year. Half my heart was missing. I hadn't slept in forever, and this fake marriage bullshit grated on my nerves.

I said the words as calmly as I could, even though my temper flared in the center of my chest. *"Tell me the truth.* Did you tear us apart? Are you keeping us apart?"

The air pulsed between me and my father, and I looked at my mother to see if she saw it. When her reaction didn't change, I cleared my throat and blinked.

I must have imagined it. I'm just tired. Really tired.

Then my father said, "We've been planning your marriage to Ivy since Marcus died. Princess Miriam was always a blip, and I'd force you two together again if it meant I'd get elected." He stood, the link between us blinding and blaring, a physical pull between my mind and his mouth. "Six years of watching you fail has made me regret every part of being your father. You were right when you said it should have been you, and standing here today, I'd drown you in the Boston Bay myself if it meant I'd get *my* son back."

I balked. Froze. Shock and disgust and utter *relief* coated my veins when the connection broke and he shook his head, blinking like he'd been in a trance. My mother gasped, dropping her wine, the shattering glass deafening and muffled at the same time.

My father had *never* talked to me like that. He'd always verbally denied his hatred for me, even as he continued to act on it.

I raised my eyebrows, and my father squared his jaw, his hands turning into fists. "What was that? What did you do to me?"

I didn't have answers because...I didn't know. "I didn't do anything."

He slammed his napkin down on the table and stormed through the dining room to the foyer. My mother locked her eyes on me, her mouth hanging open, her gaze searching for a difference in my appearance. Maybe devil's horns or a pointed tail.

I shrugged and gaslit my father, saying something like, "Well, he's obviously cut off," but that was just my dick move to cover my own ass.

"I'm sorry, Alexei," she said in Russian, shaking her head. "Your father's behavior tonight was unacceptable. He shouldn't have said those things to you."

I answered her in the same language. "Doesn't make them untrue."

"They are untrue." She dabbed at her eye with her napkin. "You are my son, and I love you."

I snorted a sad laugh. Yeah. Sure. She loved me a lot, enough to sit there and say nothing while my father admitted he'd rather kill me himself than live with me as his surviving son. To be fair, I hadn't given him much of a reason to feel differently.

Just my whole future. Just a marriage to a girl who drove me wild. Just the loss of my two favorite people.

"You are his son, too," she said. "He knows that. He's just angry. The election is wearing on him."

I swallowed down the agony that gathered in the back of my throat and pinched a cigarette between my lips, holding a lighter up with shaking hands while I inhaled on it.

No, I thought. *He believed it.* Because I *had* made him say those things. Magic had shifted around me, the same way it had while we were in the woods. I felt it. Except this time, I could control it. I could *wield* it.

"You promised I wouldn't have to do this." I switched to English now, preferring to say what I needed to in my own language. "You promised I would be free, and you lied."

"Alexei," she said.

"You never apologized for that." I kept my tone level. Clear. Concise. I wanted her to know I'd spent time considering what I had to say next. Tears burned my eyes. I could count on one hand the number of times I'd ever cried, the last time being when my brother died. But I knew the truth, and well—what was stopping me now? "I'll never forgive you for this. I am your only child, and I despise you both."

Then I stood and walked out of that hellhole like I might never go back.

I should have told Ivy. I should have figured out how to get ahold of Carter and Miri and insisted they fly home so we could figure this out. My finger even hovered over Ivy's name for a millisecond.

But in the end, I kept it to myself.

Please don't contact us again.

Maybe I was too fucked in the head about my father finally admitting what I'd always known. Marcus was the golden child in his eyes, and I was the scum on his shoes. An inadequate replacement he'd been forced to raise.

It should have been me.

It seemed easier than having to admit that whatever bees' nest we'd kicked over in Ireland had followed us back to the States. I thought if I ignored it and pretended it wasn't there, it would go away. That like the lust that had gripped us three days after midsummer, this would stop with time.

29

IVY

I wouldn't say I healed from my heartbreak so much as I simply got on with my life.

Summer faded into fall, and I started law school. We promised we'd keep in touch. We promised to call every single night. But the minute they went out there, they disconnected their phones or they blocked my number. Either on its own would have been devastating and strange, but they'd done both.

I'd reached out on social media.

I sent emails.

All of my messages went unsent. When Carter told us to leave them alone, I didn't want to believe it was him. He wouldn't do that to me. He *wouldn't*. But Lex seemed convinced our parents had nothing to do with it, and when I asked Kit to investigate, she turned up nothing.

"I have no reason to think it wasn't him." Kit sat at my computer, typing away on my keyboard while she scoured my phone for evidence of any tampering. "If it was our mother, she hired someone good. *Really* good." Kit cleared her throat and tapped ash in the crystal from her joint. "Like, better than me good."

"Is there such a thing?" Jon sat on my bed and flipped through a college notebook. Only eighteen months younger than me, he still had another two years at Yale before he had to worry about our mother's grating influence. "I thought you were God's gift to technology."

"I am, dill weed." She glared at him. "But this?" Kit shook her head at me. "I can't prove it wasn't them. But Ivy—" My little sister touched my arm in a comforting embrace, telling me she understood my pain like only a sibling could. "I can't prove it was, either."

It wasn't much, but it was enough for me to hold on to. I couldn't believe Carter didn't want me anymore. I couldn't believe Miri had abandoned me after all these years. It would hurt more than anything I'd ever been through. We'd promised each other forever. They wouldn't simply throw it away so easily.

Despite clinging to that notion, those months following their departure were dark and lonely. Had it not been for this tenuous alliance with my ~~archnemesis~~ fiancé, I wouldn't have made it through. Carter's laugh echoed through my ears and Miri's smile flickered behind my eyes. If I let myself linger on the memory for too long, I couldn't get out of bed. Short of making myself a stalker, I redirected my attention elsewhere.

I refocused on trying to upset my mother's plans. Part of me wanted to withdraw from Georgetown and disappear into anonymity. Perhaps I'd fly out to LA and track them down. Perhaps I'd hire someone to make me a fake ID and I'd never return. But it would only be a matter of time before my mother found me and brought me back. If I had any hope of winning, I needed to play the great game. For the time being, that meant going along with...whatever this was.

Days faded into weeks, and eventually, six months had passed.

Carter got cast in a popular book-to-TV show adaptation for a premium cable network. Preliminary reviews were outstanding, and critics were already calling for an Emmy nomination for Carter, which was high praise for a relative nobody. As part of her royal duties, Miri eventually returned home to the UK and had been obliged to pick a cause. She'd chosen to save the planet. Her name had started to become synonymous with Danae Enterprises, a nonprofit organization dedicated to sustainability. It ached as much as it was a relief. I liked knowing they were finding success. It made our mutual misery seem worth it.

I could almost forget I'd married three lovers in the woods in Ireland, that I'd made vows on a midsummer night and lost an entire day of my life to sex-soaked bliss. But every time I looked at my hand, I remembered how it felt to have my oath burned into my skin. Every time I woke up alone in my bed, expecting to see Carter's smiling face, I remembered how it felt to say goodbye to him. Every time I looked at Lex's teeth, I remembered what they felt like sinking in to my neck.

The dreams hadn't gone away. Sometimes I ran in the forest alone, hunting for the ruins, my feet bare on the undergrowth. Sometimes Carter ran with me. Or Miri. Or all four of us. Sometimes Ashley found me and grabbed ahold of my arms, her boney fingers digging into my biceps and her eyes wide and terrifying the way they were in the pub. She wanted to know where the ring was.

"Where'd you drop it?" she'd snarl. *"Where is it? Where is it? Where is it?"*

"I don't know," I'd say, sitting up in a cold panic with sweat on my brow and tears streaming down my cheeks.

I wanted to forget about the things that had happened to us there, but even the practical, logical side of me suspected that may never happen.

"What's going on with you?" Lex asked one morning. He stood across the kitchen island, wearing his boxers and nothing else as he sipped his coffee and smoked a cigarette.

"What do you mean, what's going on with me?" Sleep didn't come easily these days. I'd been up since four in the morning, so I was already showered and dressed by the time he'd even come out of his room.

"I can hear you shouting and moaning in your sleep."

I cleared my throat. "It's nothing."

He paused and glanced around to make sure we were alone, bringing his smoke to his lips for a deep inhale. "Is it the ruins?"

"Yeah." I ran a hand over the back of my neck and sighed, cringing against the memory. "It's probably some PTSD thing. I obviously need therapy."

He looked like he wanted to say something else, like maybe he had a similar confession to make, but the door to our apartment opened and my driver announced he was ready to take me to class. I grabbed my stuff, gave Lex one last look that asked for his silence, and left.

I couldn't deal with whatever was or wasn't between us. I simply didn't have the time or the energy anymore. I missed Carter, I missed Miri, and I had to soldier on.

Except...

I should have let it go. It was silly and irrational and *no one* believed in fairy curses, but on those nights when I woke up in a cold sweat, unable to fall back asleep, I started digging. I went down internet snake pits that led me nowhere, and some that led me to things I'd never be able to unsee. Up until this point, most of what I'd come across was too farfetched to be anything but myth. People being turned into pigs, fairies stealing human children, little winged creatures causing chaos in the enchanted forest.

Then I found an old story about two sets of lovers wandering into the woods after a fire festival on Beltane. They were gone for three days, according to the locals, and when they returned, they claimed they'd only been lost a few hours. They said they'd dined with the fairies and married each other in a great festival of love, burning their vows onto their hands.

The queen of the fairies had given them her blessing, and the king bestowed them with unimaginable fortune.

"They'd been gifted by the faire folk," the story said. *"Eternal life and*

eternal love. They made a vow. For none could stray from the rest, or they would suffer unknowable ecstasy."

We'd wandered into the woods after midsummer, but other than that, the story rang a little too close to home. I hung it on the cork board I had in the back of my closet where I'd gathered anything else I thought worthwhile — articles or whatever I could find about Siobhan and Ashley and Killwater in general. I connected different colored yarn between the people I thought I'd seen at the festival. I tacked on any fairy lore and ancient myths that came close to what we'd experienced.

But this took the cake. It was the closest I'd come to a story like ours, proof that what happened to us had *actually* happened. Deciding I'd do more research about this fairy king and queen in the morning, I showered and climbed into bed, hoping for a peaceful night.

The dream came to me like it always did. I ran in the woods, the wind in my hair and the branches hitting me in the face and on the arms. I laughed, finally free, freer than I'd ever felt in my life. Utter joy mixing in my blood, I ran faster and harder, pushing myself, intoxicated by the fresh forest air.

When I got to the ruins, I stopped short. Standing in front of it with one hand in her pocket and the other holding a cigarette was Siobhan. She looked the same as the last time I'd seen her, her dark brown hair cut short, her matching eyes just as intense and inviting.

"Hello, Ivy," she said.

"What the fuck?" I said. "I'm dreaming. This is a dream."

"I think so." She took a step closer, raising an incredulous eyebrow. "You look more exhausted than the last time I saw you. Tsk tsk tsk." Siobhan shook her head, disapproval in her stare. "You haven't been taking care of my gift."

"I lost it," I admitted, biting my bottom lip and wringing my hands. "The ring."

She pursed her lips, leaning into me. "Did you think the ring was the gift?"

Isn't it?

"What was it then?" My eyebrows furrowed as I tried to figure it out, my heart pounding, my stomach lurching into knots. "The kiss? The night I don't remember?"

She stayed frustratingly silent.

"Answer me," I shouted, clenching my fists. "What did you do to us?"

Siobhan chuckled to herself. "If you have to ask, you haven't learned the moral of the story."

"What moral? What are you talking about?"

She pulled her lips into a slow smile and *poof*...she was gone.

My eyes shot open and I jolted upright, my empty room lit only by the DC skyline and the full moon creeping in through my curtains.

It was only a dream.

Just a dream.

I swung my legs to the side and stood, pausing when something cool fell out of my lap and landed in a soft thud on the floor. The green leaves shimmered in the faint light, and when I picked it up, my heart almost stopped.

A silver ring made of ivy.

I didn't tell Lex.

I didn't know what it meant, so I kept it to myself. I prayed for Siobhan to return to my dreams and elaborate on this whole mess. She never did. The nightmares went away, and Ashley left me alone. Almost as if the ring's return had flipped a switch in my mind or put a protective bubble around me, keeping the consequences of midsummer at bay.

If the ring wasn't the gift, then what was?

I'd stare at it for hours, memorizing the shifting light in its emerald leaves and the dazzling craftsmanship of the bent silver, anticipating the moment when it suddenly did a trick.

How had she given this to me? Was she in the room? Had she disappeared before I woke?

The alarms hadn't been tripped, and the security footage outside the building didn't pick up anyone matching her description. Suffice to say, I had no good answers. Kit hadn't found anything about Siobhan despite her months of searching, and my education had started to take up most of my time. What happened to us in Ireland seemed so far away, growing further with each passing second.

I flipped a page in the ancient book outstretched in front of me, twiddling the ring between my fingers while a game show played on the TV in the background. The medieval illustration of the fairy king and queen seemed like something out of an old history text rather than figures from mythology. Expertly done. Fine detailing around the border.

Like Ashley said that first day in Ireland, they weren't pixies from Disney tales. One light, one dark, they were twin spirits, bound together for all eternity. These myths painted them as mercurial rulers, beloved by their fairy followers and feared by humans. They'd been known to take humans as consorts, inviting them into their court and feeding them the food of the fae to keep them bound to that realm forever. Together, they were the great source of all the magic in the fairy world.

I wondered if the king and queen existed. Did they know what Siobhan had done to us? What would they do if they did? Would they even care? Or would my lowly human self not fly high enough for their radar?

I thumbed the scars on my right hand, tracing over the tiny lines as I remembered the burn from midsummer. The agony had blistered through my drunken haze, and if I thought about it hard enough, I could almost still feel it simmering there, just below the surface.

"Great news for all you Princess Miriam fans," said the talking head during a commercial. "She's back in the UK and looking more regal than ever. Find out the whole story, tonight on *PuckTV*."

I took a sip of my wine, swallowing down the rising tide of angst that brewed in my chest at seeing her. They showed paparazzi shots of her crossing the street wearing a shimmery blouse and a flowing dress, not a hair out of place. The picture-perfect princess, as always.

My heart pounded, and the sinking feeling turned to cement in my gut, tears welling in the corners of my eyes. I missed her so much.

"Well, that's enough of that." I clicked the TV off and chugged the rest of my wine, wincing as it hit me right in the forehead. I focused my (somewhat blurry) attention on the ring, now sitting on the page in the book. I'd had a stressful day at school, followed by a hectic night at the law firm, and now?

This stupid ring.

Perhaps I'd had more wine than I'd meant to because the longer I looked it, the angrier I got — like I expected it to reveal its secrets to me or lead the way to Oz. When it didn't, I clamped my fingers into fists and I slammed them down on the countertop, growling "What the fuck is happening? Goddamn it."

Even in my drunken haze, twin jolts of agony echoed up my arms and down my spine.

"Ahh, shit!" I waved my hands in front of me, regretting my outburst now that I was sure I'd broken both of my pinky fingers.

That was how Lex found me. The door to our apartment opened, and he walked in carrying Chinese takeout, his tie loosened around his neck and the sleeves of his button-down rolled up to his elbows.

He narrowed his hazel eyes as he froze and assessed me, his skeptical gaze going up and down. "What's wrong with you?"

"Nothing," I said. "Just being an idiot."

He sat the plastic bag on the kitchen island before grabbing my wrists to examine whatever I was clutching.

"I'm fine." I whipped my hands away from him, and he rolled his eyes, going back to the food.

"You don't sound fine." He unloaded white plastic containers as I tried and failed to get myself under control. Head swimming, I went to the cabinet with the plates and grabbed two so we could eat, but when I turned back around, he'd paused with his eyes locked on the ring. "Is that what I think is?"

Shit.

I opened my mouth. Shut it again. I didn't know what to tell him.

"I thought you'd lost it."

"I did." I put the plates down, wishing like hell I could suddenly be sober. Two glasses of wine on an empty stomach had made me foolish and careless.

"You found it?" Narrowing his eyes, he came around the island, tracing his fingertips down the white marble as he walked. That gaze settled on me, the one that meant he knew I was hiding something. He could smell it, and now he was on the hunt.

My hand went to the X on my neck, but he shoved it away.

"Not exactly." I held his stare, refusing to back down. In my drunken state, I'd be no match for a sober Lex, but I didn't think about that. I forced myself not to tremble when he took another step.

"X, what the fuck is going on?"

Everything in me wanted to resist, to fight him, to tell him to fuck off and mind his own goddamn business.

But where had that gotten us last time?

Where had that *ever* gotten us?

"She came to me in my dreams. Siobhan." I told him everything—how she met me at the ruins, how she told me I wasn't taking care of her gift. All of it. "When I woke up, there it was."

His eyes shifted between mine while he processed this new information. "When did this happen?"

"A few weeks ago."

"Weeks?" His eyebrows rose. "So much for honesty. When the fuck were you planning on telling me?"

"I don't know, Lex." I clenched my hands into fists as I geared up to defend myself. "Do I have to tell you everything now?"

"When it comes to whatever's going on with us, yes. It affects us both."

"Not like this." I shook my head. "I'm the one having the night-mares. They gave this gift *to me.* I have to figure out how to break it."

He balked. "Is that what you think? We're in this together."

I took a deep breath, trying to control my racing heart. If we were in this together, then why did it feel like I was the only one doing anything? Why did it feel like he hadn't thought about it...about *them*...since we'd left?

No, he'd gone through this magnificent experience with me and then pulled away when it mattered most, just like he did about everything else in his life.

"I promised you." He stepped closer, lowering his voice and brushing a piece of hair behind my ear. "When we got home, I'd help you figure out what was going on. I'd help you fight this. I meant it."

I searched his face for signs of trickery.

Why was he being so sweet?

Why was he being nice?

It didn't make sense. No, he was doing this to screw with me. Six months home and he'd reverted to his old self, the guy who lived to get under my skin.

"Don't tease me." I shoved at his shoulders to stop him from crowding me up against the counter, but he grabbed my wrist, yanking me forward. My other hand went to his chest to keep my balance.

Then something happened.

The connection between us burned. Everywhere our skin touched vibrated with a power I didn't recognize, but it resonated with familiarity all the same.

Then everything went white like I'd been blinded. Visions danced in front of me, clips from a movie on a projector screen.

No, not clips.

Memories.

Lex's memories.

I saw myself as a ten-year-old child, red in the face, my hair in pigtails and my dress in tatters as I beat at Lex's head with my fists backstage behind our parents' inauguration. Rage and passion swelled in my heart, but it wasn't *my* rage and passion. It came from the visions, like they'd invoked that response in me because of the way it had made Lex feel at the time.

I saw myself the moment he kissed me on the banks of the Potomac at Marcus's funeral, the zing of the slap slicing through his face as I hit him. His shame and guilt and *awe* of me struck somewhere in my gut, and I almost toppled over.

Then the images sped up. One of us at Mount Oberon, arguing with each other on the debate team. At TWU, me standing across the fire and insinuating that I'd slept with his girlfriend. A drunken night in my apartment sophomore year where I'd been laughing at something Carter said and Lex watched us from across the room with yearning deep in his heart.

All the emotions from those experiences hit next — the stinging heat of jealousy and the icy burn of longing.

Years and years of it. Years of our friendship. Years of his complicated torment for me. For Carter. For Miri. Years of pushing it down, pushing aside, just...pushing.

It should have been me, he thought when Marcus's face appeared. *It should have been me.*

My chest caved in on itself, and I sobbed.

Then the connection stopped. The line went dead like the plug on my projector screen had been ripped right out of the wall.

I blinked, coming back to reality—one where I stood in my kitchen with my fiancé and my cold takeout and the awkward *what-the-fuck-was-that* between us.

I didn't know what to say. Had I seen his memories? Had I been able to get into his head? And if so...did he think that way about himself? Had he been hanging on to that all this time?

All this time.

"Lex," I finally murmured.

He took a long, slow breath through his nose, his jaw tightening and his body going rigid. His normally piercing eyes turned frightening with intensity and betrayal, confusion lurking behind them.

For six months, we had been living around each other. We had tried and failed to find that bright burning thing we kindled in Ireland. But there, in that kitchen, with the weight of what I'd witnessed between us, it flamed to life again.

Nowhere near as powerful as it used to be, but definitely there.

A heartbeat passed. A slow exhale coasted over his lips.

And then I pushed up on my toes, bringing my mouth to his in a crushing embrace. How could he ever have wished he'd died? How could he ever have wanted it to be him? And all those things he felt for me. All those complicated emotions.

When he put his arms around my waist and hugged me tighter, I sagged into his hold.

This wasn't the passionate fury of that alcove at Killwater nor was it the newly discovered drunken desire at the beer pong game.

This meant something different.

A partnership, perhaps. An understanding.

He broke the kiss with his hands on my shoulders, gently pushing me back so he could cup my jaw and rest his forehead on mine.

"*Tell me the truth.* What's going on with you?"

A powerful twist hit my gut, magic clinging to the air between us like suffocating humidity. The words came out of my mouth, even though I tried to stop them. I wanted to bite them back but couldn't.

"I think I read your mind," I said. "I saw our life together."

Wait...What?

Why did I tell him that?

I'd never had any problem lying to him before.

"Is that a new party trick?" Lex reached for his cigarettes, biting one between his teeth to light it. "Or have you been a better actress your whole life than I've given you credit for?"

I ignored his cruelty. There were bigger issues to deal with. "How did you make me tell you that?"

Lex cleared his throat and inhaled deeply, blowing out the smoke before saying, "Remember when I said our parents didn't have anything to do with Carter and Miri? That's how I knew."

The puzzle pieces collided in my mind faster than I could put them together. "This is what she meant. She told me she gave me a gift. This is what she meant." *Wait...our parents?* "How long have you known?"

Lex cleared his throat. "A few weeks."

I put my hands on my hips and glared at him, mocking his earlier tone when I said, "So much for honesty, right?"

He rolled his eyes and refocused his attention on our dinner. "It doesn't change anything."

"What? This changes everything."

"No, it doesn't. You're still a stuck-up law school student, and I'm still a tattooed fuck-up. These are our roles."

"That's bullshit."

He snorted out a laugh. "I agree. But what exactly are you going to do? Call Carter and Miri to tell them? Good luck getting in touch with them. Even if you do, what if they're not experiencing it? Or better yet, what if they are? Do you think that will make Carter leave Hollywood?"

The harshness in his tone made me wince.

"Do you think Miri will leave the royal family? Do you think—" His voice cracked, and he cleared his throat before pausing to get his composure back. "Do you think that will make them change their minds? Come play house with two political nightmares?"

I took a deep breath and let it out slowly, steeling my gaze against his onslaught before I whispered a solemn, "No."

"No. Then this stays between us." Lex turned to me and pinched the bridge of his nose. "I'll help you figure out what's going on. I'll do whatever research you want. I'll even help you get us out of this mess. I promised I would. But we tell no one."

"More secrets, Lucifer?"

He sighed and gave me a sarcastic smile. "It's what makes a good marriage, right?"

I scoffed, but he closed the distance between us, cupping the side of my face and sliding his hand down until it rested over my X. He traced the mark with his thumb, and that delicate touch zigzagged all the way down my legs and back up again.

"We're in this together, X," he said. "Always."

I grabbed his wrists and rested my forehead against his, a small weight lifting off my chest at the confession.

Together again.

Since the beginning.

Until the end.

30
IVY

Now

A person's wedding day was supposed to be the happiest day of their life, but trepidation rolled through my gut for more than one reason. The truth was much more messed-up than anyone would ever believe.

I couldn't marry Lex because we were already married. Both of us. To other people.

We had married them in a midsummer ceremony four years ago...*and each other.*

My mother gave me a fake peck on the cheek and announced I had fifteen minutes to get downstairs if we wanted to start this circus fashionably late.

All I could think about was *them.*

All I could hear was the sound of Carter's laughter and the trill of Miri's whisper. All I could see were future versions of Lex and me at each other's throats, desperate to hurt each other in the worst way possible because we were so sick of the fighting and the grind and the hustle. My parents had beaten each other down relentlessly over the years. I wanted no part of that.

As soon as the door shut behind my mother, I made up my mind.

"Ivy." Kit turned to me. "I debated telling you this until after the wedding, but you should know something." She took my hands. "You're not going to like it."

I raised an eyebrow.

"It's about that thing you asked me to research — that weird thing I found on Mother's firewall."

The look on her face told me everything I needed to know. "Is it what I think? Was it her?"

Kit's features dropped, and she pursed her lips, giving me a solemn nod as she explained what happened in her tech jargon, but her voice dulled to a muffle, silenced by the tumble of emotions that shot through my blood.

Rage at my family, *at the media,* for doing this to me. To all of us.

Sadness that we had missed out on so much because of it, because of the role I had to play.

Well, I was done playing it.

Fuck her. Fuck them. Fuck all of this.

I couldn't do it anymore.

After everything that's happened, they didn't deserve it. Lex's voice played in the back of my head. *"Bunch of sycophants, all of them."* He was right. Lex had always been right about everything. Screw the polling numbers. Screw the rumors. I didn't care anymore. They'd taken everything from me.

I should let this wedding go on. I should let it blow up in her face like I knew it would.

But I couldn't. She deserved my wrath, and goddamn it, I'd hit my breaking point.

Enough.

Time to tear it all down.

I turned on my heels and met my sister's sympathetic gaze.

"What?" She narrowed her skeptical blue eyes. "You look like you're about to do something stupid."

"Maybe I am."

To be continued in Book 2

WANT MORE?

Thank you for reading *Midsummer,* and if you enjoyed it, please consider leaving a review on Goodreads, Amazon, and/or anywhere else you get your books. Not only do they help other readers, but the algorithm uses reviews to promote and categorize the book.

The next book in the series, *Samhain,* releases on October 29, 2024. The third book, *Solstice,* will release November 26, 2024, and book four, *Beltane,* will go live March 25, 2025.

If you want more while you wait, I have a novella featuring Siobhan, Finn, and Donnelly. It's a 13k short that takes place before *Midsummer*. It gives a taste of what's to come and what the king and queen of fairies are actually like.

AND! AND! AND!

I've put an extra scene between Ivy and Lex at the very end of it that takes place between *Midsummer* and *Samhain*. Enjoy!

If you're interested, please follow this link: https://books.jenadoyle.com/WeWildThings

Thanks again. Keep reading for a sneak peak at *Samhain*.

SAMHAIN

I'LL FOLLOW THEE AND
MAKE A HEAVEN OF HELL...

JENA DOYLE

SAMHAIN BLURB

<u>Carter</u>

I didn't ask Her Royal Highness, the princess Miriam Stuart to come to California with me, but now that she's here, I can't imagine going through the worst heartache of my life without her.

We're different after what happened last midsummer. I can feel it in my bones. Something strange has connected us on a level deeper than we can understand.

When the lingering effects come back with a vengeance, reuniting with the two people that broke our hearts might be the only way to survive.

<u>Miri</u>

Spending a summer with Carter Scott would have been an easy feat for anyone else, but my grandmother, the Queen of England, has other plans for me: a marriage to Prince of Monaco.

I'd rather drown myself in the Thames than touch anyone that wasn't there that night in the woods. I'm already married to three other people, but I can't tell the Queen that.

One incredible night proved that even the trees keep secrets, especially when the curse they gave us hasn't left us. The fairies aren't done with us, yet.

SAMHAIN
PROLOGUE

It was a sham marriage.

I knew that. They'd both told me. We'd promised each other honesty, and I believed them. That didn't stop the throbbing ache in my chest. I used to have a heart there, once upon a time. Now, I only had a hole and a leaking sieve.

I should be there, I thought, sipping my scotch. It went down smooth and sweet, burning my stomach with enough agony to remind me I was alive, even after everything that's happened.

"It's the wedding event of the season, Mark," said the talking head on the TV, her blond hair bouncing as she stood in front of the Washington estate. "Any moment, Alexei Fairfax will take his place in front of the altar. We're told five minutes after that, Ivy will walk down the aisle. I was fortunate enough to get a glimpse of Ivy's wedding dress, and it is *to die* for."

What a way to put it. I snorted to myself as I took another sip.

How long had I loved her? How many times had I held her in my arms while she fell apart? Being here, watching it on TV instead of in person, well... I didn't know which was worse. I had endured this and much more for them, but publicly holding my tongue while they made vows to each other that they'd already made to Miri and me took an act of God.

I'm not worthy. Not yet.

"You know, Renee Calvert designed this dress himself," Mark, the other presenter said. "It took over two million dollars in diamonds."

Jesus.

I bet Ivy hated it. I bet she'd rather get married in hot garbage than walk down the aisle in some pretentious sparkling number that weighed a thousand pounds.

I took another drink and winced against my breaking heart, now racing at the mention of a countdown. Lex and Ivy would soon make legal what the four of us had made symbolic in the woods years ago, and like an itch that wouldn't go away, my fingers went to the scars on my right palm.

Matching scars, ones we all shared.

Until the end.

We'd promised a lot of things that night. Even more in the nights after it. So many promises that we shattered to pieces. And despite that, I never suspected we'd end up here. Spread to the farthest parts of the Earth. Drowning our sorrows in liquor and hopelessness and existential dread.

I thought of Miri. What was she doing to ease the pain of today?

We'd been worrying about it for so long now, a part of me felt relieved to finally stare it down.

My phone rang, my youngest sister calling for the hundredth time. My family knew how I felt about Ivy, how much today would wreck me despite the years between us. I couldn't bring myself to talk to them. I couldn't bring myself to talk to anyone. I let it go to voicemail. Again. It didn't surprise me when I got a nasty text message after that, threatening to leak embarrassing baby pictures of me if I didn't answer.

Go ahead.

I didn't care. I didn't care about much anymore. Not since it happened. Not since this curse brought us together and tore us apart.

As long as she was leaving me shitty voicemails, she was safe. They were all safe.

My phone buzzed one more time, but the name on the screen made my dead heart give half a thump.

Juliet.

"Hey, you," I said when I answered.

She greeted me with a sigh. "Hello, Romeo."

I smiled at the nickname, my heart racing. "I'm glad you called. Where are you?"

"Oh, you know. Locked in my ivory tower."

Code for her family was around. "Are you watching?"

"Of course." Another dramatic sigh. Typical Miri. "I'm sure she looks bloody amazing. And he probably looks like my Prince of Darkness. It's absolutely horrid."

"Did you talk to her?" No sense in elaborating. There could only be one *her* between Miri and I.

"No," Miri said, followed by a pause. "Have you?"

"No," I said. "Neither of them."

"I suppose we deserve this," Miri said. "You and I, for our sins."

"Don't do that to yourself." I knew what sins she meant, and of the three of us, I was the only one who knew what sins Miri kept to herself. "We're in this together. All of us."

"All of us," she said with a sarcastic laugh. "We're pathetic."

"Have you rethought my proposal?" I asked again. "Do I need to show up on my valiant steed for you to finally listen to me?"

"I can't, Romeo," she said. Another long pause, and then a much lower, "It's not safe."

"None of this is safe, that's the point. You know what's about to happen. You know we need to be together."

"That doesn't change anything."

"Juliet," I said. "Marry me. I can come get you in twenty minutes." I was still in London. I could still put the plan into action.

She let out a sad laugh. "Now, there's a ridiculous idea."

"I'm serious."

"Ivy would kill me," she said. "She would kill you, too."

"They have each other. All we have is us."

Another sigh. "I have to go. They're already listening. I wanted to make sure you were okay."

I wanted to beg her to come to me, to spend this night, the worst night of our lives, with me. Like we used to. Like the good old days. That was how we would be safe. We were stronger together, the four of us. But it wouldn't do any good.

Her family had sequestered her away from the public eye. Freedom would mean goodbye forever, and Miri didn't know who she was if she wasn't part of her family.

"Be well, Juliet," I said.

"You too, Romeo," she said. "I love you."

"I love you." When I said the words, I meant them with every fiber in my being. The love I shared with Miri wasn't the same as what I felt for Ivy, nor would it match the intensity with which I burned for Lex. But it was there, vibrant and everlasting.

"Wait, what's this?" the talking head said, catching my attention as I hung up. "I'm being told now that Ivy and Lex are missing. No one can find them in the marital suites."

I shot to my feet, alarm ricocheting down my spine.

Son of a bitch.

My phone rang again.

KEEP READING ANYWHERE YOU GET YOUR BOOKS

Acknowledgments

Dear Reader,

Thank you for reading this little idea I had during the pandemic. I'll be honest... I was inspired to write this book while I was reading *A Lesson in Thorns* by Sierra Simone. It's an amazing four book series that's super queer and poly with hints of dark academia and BDSM and all the beautiful wonderful things. It's **chef's kiss**. So if you're looking for something to get into while you wait for the next book to come out in October, I highly recommend it.

I studied *Midsummer Night's Dream* in high school and again in college. It's a wild acid-trip of a play about choice, consent, and the magical ridiculousness of love. (If you want a decent movie adaptation, check out the 90s version with Michelle Pfeiffer and Calista Flockhart.)

At the end of this series, I will dive deep into my notes on adaptation and the themes I decided to play with. But for now, know that have only grazed the tip of the iceberg on the fairy bullshit. There is so much more to come when we meet the fairy queen and king in this adaptation. Will there be shenanigans? Will there be a fairy potion? Will the king play his evil tricks on the queen? Will there be a mysterious changeling that sets the whole plot on fire?

The answer, quite simply, is yes.

I owe a lot of people thanks with this story:

To my faithful and loving beta readers — Maggie Sims, Leslie Grace, Jenn Britt, Shannon, and Sarah. I could not have made this story without you. For four years, you kept me on track, and I truly appreciate every piece of advice that led me to this final version.

To my husband, Adam, who took care of me, loved me, and consoled me through all four years of getting this on paper. We made each other into the people we are today. For better. For worse. I love you.

To my editors, Misha and Kim - A million thanks and my undying gratitude for your wisdom and support.

To my ARC readers — I know this isn't my normal thing. "But Jena! Where's the bikers?" If you can hang in there with me, I promise you that this world is the same as my Steel Roses MC. It's Aris *Washington* for a reason.

To anyone that took a chance on this story — Thank you for reading. There's three more books to come before we're done with these four chuckle-heads, and there's so much more angsty goodness in store before we get to this happily-ever-after.

And finally to the Bards themselves, especially those that history forgot — Sometimes, it takes a village to write the greatest stories of all time. Thank you to the people who gave *Midsummer Night's Dream* to us five hundred years ago so that I could be sitting here in 2024, bastardizing it all to hell, just as they would have wanted.

Cheers!

Jena

Also by Jena Doyle

<u>MIDSUMMER</u>

We Wild Things (Prequel Novella)

Midsummer

Samhain

Solstice

Beltane

<u>STEEL ROSES MC</u>

They Called Him Saint (Prequel Novella)

Crimson Chaos

Savage Saint

Oleander Oaths

Mischief Mayhem

Ruthless Reign

<u>ROYAL BASTARDS MC: HELENA, MT</u>

Blood and Whiskey

www.ingramcontent.com/pod-product-compliance
Lightning Source LLC
Chambersburg PA
CBHW022026310726
48972CB00006B/1823